TORPEDO!

Also by Harry Homewood

FINAL HARBOR
SILENT SEA

TORPEDO!

Harry Homewood

McGRAW-HILL BOOK COMPANY

New York St. Louis San Francisco
Toronto Hamburg Mexico

1 2 3 4 5 6 7 8 9 D O D O 8 7 6 5 4 3 2

ISBN 0-07-029698-7

LIBRARY OF CONGRESS CATALOGING IN PUBLICATION DATA

Homewood, Harry.
 Torpedo!

 I. Title.
PS3558.045T67   813'.54   81–20689
ISBN 0–07–029698–7   AACR2

Book design by Roberta Rezk

This book is dedicated to my daughter, Judith McCartney, and my son, Charles E. Homewood TMC USN(Ret.), both of whom have made me proud to be a father.

H. H.

TORPEDO!

CHAPTER 1

Duty aboard a U.S. Navy nuclear ballistic missile submarine can be boring. The days stretch out, each day the same as the one preceding it. The watches are stood, six hours on and twelve hours off. The crew sees only the interior of their ship and each other for weeks on end. Once clear of the land the nuclear submarine submerges deep into the element it has been built for and doesn't emerge again into the world of fresh air and sunshine until the long patrol is over and the submarine is only a few miles from its home port.

The U.S.S. *Sharkfin* was 12 hours out of the Strait of Gibraltar on course 278 degrees true, destination New London, Connecticut. There was a subdued air of festival on board. The *Sharkfin* had been at sea for more than 60 days, prowling the eastern end of the Mediterranean Sea, the computers in its sophisticated fire control systems clicking steadily as they constantly adjusted the firing trajectories for targeting the submarine's 16 nuclear ICBM missiles at cities and military installations within the Soviet Union.

Mealtimes are the occasions when the boredom of the patrol

is relieved for a little while. The cooks and bakers are experts, the food varied and plentiful, selected and prepared to appeal to eye and palate and to maintain health in an artificial atmosphere.

The *Sharkfin*'s off-watch crew streamed into their messroom for the noon meal, laughing and talking. The bright red and blue tables and benches provided a cheerful accent to the soft pastel colors of the compartment's bulkheads and the hull overhead. As the enlisted men moved to the mess tables they observed an unwritten law of segregation. Those men who had graduated from the specialized nuclear training schools ate together as a group. The remainder of the crew ate at their own tables.

"Surf and Turf," a messcook announced as he put a platter of steaming food down at one end of a mess table. "Lobster and steak and you get two kinds of pie for dessert with ice cream."

"What kind of lobster is this?" a black electronics technician asked. "This lobster doesn't have any claws, buddy."

"Florida lobster," the messcook said. "That kind of lobster doesn't have claws but it's mighty good."

A burly torpedoman broke a lobster tail in his hands and speared a piece of the white meat on his fork. He dipped it in a bowl of melted butter and chewed slowly.

"Tastes like shrimp only maybe a little better," he said. "I might just retire to Miami when I get my time in. A man could catch some of these every once in a while and eat mighty good."

"You'd better learn to speak Spanish if you go to Miami," the electronics technician said. "I read somewhere that the Cubans have just about taken over Miami, they even have street signs in Spanish down there."

The men on sonar watch on the *Sharkfin* weren't listening for the approach of an enemy. They were primarily concerned with the sonar search patterns that were being beamed out ahead and to each side of the submarine's bow. The *Sharkfin* was running at a depth of 400 feet on a course that would take it to the north of the Ampere Seamount, an underwater mountain peak that reached upward from a depth of 15,800 feet to within 130 feet of the sea's surface.

There was a chance that the *Sharkfin*'s sonar operators might have heard the whining, high-pitched noise of a torpedo racing up the submarine's wake but it was a remote chance. The *Sharkfin*'s big seven-bladed propeller was turning fast enough to drive the huge submarine at a steady twenty knots, making just enough noise to almost muffle any sound that came from directly astern. The torpedo zeroed in on the *Sharkfin*'s spinning propeller and exploded with a roar.

The force of the explosion twisted the *Sharkfin*'s propeller to one side and ripped open a hole in the submarine's stern. Water, which is not compressible, was hurled back and away from the area of the explosion. Then, obeying the inexorable laws of physics, the displaced water smashed back in a giant water hammer that opened wide the hole that the explosion had torn in the submarine's stern.

Driven by the tremendous pressures of the sea, more than 12 tons to the square foot, at 400 feet, a ram of water roared into the *Sharkfin*'s air-filled hull and raced forward through the ship. The air ahead of the water ram was suddenly compressed, much as the air in the cylinder of a diesel engine is compressed by a piston until it ignites spontaneously. When the compressed air ahead of the water ram reached the Crew's Messroom its temperature was already above 3,000 degrees Farenheit. The *Sharkfin*'s crew died, their lungs seared to wet ash, their flesh incinerated on their bones before the water ram reached them.

The stricken submarine shuddered and slowed, its interior utterly still, filled with water. A silent blizzard of charred paint flakes eddied throughout the ship, swirling in the darkness as the *Sharkfin* coasted downward on a long, planing descent into the black sea.

Three miles astern of the *Sharkfin* a sonar operator on a submarine turned to his Division Officer.

"The weapon was tracked into the target, sir. An explosion was heard. The target's propeller noises stopped after the explosion. We echo-ranged on the target. It increased depth steadily. We lost contact when the target was at a depth of twelve thousand feet. The target was definitely sinking, sir."

The Sonar Officer nodded and spoke briefly into a telephone. In the ship's Command Center the ship's Captain put down his telephone and turned to his Navigator.

"Chart the operation as for a practice firing of a torpedo. Our course, target's course, track distance, the usual things." He paused and thought for a moment.

"Estimate the target's angle of descent to the bottom. Begin with a ninety-degree down angle and open that up at five-degree increments. Put that into the computer and give me an estimated area on the bottom where the target is resting."

"I'd guess a descent angle of about forty-five degrees," the Navigator said. "Provided all her watertight doors were open, sir."

"They should have been open," the Captain said. "He had no reason to suspect anything and it was time for the noon meal."

"It's nice to know the weapon worked perfectly." The Gunnery Officer, a young, heavy set man with a small blond mustache smiled self-consciously.

"In time of war your weapons had better work perfectly," the Captain said. "We are not at war. Not yet. We can only hope the target is down in water so deep the other side can't find her. If they do find her God only knows what kind of an international stink will be raised or what will happen to us if our masters decide they can't take the heat and say we acted without orders." His deep-set, somber eyes turned toward the Navigator.

"Set a course back to our regular patrol area. Secure from Battle Condition One. Tell the cooks to serve the noon meal."

His eyes blinked twice and he turned and ducked through a bulkhead door opening.

"And hope the other side doesn't come after us while we're eating our dinners," he muttered to himself as he entered his small cabin.

CHAPTER 2

The icy air of Moscow's December seeped in around the window frames of the gray stone building at Two Dzerzhinsky Square. In a third-floor office the shabby green walls, spotted here and there with faded beige patches where the scabrous paint had flaked off, gave off a cold, clammy smell. Igor Shevenko, the head of the First Directorate of the KGB, the division responsible for clandestine intelligence operations outside of the Soviet Union, opened a fresh pack of Kool cigarets and lit one with a Zippo lighter. He unfolded a copy of the *New York Times* and turned to the sports section, looking for the scores of the previous day's professional football games. He smiled as he read a story about the New York Jets; Joe Namath had thrown four touchdown passes and if the Jets won one more game they were a cinch for the Super Bowl. He looked up as his aide came in with a tray holding two steaming mugs of coffee and a plate of French pastry.

"Can't you get those lazy bastards in the basement to send up some heat?" Shevenko growled. "These radiators have about as much warmth in them as my wife. By the Beastly Beatitudes of Balthazar B., if I don't get some heat up here I'm going to send everyone in that basement to Siberia."

"Beastly what of what or whom, sir?" Stefan Lubutkin's thin face was a study in confusion.

"You've never read J. P. Donleavy? You're not properly educated, Stefan. Marvelous writer, Donleavy. A New York Irishman. He reminds me of the way I used to write when I was taking my doctorate at Columbia in New York. Now what in the hell do we have to do to get some heat up here?"

"The approved method, Comrade Director, is to write a letter in triplicate and send it by post to the proper bureau. The way the mails are these days that could take from four days to two weeks.

"The bureau that receives the letter will then call a meeting to decide if they are indeed the proper people to consider your request. If they are, they will then schedule another meeting to take up the request. The odds are that they will then write a letter to us, in triplicate, advising us to form a committee and study the problem and keep them advised. By that time, Comrade Director, it will be summer and the problem will be solved."

"One of these days your sense of humor is going to cost you your balls," Shevenko growled. "I don't want to write letters or form committees. I want heat."

"It is taken care of, sir. I gave the chief engineer a bottle of your American vodka. He prefers it to our own brands, says it has more bite." As he placed the tray on Shevenko's desk the radiators began to clank and hiss.

"About time," Shevenko grumbled. "Now what about that stupidity in London? What's been done about that idiot who used a truck to mash our would-be embassy defector into strawberry jam against some brick wall or other?"

Lubutkin pulled a chair across the worn carpet and placed it in front of the desk. "Not just some brick wall, sir, it was a wall around a formal garden. A nice poetic touch, I'd say. The idiot you referred to worked, as you know, as a gardener on the palace grounds."

"Poetic touch your ass," Shevenko said. "It was a mistake to liquidate the defector in that way, in front of witnesses. The idiot was lucky to get away without being arrested. The defector should have been brought back here where we could have emptied him like a garbage pail. What did that fool who drove the truck expect, a medal, a promotion to the Wet Squad?"

"I don't know, sir. Perhaps he will get his reward in Heaven, as they say in the West."

Shevenko cupped his hands around the mug of coffee, relishing the warmth. "Was it done in such a way that the London police will think it was an accident?"

"The subject in question was a heroin addict, sir. I arranged that he get some pure heroin. He died of an overdose. His body wasn't used to the pure drug."

"Pure heroin?" Shevenko's voice rose almost a half octave from its normal deep bass. "You ordered money spent for pure heroin? You're dumber than you look, Lubutkin. Your father must have mated with a jackass. Or would it be a jenny? No matter. Why didn't you have him run over by a car or mugged and dropped off a bridge into the Thames?"

"We gain twice, sir. We are rid of an agent who was no longer useful. The stories of his death, he was a British subject as you know, will underline the decadence of a society that uses drugs." He looked meaningfully at the plate of pastry. Shevenko nodded his head and Lubutkin reached for the plate.

"I wish you'd stop playing the international spy, Stefan. You're not cut out for it. Your genes aren't right. Keep things simple. It's bad enough when our friends on the other side play spy games and get things so messed up we can't do our work. Keep it simple and keep it cheap. I have enough trouble now with the people who dole out the money." The clear blue eyes focused on Lubutkin.

"Now the other matter, Stefan. The one that none of us could keep simple?"

"The submarine captain reported that he carried out his

orders. He sent the co-ordinates of the area on the ocean bottom where his target is resting. The water there is very deep, thirteen thousand feet, Comrade."

Shevenko bit into a Napoleon and wiped the creamy filling from his lips with a Kleenex he took from a box that stood on his desk. "The submarine captain is on his way here?"

"Yes, sir. All that information is in the morning folder that I brought in with the newspaper, sir." His voice held the faintest tinge of reproach that his chief had chosen to read the *New York Times* before he looked in the folder Lubutkin prepared for him each morning.

"Our leaders have done some stupid things in the past," Shevenko growled, "but this is one of the more stupid. Those damned admirals get their hands on a new weapon and they can't rest until they're tried it out under what they like to call combat conditions. Never forget one thing, little Stefan; if you give a man a target pistol as a gift he won't rest until he has found a target to fire at. Testing weapons makes noise and noise disturbs the status quo."

"A target that is now deep under the sea isn't likely to make much noise, sir," Lubutkin smiled slyly.

"Don't underestimate the Americans. That windbag they call a Secretary of State could probably fill his lungs and dive to the deepest part of the ocean and find their missing submarine. Now take this down.

"I want you to schedule a meeting for tomorrow afternoon, as soon as possible after the arrival of the submarine captain. I want the meeting to be held here and I want the submarine captain and Admiral Zurahv and his aides to be there, also old Plotovsky. He may be getting a little senile but he's still a power in the Politburo and he was against this operation from the start. If you have any trouble getting him let me know and I'll take care of it. I want him there to maybe throw a little scare into the admirals.

"I want that woman we have, the expert in American affairs, the one with the big bosoms. Tell her I want her there as an observer. Looking at her might make the meeting bearable."

"I agree, sir, the lady is handsome." At Shevenko's nod he placed a Napoleon on a square of Kleenex and carried it into his office. Shevenko broke the seal on the folder with a thick thumb and let its contents spill out on his desk.

"That Joe Namath," he muttered as he pushed the *New York Times* to one side. "He lives as we would all like to live. Do your job spectacularly and romp with beautiful women in your off time. Which reminds me." He punched a button on his desk and Lubutkin's head appeared around the edge of the doorway between their offices.

"Send a message to Fidel. I want two tickets for the Super Bowl game, good seats, as soon as they are available. I want transport from Havana to Miami and I don't want to come ashore through a mangrove swamp in the Florida Keys. Tell him to route me through Mexico City to Miami and return the same route. I want a good hotel on Miami Beach, a suite, for three nights."

"Isn't it a little soon, sir? If I remember, that game is played late in January."

"I know when it's played. Fidel is like all our sacred Cuban brothers, he's completely disorganized." Lubutkin nodded. Shevenko began to read the report from the submarine captain who had torpedoed and sunk the U.S.S. *Sharkfin.*

Vice Admiral Michael P. Brannon, Commander, Submarines Atlantic, turned at the door of his quarters and used his bulk to shield his wife from the wind.

"You'd better get inside, Gloria, this wind is cold. I'll try to be home by eighteen hundred. If I'm going to be late I'll phone." He bent and kissed her upturned mouth and went down the steps to the sidewalk, carrying his heavy frame with an erectness that belied his age and the crushing weight of responsibility that went with his job. His driver smiled a greeting as he held open the car door. The driver trotted around the car and settled himself behind the wheel and the car moved off, the blue pennant with three white stars on it that flew from a front fender snapping in the cold morning wind.

The outer, or E-Ring of the four-story Pentagon building is the area where the offices of the nation's defense chiefs and planners are located. The offices are large and comfortably furnished. Depending where in the E-Ring an office might be located, a sweeping view of some of the nation's history is visible; the dome of the nation's Capitol, old Georgetown, the Lincoln Memorial or, in summer, the lush greenery along the historic Potomac River.

The office suite occupied by Vice Admiral Brannon was luxuriously furnished in keeping with his rank and his position as ComSubLant. The General Services Administration saw to it there were comfortable sofas, chairs, coffee tables, and a massive walnut desk with a high backed swivel chair for the Admiral. Within arm's reach of the swivel chair there was a taboret with a carafe of ice water and glasses. The walls were decorated with a large picture of the President of the United States and framed color photos of the submarines, the submarine squadrons, the heavy cruiser, and the battleship Mike Brannon had commanded during his long naval career. A corps of yeomen worked in the three outer offices of the suite under the supervision of a dour Chief Yeoman who wore seven gold hash marks on the left sleeve of his uniform jacket denoting twenty-eight years of honorable service.

Admiral Brannon paused at the Chief Yeoman's desk in the outer office. "Good morning, Chief. Any word on the *Sharkfin* come in overnight?"

"Negative, sir. Admiral Olsen is waiting for you in your office. Coffee will be ready in a minute, Admiral."

"Thank you. You'd better get a sweet roll for Admiral Olsen. He's always hungry and nothing he eats puts an ounce on him." Brannon went into his office as Rear Admiral John Olsen turned away from the office window.

"Good to see you, John. The Chief said there was nothing on *Sharkfin*. That right?"

"No word, Mike. As of zero eight hundred today, in a

few minutes, she'll be sixty-eight hours overdue with her position report. Aircraft search out of Spain and the Azores is negative. We're calling her on all bands every five minutes, alternating from Rota and Washington. No answer."

"She could have a breakdown in her communications gear," Brannon said. There was a light tap on the door and a yeoman came in with a tray holding a carafe of coffee, cups, a can of condensed milk, sugar, and a huge sweet roll. He put the tray down on a coffee table and closed the door quietly behind him as he left the room. Brannon carefully measured half a teaspoon of sugar into his coffee and then poured in evaporated milk until the liquid was a creamy yellow. Olsen bit into the sweet roll and chewed rapidly.

"She's got too much redundancy in communications for a breakdown to be the cause of not reporting," Olsen said. "The only thing I can think of is a major breakdown in her nuclear power plant and that she might be somewhere on the bottom, trying to make repairs."

"That won't wash," Brannon said. "Water's too deep for her to be on the bottom. Way too deep."

The two men, shipmates during World War II when Mike Brannon had commanded the U.S.S. *Eelfish* and John Olsen had been his Executive Officer during six harrowing submarine war patrols, looked at each other, each sensing the other's concern.

"Let's go down to the Black Room," Brannon said. He turned and stretched, reaching for the console of buttons on his desk top.

"You don't have to call them," Olsen said. "I did that a little while ago. I asked Captain Steel to meet us there."

Brannon frowned. "You think that was necessary at this point?"

"He's an important man in the Navy, and still very powerful, Mike. He may not be able to contribute very much at this stage but if he isn't kept informed he'll raise so much hell that life won't be worth living."

"I suppose you're right," Brannon said. He drained his coffee cup and stood up, his mind on the abrasive Captain Herman Steel. "I just don't much like that man, John."

"Who does?" Olsen said as he unfolded his long, lean length from a sofa. "He doesn't even have a wife or kids to like him. He's just a mean, nasty, son of a bitch but he's our son of a bitch and God help us."

The Black Room in Operations was well named. Three of the four walls were made of thick glass. There were no lights in the room except for one red light on a desk in the center of the room and a glowing ruby tip on the end of a microphone that sprouted out of the desk top on a long flexible stalk.

"You took your time getting here." The rasping voice of Captain Herman Steel was loud in the quiet dimness of the room. "I've got better things to do than to stand around and wait for people who can't begin their day's work until they've poisoned their systems with coffee. Caffeine is a drug. It dulls the brain. I see evidence of that every day when I have to deal with coffee-swilling, seagoing types."

"Good morning, Captain." Mike Brannon's voice gave no evidence that he was aware of the rudeness of Captain Steel's remarks. "I thank you for coming down here on such short notice. I know you have a busy schedule." As his eyes adjusted to the room's gloom Brannon saw that Captain Steel was watching Brannon closely.

Commander John Fencer, the officer in charge of the Black Room, moved out of the gloom to the desk. The red light illuminated his square, compact form and made deep shadows under his eyebrows. As he turned to face the three men the red light cast an eerie sheen on his close-cropped blond hair. He touched a finger to a button on the desk top.

"Standing by, sir." The voice came from a speaker built into the desk.

"Please display the western half of the Mediterranean, the Strait of Gibraltar and the eastern half of the Atlantic," Fencer said crisply. He turned with the others to face a glass wall that began to glow faintly and then lit up with a detailed nautical chart of the requested areas.

"Please chart the course of the U.S.S. *Sharkfin* up to and through the Strait and beyond and lay down her designated course after her last position report." A black line appeared in the Mediterranean and moved through the Strait of Gibraltar and out into the Atlantic, veering slightly to the north as the line moved out to the edge of the chart.

"Thank you," Fencer said. "Now indicate the points where *Sharkfin* made her known position reports."

A black X showed on the chart in the Mediterranean and another black X appeared on the chart on the course line to the west of the Strait. Fencer looked at a paper he held in his hand, tilting it to catch the dim light.

"Assume speed to be twenty knots made good over the ground. Indicate where on the course line *Sharkfin* would have made her next position report." A black O showed on the course line. The desk speaker rattled.

"*Sharkfin*'s last position report was made just before she crossed the outboard edge of the SOSUS network, sir."

"What other information do you have from SOSUS, Commander?" Brannon turned to Captain Steel. "SOSUS is our network of ocean bottom sensors, Captain."

"I'm aware of that," Steel snapped. Brannon shrugged and turned to watch as a red line appeared on the chart just south of the Strait of Gibraltar. The red line moved northward and then joined the black course line of the *Sharkfin*. The red line followed along the black line and then stopped. It reappeared, moving on a reverse course and veering to the southeast, away from the black line. The red line continued in that direction until it neared the west coast of Morocco, where it formed an elliptical loop.

"The red line is the track of a submarine, not one of ours," Fencer said. "The break in the red line is where the other submarine passed out of the SOSUS area. It then returned and proceeded to the area where it has been on patrol. That area is shown as the elliptical loop on the chart, Admiral."

"Do you have an ID on that other submarine?" Brannon asked.

"Yes, sir. We have a positive footprint confirmed by visual observations off Algeria, in the Med. She's a late model Soviet nuclear attack submarine. I must point out, Admiral, that Soviet submarines often follow our submarines and surface ships. Our submarines follow their ships. It's a rather common practice, sir."

"But they don't usually follow one of our ships that far, isn't that so?"

"Yes, sir," Fencher answered.

"Thank you, Commander. Please give my thanks to your staff." Brannon turned to Captain Steel. "I'd like to see you in my office, sir, if you have time?"

"I don't have time," Steel snapped. "A congressional committee takes precedence over a vice admiral, I believe. I have to testify this morning. I can give you forty-five minutes this afternoon. At fourteen hundred. In my office." He turned and left the Black Room, his steel-shod heels ringing on the tiled floor.

Brannon's Chief Yeoman brought fresh coffee into his office. He put a list of telephone calls to be answered on the desk and left.

"Care to drug your system with a little poison?" Olsen asked as he poured the coffee. "The arrogance of that man! You'd think he flew three stars and that you were a snot-nosed ensign! I don't know why you don't lower the boom of rank on that man, Mike, I really don't."

"Don't let it bother you, John," Brannon answered. He stirred his coffee slowly. "I don't let it bother me and I've been exposed to him for three years. You've only had that pleasure for the last six months.

"The Chief of Naval Operations gave me two major priorities when he assigned me to this job three years ago. One was to carry out the responsibilities of the office and God knows, that's a heavy load. The other was to try, as subtly as I could, to restore the morale the submarine Navy has lost over the years and to increase the re-enlistment rate in nuclear submarines. The re-up rate had fallen to an all time low and cash bonuses for re-upping weren't doing the job.

"To carry out that second priority I had to begin countermanding a lot of the directives that Captain Steel had put out. The sort of directives that coddled the graduates of the nuclear power training schools he had set up. I had to do that in such a manner that Captain Steel didn't get his ass in an uproar and go running to the Congress to demand my head on a platter alongside the head of the Chief of Naval Operations.

"What did they teach us in War College? Know your enemy. Study your enemy. Understand him. I did that. I wound up not liking the man any more than I had but I did gain a lot of respect for him. He took an awful hazing at the Academy because of, well, call it ethnic bigotry. That same bigotry that Rickover had to deal with as a Jew. It gave the two men a common ground. That's how they were able to work so closely together.

"Rickover had only one weapon he could use against the bigotry—his brain. He used it. He took the reality of the atomic bomb and the concept of nuclear power from that bomb and he literally created the nuclear submarine Navy all by himself and Steel has done nearly as much bringing the Navy up to date."

"Don't forget how he did that," Olsen said dryly. "He sucked up a lot of powerful members of the Congress and when he had them in his hip pocket he sucked up to presidents, their

White House staffs and to the press. He became a little tin god, untouchable.

"Once the nuclear submarine Navy was underway he coddled, that's your word and it's a good one, he coddled the nuclear school graduates until damned good submariners who hadn't qualified to go through his schools got so fed up they either didn't re-enlist or if they had a lot of time to serve they tried their damndest to get off the nukes. I know of cases where some of them offered as much as a thousand bucks to get a swap. I had to live with that in my command in Pearl Harbor and it almost drove me crazy."

"I know," Brannon said. "It's taken me the better part of two years to get rid of the worst of the petty stuff. There's still a hell of a lot to be done, a hell of a lot and it's got to be done carefully and slowly." He looked at Olsen, his dark blue eyes boring into the other man.

"Why do you think I asked for you as my Number One when Roger retired? I want someone I can trust to carry on the work. Someone who can make this nuclear submarine Navy into the same sort of submarine Navy we had in World War II and after the war. An outfit that good men will try their damndest to get into and will never want to leave. Captain Steel has been passed over for admiral but I know that he's got a scheme going that's going to override the Navy's rules and give him his big star. I've only got another year and a bit in this job and then they'll pipe me over the side. They don't let you stay past the age of sixty-two. Unless you're Captain Steel, of course."

"He must hate you with a passion," Olsen said slowly. "And he'll hate me just as much. Fine shipmate you are, Mike, letting me in for this."

"I don't think he hates anyone," Mike Brannon said. "He's too intelligent to waste emotion on hatred. I think he sees me as a problem he has to solve with his intellect."

"Oh, sure," Olsen said. He refilled the coffee cups from the carafe. "I can name two or three admirals he got rid of.

Damned good men who didn't want to go, either. But he got nasty about them and they went."

"That was early, when he was starting to build his power base," Brannon said. "He had to show his power so he could do the things that he wanted to do. He's too good a politician now to try that sort of thing." He pushed a button on his desk and his Chief Yeoman came in, a stenographic pad and pen in hand.

"Would you call the director of the CIA and ask him to sit in with me in a meeting in Captain Steel's office at fourteen hundred today? Tell him I apologize for the short notice but I consider the meeting important."

"Talk about politicians," Olsen said, "Didn't Steel try to torpedo Admiral Benson when the President proposed him as head of the CIA?"

Brannon nodded. "That's one of the very few times Mr. Steel ever ran up on a reef. Johnny Benson had a hell of a record as a pilot and as a carrier skipper and when he made admiral he showed his colors as an administrator.

"I wasn't playing politics asking him to sit in on the meeting. I'm worried about something else, John." He rose and walked over to the window and stood looking down at the tree tops whipping in the wind.

"We've never had a nuclear power plant failure in a submarine that I know of. We've got our hands full in Vietnam right now and what I'm damned afraid of, old friend, is that the Russians have decided to take advantage of our problems in Vietnam and restart the Cold War. Only this time the theatre isn't Europe, it's our area, the deep sea."

CHAPTER 3

His long membership in the Politburo entitled Leonid Plotovsky to sit at the head of the table in the third-floor conference room in the KGB headquarters. The radiators hissed and rattled as the building engineers, alerted by Stefan Lubutkin that a senior member of the Politburo was in the building, sought to keep the third floor warm enough to prevent a complaint from the old Communist street fighter.

To Plotovsky's right sat two admirals of the Soviet Navy, their uniform jackets bedecked with metals. To his left, one chair removed from the end of the table, sat Submarine Commander Nikita Kovitz, his square face solemn, his deep-set eyes wary. His face showed the strain he had been under during the flight from Tripoli to Moscow. He had spent the long hours of the flight worrying about the meeting that was now about to begin.

To Kovitz's left sat Stefan Lubutkin, a pad of paper and a gold Cross pen on the table in front of him. Lubutkin kept his eyes lowered, looking at the pen, a gift from Igor Shevenko. Farther down the table Sophia Blovin, her prominent breasts encased in a tight sweater, sat next to Shevenko.

Plotovsky cleared his throat and looked around. He saw the white enameled cuspidor that Shevenko had ordered Lubutkin to place beside his chair. He hawked noisily and spat into the cuspidor.

"Begin," he ordered.

"As you know, honored Comrade," Admiral Aleksandr Zurahv said, "we have been greatly concerned with the American capability to strike at almost every one of our cities with nuclear missiles fired from their submarines. We are vulnerable to that threat from every quadrant of the compass except the north.

"We have devoted great energy to find a means to neutralize that threat. We have had some success. The development of our own nuclear ballistic missile submarines gives us a means to strike at American cities from the sea. Another success has been the building of a new class of nuclear attack submarines which are very fast and can go much deeper than previous submarines of that type.

"We realized that to make these new attack submarines a real threat to the American missile submarines we needed a new weapon, a torpedo, that would have great range and yet could be fired at a target close to our own submarines." He paused and filled his great chest with air and let it out slowly.

"I must at this point, Comrade Plotovsky, give you a little background that you might not have. The Americans have armed many of their torpedoes with nuclear warheads. We can do the same thing. When one does that the torpedo must be exploded at least six to eight miles away from the submarine that fired it or the submarine will be destroyed in the nuclear explosion. At such great distances one sacrifices accuracy.

"We wanted a new type of torpedo that would seek out the enemy through the sounds the enemy ship makes. It should be armed with a non-nuclear warhead. Using a non-nuclear warhead means the torpedo can be fired at a target that is fairly close to the firing submarine, thus increasing accuracy to a high degree. We have developed such a torpedo with an entirely new type of sonar reading device that will not confuse the noise our submarine makes with the noise of the enemy submarine." He paused as he saw Plotovsky's forehead wrinkle.

"Existing models of sound-seeking torpedoes have a weakness, Comrade. Often the torpedo, after being fired, would hear the noise its own submarine was making and would circle around and attack the ship that fired it. With our new torpedo we can program it ahead of time with the sound patterns of the ship that will be firing it and it will ignore those programmed noises and seek out the noise of an enemy ship, for example, an enemy submarine."

"Speak precisely," Plotovsky said. He hawked and spat noisily into the cuspidor. Sophia Blovin shuddered slightly and Shevenko smiled to himself.

"Politically speaking," Plotovsky wiped his mouth with the back of his hand. "Politically speaking we are not at war with anyone so we have no enemies, as that word is commonly used."

"A matter of habit, Comrade," the Admiral said. "Like all true Party members I consider all nations, all peoples who oppose us in any way as an enemy."

"Go on," Plotovsky said.

"The development of this new weapon gave us a countermeasure against the American nuclear threat but it was a countermeasure on paper only. Unless we found a way to test it under actual combat conditions." The Admiral's small eyes, almost buried in heavy pouches of flesh, squeezed shut and then opened.

Plotovsky raised a thin hand, the age spots on the back of his hand standing out clearly in the harsh fluorescent lighting. "This is information that was not brought out at the Politburo meeting where the testing program was discussed. I will take up that omission with you later." He turned toward Captain Nikita Kovitz.

"I presume that the weapon has been tested and you are the one who did the testing?"

"I was given orders, Comrade." The words came slowly

from Captain Kovitz. "I have the habit of loyalty, sir. I am loyal to my Party, to my nation, to my superior officers. I carried out my orders, Comrade Plotovsky."

"Which were? Please speak precisely, Captain."

"I was told that on a certain day and at a certain time a submarine would clear the Strait of Gibraltar on a certain course. I was ordered to track, to follow, sir, that submarine for several hours. If I were detected during the tracking period I was to break off the operation and retire at high speed. If I was not detected I was to close to a specified firing range and test fire the new weapon.

"I closed to the prescribed firing range," Kovitz said stolidly. "I test fired the new torpedo."

Plotovsky had closed his eyes. His thin hands rested on the table top.

"The weapon was fired," Captain Kovitz continued, his voice low. "Our sonar operators reported that the weapon ran toward the target at what is called the search mode speed. It was heard to increase speed when it detected the noise from the target's propeller. The weapon exploded precisely when it should have, given its speed and distance to be traveled. The target's propeller noises stopped after the explosion. Our sonar operators echo-ranged on the target, that is, sir, they sent out sound beams against the target. The target was tracked down to a depth of two thousand fathoms. It is my considered opinion, sir, that the target was destroyed. No submarine can survive at a depth of two thousand fathoms, sir."

"Your target was an American ballistic missile submarine?"

"I do not know that, Comrade. I never saw the target."

"Then it is possible that you fired this new weapon at a Soviet submarine, is it not?" Plotovsky's fierce eyes opened with a snap, staring at Captain Kovitz. Kovitz reached into the sleeve of his uniform jacket and pulled out a clean white handkerchief. He mopped his face and looked across the table at Admiral Zurahv. The Admiral smiled.

"Comrade Plotovsky," Admiral Zurahv said in his heavy

voice, "one must break eggs to make an omelet, as the saying goes. You broke many eggs for the good of the Party, the nation. A good omelet is worth the price of a few broken eggs. We have developed and tested a weapon that could save our nation from a nuclear holocaust."

"I see," Plotovsky said in a mild voice. "But if you will, Admiral, consider this possibility.

"Let us assume that the target you tested your weapon on was an American submarine. The Americans will know, soon enough, that one of their submarines is missing. They will search for it, won't they? And if they find it and determine how it was lost do you think they will blame the North Vietnamese?" Plotovsky began tapping the table top with a thin forefinger. The clicking sound of his brittle fingernail hitting the table hung in the air.

"What interests me, Admiral, is the price of your omelet."

"The test site was carefully chosen, Comrade." Admiral Zurahv's heavy lips parted and showed a row of tobacco-stained teeth. "As Captain Kovitz said, the target is on the bottom in two thousand fathoms of water."

"Two thousand fathoms is twelve thousand feet," Plotovsky's voice was soft, pedantic. "The oceans have been explored, by the Americans among others, to much greater depths, to depths three times two thousand fathoms. In a submersible vessel with windows and lights and manned by men, Admiral, men who can see and evaluate what they see.

"One must then assume that the Americans have the means to find their submarine and once they find it to learn how it was sunk." He paused, his lizardlike eyes staring at Admiral Zurahv. When he spoke his voice was like the crack of a whip.

"You have committed an act of war, Admiral! You have acted politically and you have no authority to make political decisions or acts! That is the province of the Politburo!"

"The Politburo authorized the test," Zurahv said.

"For some years now," Plotovsky's voice was again soft, "we have had eleven members in the Politburo. There is wisdom in the odd number. If a vote results in a tie, five to five, Comrade Brezhnev as First Secretary can cast the tie-breaking vote. When your project was voted on one member was sick and did not vote. The vote was five to four in favor of the test. Comrade Brezhnev did not choose to vote and cause a tie." He stood up, his hands braced against the top of the table.

"I led the minority, sir. I will call for a special meeting of the Politburo to consider the situation you have created. If I were you I would not depend on a confirmation by vote of your action. You will be given the opportunity to explain your actions." He turned to look at Captain Kovitz.

"I advise you, Captain, to read the accounts of the Nuremberg War Trials. Blind obedience to orders from a superior can be dangerous." He turned and shuffled out of the room. When the door closed behind him Admiral Zurahv shrugged and smiled at the people around the table.

"Once he was a great hero, a fearless man. Now he is old. He fears progress and the changes it brings, the technology that gives us progress." He stood up and smoothed his uniform jacket over his vast belly, smiling at Sophia Blovin.

"It is a pleasure to meet you, young lady. I hope to see you again. Captain Kovitz, I would like you to come with me to my office to discuss your report. We have made arrangements for your lodging tonight. You will be flown back to your ship tomorrow." He smiled genially at Shevenko and bowed slightly toward Sophia Blovin. He left the room followed by the other admiral with Captain Kovitz bringing up the rear.

Shevenko pushed his chair back and stood up and pulled Sophia's chair back as she stood. "You have made an impression on Admiral Zurahv," he said with a grin. She shook her head, her smile faint.

"I trust that you won't consider this meeting a waste of your time," Shevenko said. "Without doubt you will be called on to appear before the meeting that Plotovsky mentioned to give your impression of what effect this incident will have on the American political and popular mind. I reasoned that if you could see the shape of the clouds that are forming you could better prepare yourself for that meeting."

Sophia drew a deep breath and the fabric of her sweater stretched dangerously. "I appreciate your concern for me, Comrade Director. I would like to talk to you about what areas of research I should follow."

"Dinner this evening?" Shevenko whispered as he pushed the chairs back to the table. She smiled and nodded and Shevenko went to the door and held it open for her, letting his elbow brush gently against the swell of her breast as she passed him.

Captain Steel's office was as austere as the man. A battered desk stood at one end of the room. Although the Captain's office was in the E-Ring he had resisted the efforts of the GSA to furnish the office according to the GSA directives. When meetings were held in Captain Steel's office his Chief Yeoman brought in folding metal chairs and lined them up in front of the desk Captain Steel had first sat behind when he had been ordered to Washington.

Vice Admiral Brannon and Rear Admiral John Olsen were waiting in Steel's outer office when Rear Admiral Benson arrived with Bob Wilson, his senior aide. The three admirals shook hands and Benson introduced Bob Wilson to Brannon and Olsen. The Chief Yeoman in charge of the office looked agonized as he glanced at his wrist watch.

"It's thirteen fifty-seven, Admiral Brannon. Captain Steel told me your appointment was for fourteen hundred hours, sir."

"It's all right, Chief," Brannon said. "We don't mind waiting." He turned to talk to the other men as the Chief Yeoman watched the second hand on his Rolex click slowly toward two P.M. At thirty seconds before the hour he opened the door to Captain Steel's office.

"Vice Admiral Brannon, Rear Admirals Benson and Olsen and Mr. Robert Wilson, civilian aide to Admiral Benson, sir." He stood to one side as the party entered the office and then closed the door. Mike Brannon chose a metal chair at the end of the row of four chairs and sat down cautiously, testing the chair to see if it would hold his bulk.

"Good afternoon, Captain," Brannon said. "As you know, *Sharkfin* is seventy-four hours overdue with her regular position report.

"Several possibilities exist as to why *Sharkfin* has not reported. One is that she suffered a communications breakdown. That is not a very solid assumption since all nuclear submarines have ample redundancy in comunications. Another possibility is that she may have suffered a breakdown in her nuclear power plant and is on the bottom, trying to make repairs."

"No nuclear power plant in any nuclear submarine has ever failed." Captain Steel's voice was dry, rasping.

"Acknowledged," Brannon said. He drew a long breath.

"There is also the possibility that *Sharkfin* was attacked by the Soviet submarine that tracked her."

"You can assume anything you wish," Steel said. "I am an engineer. I am not a gossip or a rumor monger. If *Sharkfin* is down the probable cause of her being down is a manpower failure. We have too many enlisted men on nuclear submarines who have not been through my training schools. Any one of those enlisted men could have made a fatal mistake that could cause the loss of the *Sharkfin*. Or any other nuclear submarine."

"That ground has been gone over time and again," Brannon said. "You know why every enlisted man aboard nuclear submarines is not a graduate of the Navy's nuclear training schools. We can't recruit enough men who are able to pass the tests to qualify for the nuclear schools. We can't even coax enough qualified submarine men to go to the schools. We are forced to fill out the crews on the nukes with men who even if they haven't been to a nuclear school are damned good submariners."

"I know how many times that specious argument has been

raised and I know who is chiefly responsible for raising it," Steel said. "I presume you didn't come here to resume that argument. Please get to the point."

Brannon sensed John Olsen tensing beside him and cleared his throat.

"If the *Sharkfin* has been lost to an unprovoked enemy action then all of our nuclear missile submarines might be in danger from continued unprovoked attacks."

"You have no proof of such an unprovoked action," Steel snapped. "You're jumping to a conclusion, sir. You are, I believe, addicted to reading spy stories, are you not? Is that why you brought these two spies with you?"

Mike Brannon felt the anger rising in him and fought to hold it back. "Captain Steel," he said, keeping his voice level, "we are here to do you the courtesy of keeping you informed. Admiral Benson might be able to give us some information we do not know. Mr. Wilson has spent his adult life working in the CIA and he is the Agency's ranking expert on Soviet clandestine operations. You might learn something you don't know. So might I."

Captain Steel looked at the battered Timex he wore on his right wrist. "You have a few more minutes left of your time." He lowered his head and stared at his desk. Admiral Benson nudged Wilson.

"The Soviets have a new attack submarine," Wilson began. "Our information is that these new submarines are very fast, faster than ours." He stopped as Captain Steel raised his head.

"I know that," Steel said.

Wilson flushed. "We also have information that the Soviets have a new type of torpedo that has a sophisticated sound system in it to search for targets."

"How long did you serve in submarines? How much experience have you had with torpedoes? When did you first hear about this new torpedo?" Steel's voice was harsh.

"The answer to the first two questions is none. Four months ago is the answer to the third part of your question."

Steel looked at Wilson and then at Brannon. "I knew about

their new torpedo six months ago. I have work to do. Keep me informed, Admiral Brannon. I will see to it that the President and the chairmen of the appropriate congressional committees are informed at the proper time."

Brannon stood up, his normally genial face suddenly hard. "I will be the judge of when and if the President or anyone else is informed, sir. Keep that in mind." He wheeled and left the office, Olsen following him. They heard Steel's snickering laughter as they went through the door.

Brannon's yeoman had hot coffee and a platter of doughnuts waiting for Brannon and Olsen when they got back to Brannon's office.

"How do we retaliate?" Olsen asked.

"I don't know," Brannon said. "What I do know is that we have to find the *Sharkfin* and find out what happened to her." He sorted through a stack of papers on his desk.

"The *Medusa* is in Rota for rest and minor ship repair. She's an oceanographic survey ship and she's got enough bottom-charting sonar gear on her to find the *Sharkfin* if anything can. Get a message off to her skipper. I want her at sea as soon as possible." He went over to a chart of the world that dominated one wall of his office, a pair of dividers in his hand.

"She's only a few hours steaming from *Sharkfin*'s course line. Send her orders to chart the bottom along that line from *Sharkfin*'s last position report for, oh, two hundred miles. If she picks up anything that gives a return indicating metal of any size on the bottom I want to know about it at once."

"You want to tell her skipper what he's looking for?"

Brannon chewed his lower lip. "No, but I guess we have to. Get latitude and longitude and *Sharkfin*'s course from Commander Fencer." He went through another stack of papers on his desk.

"Send a priority message, 'Captain's Eyes Only,' to the *Devilfish*. She's in Holy Loch. Tell her skipper to get underway at once. Give him a patrol area one hundred miles west of Gibraltar. Tell him to make all possible speed in getting to the patrol area. Put him directly under my command. I want position reports from him pre-dawn and after dark. He is to operate without being observed." He turned and walked to the window. A burst of sleet hammered against the glass.

"If I remember an information memo a while back," Olsen's voice was low, "if I remember, all the submarines at Holy Loch have been given the modified SUBROC nuclear missiles, that right?"

"Yes." Mike Brannon answered.

CHAPTER 4

The U.S.S. *Devilfish* moved slowly westward from the coast of Scotland. The weather was foul, as it so often is in that latitude, with low storm clouds and an icy, stinging rain. The winds were out of the northwest and were kicking up a rolling chop that could be felt by the crew of the *Devilfish* as the submarine moved through the water, 100 feet beneath the surface. The sonar operators on duty were watching the fathometer screens intently as the sonar beam probed the sea bottom, searching for the edge of the 100-mile-wide, 14,000-foot-deep trench that scarred the ocean bottom and led southward to the deep abyssal plain on the eastern edge of the great Mid-Atlantic Ridge. The white-line picture of the sea bottom on the display screens changed suddenly as the submarine passed over the edge of the chasm. The sonar operator picked up his telephone and notified the Officer of the Deck of the change of depth under the ship's keel.

The OOD put down the telephone and looked at the night order book and the navigation chart. "Stand by for a change of course and depth in five minutes," he said. He checked his watch and waited for five minutes.

"Five degrees left rudder," he ordered. "Come left to new course two two zero. Make depth five zero zero feet. Two degree down bubble." The helmsman, seated in a comfortable chair with a control stick, not unlike the joystick of an old-fashioned airplane sticking out of a chair arm, repeated the orders and moved the control stick gently forward and to the left, his eyes on the dials in front of his watch station. The *Devilfish* began a gentle turn to port and began to slide down deeper into the sea.

"Increase speed to seventy-five percent of the max reactor output," the OOD said. The helmsman repeated the order and the submarine vibrated slightly as the nuclear power plant began to pour enormous quantities of superheated steam to the turbines that drove the propeller shafts.

"Steady on course two two zero, helm on automatic. Depth is five zero zero feet, depth on automatic. Making turns for seventy-five percent of maximum reactor output, sir," the helmsman said quietly. The OOD acknowledged and entered the change of course, depth and speed and the time in the log book. He sent a messenger to inform the Captain and the Executive Officer of the changes.

The *Devilfish* was in her element now, free of the surface effect of the sea, free of the turbulence caused by bow waves and propeller slippage. As a submarine goes deeper and deeper into the sea the increasing pressure of the sea itself eliminates turbulence along and around the ship's hull. The same pressures of the sea eliminate the cavitation, or turbulence, around and behind a ship's propeller, reducing slippage and noise to almost zero. The sea outside the submarine's hull, exerting a pressure of 222 pounds to the square inch at 500 feet against the subtly contoured cylindrical hull becomes an ally, enabling the submarine to go faster and more quietly than if it were cruising under equal power at a depth of 100 feet.

The *Devilfish* was one of the U.S. Navy's new nuclear attack submarines. She had been designed for one purpose, to seek out and destroy enemy submarines. She was equipped with a staggering array of sophisticated sonar gear. Like the predator sharks that prowl the ocean and detect the irregular swimming vibrations of a sick or wounded fish by means of a line of sensory nerves down each side of the shark's body, the *Devilfish* had a lateral line of sonar sensors down each side of its sleek black hull. Other sonar sensors were located in the submarine's bow and stern areas, along its keel, on the decks and on the sail, or bridge structure. All of the sensors and transmitters were connected electronically to computers that analyzed the sounds received and displayed the analyses on video screens and printed the analyses out on paper. Other computers, which were part of the fire control systems of the *Devilfish,* were connected to the sonar computers so that a target, once detected and identified, could be analyzed, its course, speed, distance, and depth determined and then the target could be tracked and destroyed.

The armory of weapons on *Devilfish* was awesome. In her torpedo tubes and torpedo reload racks were torpedoes much smaller and far more sophisticated than the steam-driven torpedoes of World War II. All the torpedoes were fitted with nuclear warheads, and some carried within their afterbodies miles of thin wire that connected the torpedo to the submarine after it had been fired. The wire contained communications circuits so the ship's fire control computers could guide the torpedo as it raced away from the submarine, change its course, speed and depth, set its search patterns, and explode it precisely at the right time, even though the torpedo might be as much as ten miles distant. In addition to its torpedoes the *Devilfish* carried SUBROC missiles with nuclear warheads. The missiles, when fired underwater, surged to the surface where powerful rocket motors launched them into the air and toward a target too distant for the torpedoes to reach.

The message that had arrived the previous evening, addressed to Lieutenant Commander Robert R. Miller, "For the Captain's Eyes Only," had been succinct. It ordered Captain Miller to proceed with all possible speed to a patrol area 100 miles west of the Strait of Gibraltar, to report his position every 12 hours and to proceed without being detected. Captain Miller looked at the chart on his cabin table. At normal submerged cruising speed the 2,100 mile trip would take about four and a half days. At 75 percent of the nuclear reactor output, considerably less than four and a half days. He looked up as his Executive Officer stepped into his cabin.

"The messenger of the watch just told me the OOD reports we're on course two two zero, cruising at five hundred feet and the reactor is putting out seventy-five percent of its max output, sir. I told him I'd give you the word." Lieutenant John Carmichael slid into a chair and lit a cigaret.

"Thank you," Miller said. "What's the weather like topside?"

"Rotten," Carmichael said. "Rain and some sleet that might turn into snow. Wind's building up but it won't affect the current down here. The North Atlantic current funnels up this big trench but it's rated at only one, one and a half knots." He looked at his Commanding Officer.

"Any idea of what this exercise is about, sir? That is, if you can say."

"Beats me, John." Miller took the message out of his shirt pocket and handed it to his XO. "I thought that it would be orders to send us after that Russian missile sub that crossed the SOSUS array between Britain and Greenland. He's probably heading for home. I was looking forward to a game of hide and seek in the dark with him and then letting him know we'd tagged him. God knows, we need the practice. It's been months since we've had a chance to play tag with one of their missile subs. I guess that Dick Reinauer on *Orca* will have the fun now that we're heading south. Read the message and keep it to yourself."

"Sort of strange," Carmichael said as he read the message. "This takes us out of the Holy Loch command and puts us directly under ComSubLant. Why tell us to maintain a state of full preparedness? We're always that way. Sounds like something big might be cooking, Skipper, don't you think?"

"I don't know what to think because I can't think of anything big that might be in the wind," Captain Miller said. "You'd better put orders in the log that we'll slow down and do a full sonar sweep before we go up to make a position report. When we do go up I want a radar sweep before we begin transmitting."

"I'll do that now, sir," Carmichael said. He rose and stubbed out his cigaret in an ashtray.

"Better pass the word to all hands that we're on a special training exercise," Captain Miller said. "This is the first time since I've had command that I've been right under ComSub-Lant's thumb and I don't want any foul-ups. That big Irishman in the Pentagon can cut you off at the knees just by looking at you."

Carmichael paused at the entrance to the cabin. "I didn't know you ever served with the famous Iron Mike Brannon, Skipper."

"I didn't. I was at PCO school learning how to be a skipper and he came over to lecture us on evasive tactics when under attack and how to maintain crew morale on long war patrols. He made quite an impression. He had one hell of a war record in submarines in World War II."

"Those were the old days," Carmichael said with a grin. "Diesel submarines and primitive sonar gear. Things are different now."

"This is a submarine, John, and we're submariners." Captain Miller said. "Iron Mike is a submariner. He's also a Vice Admiral and he's ComSubLant. I want everyone on their toes."

The messenger of the watch on the U.S.S. *Medusa* knocked twice on the steel door of the Captain's cabin and waited. He heard the command to enter and he stepped into the cabin.

"Priority message, sir," he said. Captain Fred Lutz turned in his chair and pushed the letter he had been writing to one side.

"Thank you," he said. He opened the envelope as the messenger closed the door behind him. He pulled out two sheets of paper. On the top sheet in the Communications Officer's neat handwriting were the radio call letters of the *Medusa* and the call letters of the originating station, time and date. Below it the Communications Officer had stopped decoding after the words "Captain's Eyes Only." The second sheet was the coded message. Lutz stretched over his desk and opened his safe and took out a code book. When he had finished decoding the message he picked up the telephone and dialed the Quarterdeck.

"Captain here," he said. "Please give me the status of the liberty party." He waited, seeing in his mind's eye the OOD counting the empty slots in the liberty card board.

"Twenty-six enlisted men still ashore, sir. No reports of any incidents from the Shore Patrol. All officers are aboard. Liberty is up at midnight, ah, two hours and five minutes from now. Last liberty boat should be alongside at zero zero twenty, Captain."

"Thank you," Lutz said. "Please have the messenger notify the XO that I'd like to see him in my cabin at once."

Lieutenant Commander Bruce B. "Blighty" Lee walked into Captain Lutz's cabin and sat down in a chair. "You pulled me out of a four spade bid, doubled and redoubled that I couldn't have made if I'd had a gun. Old Fuzzface Martin is going to be chewing his beard. He had me set for sure. What's up, sir?"

"Before we get to that, Blighty, give me a rundown on how ready we are for sea."

Lee rubbed his forehead in thought. "We topped off the fuel tanks two days ago. Stores came aboard yesterday. All shore-side repair work was finished day before yesterday. Still some minor stuff, painting, that sort of thing to do. Nothing important. We can go any time you say, once the liberty party comes aboard, sir." His eyes questioned Lutz, who handed over the decoded message. Lee read it and looked up, his face grave.

"They don't give us any reason for their thinking a submarine might be on the bottom."

"Probably a matériel failure if there is one on the bottom," Lutz said. "I can't think of any other reason."

"That 'Captain's Eyes Only' thing makes it sticky," Lee said. "Harold Hahn and Chief Klinger are probably the two best sonar people in the Fleet but if they don't know what they're supposed to be looking for," his voice trailed off.

"I know," Captain Lutz said. "We're going to have to think of something. Lieutenant Hahn is damned sharp. The Chief, too."

"An aircraft, maybe? Could we say that? Say we've been asked to search for an aircraft that's down on that course line? Aircraft are pretty big."

"Might work," Lutz said. "Worth a try anyway. Except for one thing; if we find the submarine we're going to have to take pictures and the Chief and his people in Sonar and Hahn in Charting and the Bridge crew are all going to know what's down there." He shrugged. "ComSubLant wants complete secrecy. Well, we're at sea so no one can mouth off in a bar ashore. He's got to know that if we find his submarine the crew is going to know it. After that, it's his worry." He reached for the message.

"Write down the latitude and longitude co-ordinates and lay out the course line of the *Sharkfin* and her last position report. We'll start the search there. Notify the Port Authority and the SOP that we'll be getting underway at zero two hundred. Set the sea detail at zero one hundred. It shouldn't take us very long to get on station."

The sonar compartment on the *Medusa* was located deep in the bowels of the ship. The compartment was large and crammed with the sophisticated electronics needed to probe and chart the bottom of the oceans. Set into the *Medusa*'s hull were dozens of sonar transmitters and receivers to send out directional sonar beams from the ship and receive them when they bounced back off the bottom. The returning sonar signals were fed into audio circuits and video screens so the sonar operators could see and hear them and into computers that analyzed the sonar echoes and printed out the depth and configuration of the sea bottom.

The four walls of the sonar compartment, or bulkheads, as walls are called at sea, were covered with a maze of dials, switches, and controls. Against one bulkhead there was a long desk with swivel chairs bolted to the deck in front of it. In the center of the desk there was a large video screen that was flanked by smaller screens on either side. Along the desk top were sets of controls that enabled the sonar operators to mass all of the sonar transmitters to send out simultaneous sound beams at one time, to use selective banks of transmitters or a single transmitter. The compartment was kept dimly lighted with red lamps for the convenience of the sonarmen on watch who sat in their swivel chairs studying the video screens.

Chief Sonarman John Klinger, a heavy set man with seventeen years of service in the Navy, sat in front of the large master video screen. He sensed rather than heard Captain Lutz walk into the compartment and he half turned in his chair. He pushed one of the big mufflike earphones he wore up on his temple.

"Nothing yet, Captain. I'm using a bank of transmitters up forward in a wide angle scan. If they pick up anything we can go to concentrated scan. I've got a scan going amidships, one hundred and sixty degrees to each side from the keel to give us a fan over the bottom."

"What's the bottom look like?" Lutz asked

"We're getting a mushy return, sort of, sir. Lot of sediment down there on top of solid rock. We're in deep water now, eleven thousand feet and getting deeper."

"A plane fuselage would show up, you think?"

"Oh, hell yes, Captain. The metal fuselage would give off a bang in the earphones like you hit a dishpan with a hammer. If the pilot was on course when he went down we should find the plane. Provided he didn't lose a wing when he went into the water and went skewing way off to one side."

"Very well," Captain Lutz said. "The minute you get anything inform the Bridge and Charting." He touched the Chief Petty Officer on the shoulder and left the compartment.

In the middle of the afternoon watch on the second day of the search the telephone on the Bridge rang. "Sonar reports a solid metal return at fourteen hundred twenty hours and seven seconds, sir." The Quartermaster of the Watch turned to the OOD.

"Notify the Captain," the OOD said. He made a small X on the course line on the chart. Captain Lutz, breathing hard after running up the steep ladders to the Navigation Bridge, bounced into the Chartroom.

"Right here, sir," the OOD said. He pointed at the X on the chart.

"Reduce speed to four knots if you can maintain steerageway," Lutz said. He picked up the telephone and dialed the Sonar Compartment.

"We're slowing to four knots, Chief. Use the after scan as long as you have contact. We'll go ahead on this course until we can make a turn and then come back down along the reverse course. I'll let you know when that is. As soon as you get contact again we'll drop sonar buoys." He turned to the OOD.

"Tell the First Lieutenant I want sonar buoys ready to drop when we come about on the reverse course. I want the paravane rigged for a camera and floodlight drop, deep drop, about thirteen thousand feet. Tell Mr. Hahn in Charting that I want a bottom charting and analyses as soon as we come about on the reverse course. Get Mr. Lee up here on the double, we've got some tricky navigating and ship handling ahead of us."

"Has Sonar found the plane, sir?" the OOD asked as he reached for the telephone.

"I don't know," Captain Lutz said. "They've got something down there and we've got to check it out."

In the Sonar Compartment Chief Klinger was staring at the computer readout, a puzzled expression on his heavy face. "Damned computer says the target on the bottom is over four hundred feet long. We hit it with a wide scan but there's no indication of any wingspread on the aircraft. Either he lost both wings or else," he rubbed his chin, "maybe we got the hull of an old freighter down there, something that was sunk in World War II." The telephone by his elbow rang and he picked it up.

"Aye, aye, sir." He turned to the men on watch.

"The Old Man's swinging around to run back down the course. They're standing by to drop sonar buoys as soon as we give them the word we've got the target again. I want all you clowns to sharpen up." He settled in front of his video screen and pulled the big earphones down over his ears.

The *Medusa* made a long sweeping turn and came back on the reverse course, steaming slowly as the sonar beams probed the ocean bottom. The forward scanning beams picked up the target to the port side and Chief Klinger snapped crisp instructions to the Bridge to alter course slightly. As the *Medusa* passed over the target the sonar buoys were dropped to go arrowing down to the bottom and begin their steady beeping. With the sonar buoys in place the target was marked, easy to find for the camera run.

On the After Well Deck a Chief Boatswain's mate and his crew of seamen had rigged a paravane on a long boom that would be swung over the side of the ship. The paravane would swim out to one side of the ship as it moved through the water. The camera platform, studded with powerful floodlights, would be lowered from the paravane. The Chief checked the maze of rigging cables and spoke into his telephone.

"Ready to make the camera drop, Bridge. Camera and floods have been checked out. Everything four oh. We've got enough cable rigged for a thirteen thousand foot drop."

In the Chartroom on the Bridge Blighty Lee worked with his dividers and parallel rulers, guided by Chief Klinger's reports on the sonar buoy bearings. The *Medusa's* helmsman spun his wheel in response to Lee's quick orders and the *Medusa* came about in a turn and steadied on course. Lee turned to Captain Lutz.

"We're far enough to the east of the target to make the

camera drop, sir. We can hold a steady course at four knots in this sea. Camera drop should take twenty-five minutes." He pointed to the course line on the chart. "We can have the camera in position when we're about a half mile from the target. We can start taking pictures then, just in case there's any debris along the course line that might be important."

"Very well, Blighty," Lutz said. "It might be a dummy run. Chief Klinger said the object on the bottom shows a length of over four hundred feet on the computer readout but he saw no evidence of aircraft wings. He thinks we might have an old freighter that was sunk in World War II down there."

The Officer of the Deck, a young Lieutenant, shook his head. "Awful lot of work for the deck force if it's only some old wreck down there." Lutz and Lee looked at each other. Lee picked up the telephone and ordered the Chief Boatswain's Mate to make the camera drop.

A sonar device on the camera platform beeped steadily as the camera and light platform dropped into the sea. A sonar operator who was ranging on the camera platform studied his video screen and computer readout. The long minutes went by as the cable unreeled and let the camera platform and the floodlights drop ever deeper into the sea. The sonar operator who was watching over the camera platform's depth turned to Klinger.

"Camera platform is at one one zero feet from the bottom, Chief."

"Belay lowering the camera platform," Klinger said into his telephone. "Bridge, camera platform is now one one zero feet from the bottom."

"Very well," Lee answered. "We're making a camera run now. Floodlights are on. Camera is on. I want a full analysis and a bottom charting white-line printout, Sonar and Charting, keep in contact and report anything you see."

Far below the *Medusa's* keel the bright glare of the floodlights illuminated a world that had never before seen light. Small fish with great gaping mouths full of teeth charged at the lights and then turned away. On the sea bottom vast areas of tube worms unfurled in the light, writhing in the slow bottom current. Chief Klinger watched his video screen intently, his whole being concentrated on the pictures the camera was sending back.

"That's a ship's screw!" Klinger rasped into his telephone. "That's got to be a submarine, Bridge! You getting the picture I'm seeing? I'm seeing a submarine with its screw bent off to the port side and I'm damned sure there's a big hole in her stern! That's the sail coming up now, Bridge. That's a submarine!"

"Affirmative, Chief," Lee's voice was calm. "We'll keep taking pictures until we run past the target and then we'll come about and make a run down the reverse course and take pictures. Then we'll get into position again and run on this course and take another set of pictures. How much battery time in those sonar buoys, please?"

"Twenty-four hours, sir." Klinger answered. "Way I saw it, that submarine is on almost an even keel. I think we can get a better picture of the hole I think I saw in her stern if we come back on course a little bit to the starboard of this course run."

"Very well, Chief, will do." Lee turned to the Officer of the Deck. "It wasn't a freighter after all. Let's make the same turn we made before and we'll come back down on the reverse course. I want to get some good pictures of her number on the sail for identification. Move it, damn it, give the orders. You're the Officer of the Deck, you're not here for a pleasure trip."

In the Sonar Compartment one of the men on watch lit a cigaret. "Fucking aircraft we're looking for, hey? That was an SSBN, Chief. I saw the fucking missile hatches plain as day."

"You want to make Chief some day?" Klinger growled. "You, all of you, button your damned mouths when you leave this compartment. There's something screwy going on and those people in Officer's Country aren't giving us the word the way they should. Until I give you the word all of you keep your fucking mouth shut. That's an order."

CHAPTER 5

Vice Admiral Mike Brannon sat at his desk contemplating the lunch tray that had been brought in to him. A dish of cottage cheese topped by a half a peach, two squares of dry toast, and coffee. He made a face and began to eat. There were times, he thought, when the Navy intruded itself too much into a man's personal business. When you passed the age of sixty eating should be a pleasure, not a duty. But the doctors at Bethesda had impressed on Gloria Brannon that the Admiral was carrying too much weight and had to lose twenty-five pounds. Her orders to the Admiral's staff had been clear; the Admiral was on a diet. The staff obeyed orders.

He pushed the tray away as his office door opened. "Priority message from the *Medusa*, Admiral. I cleared the office area of personnel before I ran it through the decoding machine, sir." The Chief Yeoman laid the message on the desk and picked up the tray. "I called Admiral Olsen's office, sir. He's on his way here."

"Thank you, Chief," Brannon said. He read the message through. He was reading it for the second time when John Olsen walked in and closed the door behind him.

"They've found the *Sharkfin, John.*" Brannon's face was grim. "She's on the bottom, right on her course line. Captain Lutz of the *Medusa* says they've got excellent pictures, lots of them."

Olsen looked at Brannon's harsh face. "What do the pictures show, does he say, Mike?"

"Her screw's twisted off to the port side and there's a big hole in her stern. She's on an even keel. Lutz says there's no mistake about the hole. It's there, in her stern. He made four camera runs. The hole shows up clearly." He glared at Olsen. "Just what in the hell could have twisted her screw off to one side and holed her in the stern?"

"It couldn't be anything she hit running submerged," Olsen said.

"I think she was hit by a weapon," Brannon grated. "Lutz says in his message that he's ordered a chopper out of Rota to meet him and pick up the pictures. *Medusa* has a chopper landing pad. But he hasn't got any authority to order the pictures sent here by special courier plane. See the Chief and get that order off in my name at once and find out when the plane will be here.

"I want you to meet the plane and pick up the pictures and bring them here. I want to see Captain Steel now, right now." He picked up the message and read it again as Olsen went into the outer office. He was at his wall chart when Olsen came back into the office, trailed by Captain Steel.

"The *Medusa* has found the *Sharkfin,* Captain," Brannon said. "I need your engineering opinion. We'll have pictures by tomorrow but *Medusa* has told us what the pictures show. *Sharkfin* is on the bottom on an even keel. Her screw is twisted or bent off to the port side. There's a hole in her stern area."

"Is he sure it's the *Sharkfin?*" Steel asked.

"He's got pictures of her number. No doubt. What I'd like to know is, would it be possible for the propeller shaft to burst its bearings or something and run wild and tear up the stern, twist the propeller off to one side?"

"No." Captain Steel said.

"My thought also," Brannon said. "The only other thing that comes to mind is that *Sharkfin* was hit by a weapon that destroyed her screw and blew a hole in her stern."

"You may be right." Steel's tone was grudging. "I told you it wasn't a failure in her nuclear power plant. We need the pictures to make a reasonably accurate analysis. If the pictures bear out your supposition, Admiral, then you've got a very serious problem facing you. You'd better solve it quickly. I won't have my nuclear submarines interfered with by anyone or anything."

Mike Brannon came out of his chair, his face darkening with rage. "Now you get one thing straight, damn it! The nuclear submarines are not *your* Goddamned submarines! They belong to the Navy. And you hear this; I care a hell of a lot more about the hundred and twenty or so sailors who were on the *Sharkfin* than I do about the ship. Is that clear, sir?"

Captain Steel stared at Mike Brannon. "You make it perfectly clear, Admiral. But the problem remains. Someone destroyed the *Sharkfin*. And its crew. And that someone has got to be stopped. I'd rather not say any more until I have seen the pictures."

"Tell your office to notify my Chief Yeoman of your schedule tomorrow. I expect to have pictures then. I'll notify you as soon as they arrive." Brannon turned to John Olsen as Steel left the office.

"You get the message off to Rota?"

Olsen nodded. "Good Chief you've got out there. He had them on the line, waiting, when I went out there. They've got a plane available. It will land at Andrews tomorrow at zero six hundred. I'll be there." He picked up the message and read it.

"The way this reads, Mike, it had to be a weapon. Probably a sound-seeking torpedo fired at her screw. Think it could have been that Soviet attack submarine that tracked her out of the Strait of Gibraltar?"

"I think so," Brannon said. He went to his office door

and opened it. "Chief, please notify Admiral Benson and Mr. Wilson of the CIA that I would appreciate it if they could be here in my office at zero eight hundred. We have information of great importance for them. Notify Captain Steel's office that I expect him here at ten hundred tomorrow. I want you here by zero seven hundred at the latest. I expect to be here at zero six thirty."

The Agency limousine eased out of the Pentagon parking area and began the long trip back to the CIA headquarters. Wilson pushed a button that slid a glass partition between the driver's area and the rear seat and turned to Admiral Benson.

"Those pictures were scary," Wilson said. "They don't leave much doubt about what happened to that submarine. What I'd like to know is, how well do you know Admiral Brannon? He's Irish and like a lot of the Irish he's keeping his feelings to himself but he's boiling inside. What's he likely to do?"

"He's submarine, I was aviation," Admiral Benson said slowly. "I don't know him that well. I know his record, his reputation. He's tough. He's direct. He's a decent man, a hard worker. But what will he do? I think that's pretty clear, Bob. He's got to take this to the President."

"Maybe," Wilson said. He lit a cigaret and watched the smoke swirl away in the car's ventilation system.

"What else can he do?" Benson said. "The pictures are excellent. *Sharkfin* was hit by a weapon fired by a ship from an unknown nation. He's only got one course of action to take, to go to the President."

"Then why did he order an attack submarine to leave Scotland at the same time he ordered that *Medusa* ship to start searching for the *Sharkfin?* Why did he order that attack submarine to go to the area where the *Sharkfin* was sunk and to obey only orders that came from him, from Brannon?"

"Who said he did?"

"We monitor every radio circuit going, you know that," Wilson grunted. "He gave those orders. You give me your guess and I'll give you mine about why he did it. I think he's going to go after that Soviet submarine and sink it."

"He couldn't!" Admiral Benson protested. "His whole career would go down the drain. It's unthinkable!"

"So?" Wilson said. He pushed a button that lowered the window on his side of the car and flipped his cigaret butt through the opening. He raised the window and looked at Benson.

"Admiral Brannon's been in Washington for about three years. He knows the score, as you Navy people say."

"What's that supposed to mean, Wilson?" The CIA Director's voice was suddenly sharp. "I've kept it to myself but you sometimes annoy the hell out of me when you put on that old Washington hand attitude. I know I'm relatively new to Washington but I'm not a complete idiot."

"I apologize, Admiral," Wilson said. "I didn't mean it that way. What I mean is that we've lived in different worlds. In your world, the Navy, you expect people to be loyal, to do a good day's work, to respect rank, that sort of thing. You assume that people can be trusted, especially if they've got rank. In my world, I expect people to be shitheads, if you'll excuse the word.

"What I meant was that Admiral Brannon's been in Washington in a damned tough job long enough to have been stabbed in the back, lied to, and he's learned the score. He knows, I know, that if he takes this to the President—and he may do that, I'm not saying he won't—but if he takes this to the President he knows what will happen.

"What will happen is there will be meetings, a lot of crisis meetings. You can't keep crisis meetings secret in this town. The press will begin to snoop around and you can bet your last dollar that some son of a bitch who spends a lot of his time kissing the President's ass will leak the story to some reporter. And within a few days the whole damned world will know we lost the *Sharkfin*.

"Once the story gets out we won't be able to do a damned thing. The Russians will offer their sympathy and deny everything. We'll be left with egg on our chin, a submarine on the bottom of the ocean, and a lot of good American sailors dead." He lit another cigaret.

"Uncle Sam, the patsy," he growled.

"You believe that?" Benson said.

"I've seen it happen before. The Cuban invasion project is a good example. That was supposed to be absolutely secret. But there were too many meetings, too many people in the damned project. Little things began to leak out. James Reston of the *New York Times* got the whole story weeks before the invasion.

"Happens that Reston is an honorable man. He went to his editors and told them they shouldn't print the story. Might have been better for all of us if he had gone ahead and printed it. That might have killed the damned project." He hunched down in the upholstered seat.

"Brannon knows his way around this town. I have to assume that he knows a little about how the Soviet mind works. If he did order that Soviet submarine wiped out—well, that would be about the best message you could send to the Kremlin. They'd understand that sort of action because that's how they work."

Admiral Benson fiddled with the snaps of the briefcase he held in his lap. "If we suspect he might go after that Soviet submarine, and I don't for one minute think he will do that, but if we did suspect he might we'd be honor bound to go to the President and tell him."

Wilson glanced at Admiral Benson out of the corner of his eye. "And if we did that and Brannon didn't do anything his name would be shit with the President and the Joint Chiefs."

"But if we just sit here and do nothing we're right in the middle!"

"Comes with the territory," Wilson said. "There might be a way around this whole thing, though."

"How?"

48   Harry Homewood

"If we assume the Soviets did sink our submarine, and I'm damned sure they did, they had to have a reason because they don't do things that serious without some reason. Maybe I can find out the reason. I'd need several days to do that, if I can even do it. You'd have to stall Brannon, convince him not to throw the baby out with the bath water while I try."

"I don't know how you expect to do that. We haven't got a single good agent inside of the Soviet Union who is far enough inside the system to know that."

"We don't, sir, but Israel does. Dr. Saul, he's the head of the Mossad, he might know. He's got the best penetration into the Soviet Union of any of us and he's a friend."

"I didn't think of Israel," Benson said slowly. "But if he knows he should have told us by now. We're his best ally."

"That isn't the way the game is played," Wilson grunted. "If it's okay with you I'll go to Tel Aviv and see him. He owes me a few favors. If he knows he'll tell me. I'd like a couple of those pictures Admiral Brannon gave you of the *Sharkfin* to take with me."

Admiral Benson sat quietly, looking out the window, turning the problem over in his mind. He opened and closed a snap on the briefcase and the sharp metallic sound hung in the air.

"I'd better send you an interoffice memo telling you to go to New York, to the United Nations for some talks. That would account for your absence from the office." He looked out the window at the wind-scarred countryside. "I'll get back to Mike Brannon, tell him to stand pat for a few days." He drew a deep breath and let it out slowly. "You know, running a carrier division was a hell of a lot more fun than this job."

Seated in his office with a cup of coffee Wilson looked at his watch. Ten in the morning, Washington time. Five in the afternoon in Tel Aviv. Isser Bernstein, a.k.a. Dr. Saul, would be in his office. No chief of Israel's Mossad, its famed intelligence service, ever went home early. He reached for the scrambler phone and asked to be connected with Dr. Saul's office.

"How's your health, my friend?" Dr. Saul's hearty voice boomed through the mechanical artificiality of the scrambler.

"Not so good, Doctor. Bad attack of nostalgia, I think. I desperately need to see someone."

Wilson sat back in his chair, visualizing the man at the other end of the telephone connection. A short man with a tanned bald head ringed with a fringe of gray hair that matched his small goatee and precisely trimmed mustache. Isser Bernstein was a former Irgun terrorist who had helped form the Mossad in 1945. In the years since he had risen to be its chief and had become a legend in the world's intelligence circles.

"Nostalgia can sometimes be difficult to treat." Bernstein's voice was solemn.

"I know," Wilson said. "I think you're the only doctor who can help me. Do you remember our mutual friend, the one who smokes Kools and who went to a university in New York?"

"Ah, yes. Not a person to help sick people."

"I know but I have to see him if I am to be cured of what ails me. I'd like to do that in your consulting room. Soon. Very soon, Doctor."

"So you suffer also from anxiety. Be calm. Don't drink too much coffee. I will see what I can do."

The call came the next morning from the Israeli Embassy in Washington. A man's voice instructed Wilson to be in New York that afternoon, that a seat had been reserved in his name on El Al Airlines. The man hesitated a moment and then said, "Dr. Saul advises you eat a light lunch, sir. The cuisine on the airline is famed for its excellence. You will be met upon arrival."

When Wilson walked into the terminal at the Lydda Airport the next day he saw Isser Bernstein's secretary waiting for him at the Customs barrier. They smiled at each other and she nodded at the Customs agent who bowed slightly to Wilson.

"Nice to see you again, Naomi," Wilson said. "You get more beautiful every time I see you."

"And you flatter without reason just as much as you always did. It's been more than two years since that weekend in Athens and you never wrote me, not once."

"People in our business don't write letters, you know that. You broke my heart when you told me you wouldn't marry me."

"People in our business don't marry," she said primly. He followed her through the crowded terminal, his trained eye picking out the unobtrusive men who were ahead of them and back of them as they moved through the crowd. Naomi led him to a battered Fiat parked in a No Parking zone. He cramped himself into the bucket seat beside her and reached for his cigarets.

"How's the good doctor, and do you mind if I smoke?"

"He's fine and I do mind. Cigarets give you cancer, don't you know that?" She pulled the car out into the traffic behind a Mercedes with four men in it. "There's another car behind us," she said. "Even here at home Dr. Saul takes no chances."

Twenty minutes later the Fiat pulled up in front of a house surrounded by a high whitewashed wall with sharp spikes studding its top. Two men opened a heavy iron gate and came trotting out to the car. One of the men opened the car door on Wilson's side and extended a hand to assist him out of the car.

"Welcome home, Mr. Wilson," he said, his teeth gleaming in his dark face. "The doctor is inside the gate."

"My old friend from the wars!" Isser Bernstein wrapped his arms around Wilson in a hug. "How is it you grow old and ugly with the years while I get ever more handsome and youthful?" He stepped back, his eyes shrewd. "And how is life for you these days with that airplane jockey your president put at the head of your company?"

"He's a good guy, very bright," Wilson said. "He's hung up on things like loyalty and trust and honesty."

Bernstein shook his head as he led Wilson into the house. "None of those are qualifications for our work. One must be a thief and a liar and have no sense of shame. Which is why we two are such a great success. Come into the kitchen, I must talk with you before Shevenko gets here. We've got a few minutes.

"I have to impose a condition, my friend. This is a very delicate thing you have asked me to do and I have done it. Now I must insist that I sit in on your talk with Shevenko. Moise, you remember Moise Shemanski, he's still my right hand man, he'll sit with me."

Wilson shook his head. "I'd rather not, Isser."

"So I'll leave you alone with Shevenko. Do you know if the room is bugged? No. But you might suspect so you go for a walk in the garden to talk. I can listen to you with a Big Ear. You gave us our first Big Ear and we have made many since then. So what do you want to do? Better to have Moise close by in case that Russian bear decides to give you a hug."

"You've got a point," Wilson said. "We'll do it your way. But don't interrupt unless I ask you to do so."

"Who interrupts? I don't like talking to that bastard."

The meeting was held in the kitchen. Wilson and Shevenko sat across from each other at the kitchen table with cups of steaming coffee in front of them. Isser Bernstein and Moise Shemanski, a burly, taciturn Pole who had escaped from a Nazi concentration camp in 1944 and made his way to Israel, sat in wooden chairs against one wall of the kitchen.

Shevenko raised his coffee cup as if offering a toast. "We meet again, Bob. It was worth the long trip just to see you." He sipped at his coffee. "I might say also that it is almost worth the trip to taste this coffee. You would not believe the coffee we get in our building at home. It must be the water, not even the best American instant coffee tastes very good."

"You know why I want to see you," Wilson said.

"I am not good at guessing games, my friend. Tell me."

"One of our ballistic missile submarines was attacked and sunk by one of your submarines. The attack took place in the Atlantic, west of the Strait of Gibraltar. That was a deliberate act of war, Shevenko."

"A very serious charge, Bob," Shevenko said slowly. "More serious because it is made in the presence of our mutual friends. What is the basis for such a charge?"

Wilson opened his attache case and pulled out several eight by ten black and white photographs. He spread them out on the table in front of Shevenko.

"You can have two of these to take home with you. Take your pick. It's not conjecture, Shevenko."

The Russian studied the pictures. "What astounding clarity!" he said in a low voice. "At that depth!" He looked at Wilson and slowly slid two of the pictures over to one side. "I may have these? Thank you. I know of an admiral or two who are going to come down with a bad case of diarrhea when they see these pictures." He raised his coffee cup and sipped slowly, his eyes steady on Wilson.

"Give me a reason for this insanity," Wilson said.

"Between sane men there can be no reason, no rationale," Shevenko answered. "I was against the operation from the beginning. I argued against it as long as it was politic for me to do so. We have as many fools in our Politburo and our military as you do in your Congress and Pentagon. Maybe more."

"That's no answer," Wilson said.

"Because there is no answer," Shevenko said. "No answer that will satisfy you or would satisfy me if I were sitting in your chair." He shrugged his heavy shoulders.

"The only thing I can offer you is the truth, a rare commodity in our business but often useful. Your nuclear ballistic submarines, which you call a nuclear deterrent, are to us a nuclear threat. Our cities could be subjected to holocaust, a word our hosts know very well."

"Doesn't wash, Shevenko. Your side has nuclear ballistic missile submarines."

"Of course," Shevenko said. "But you don't see through our eyes. We have the longest border in the world and most of it is landlocked, not available for submarine ports. We have only two major submarine ports, one in the north on the Kola Peninsula. In order to get to the Atlantic our submarines have to pass between Britain and Greenland." He leaned back in his chair and smiled his thanks as Moise brought a hot pot of coffee from the sideboard.

"We know, my friend, that you have sown the bottom of the sea with listening devices so that you will know when one of our submarines makes the passage to the Atlantic and we know, as well, that you have mines laid so that if you wished you could blow our submarines up before they ever got to the open waters of the Atlantic." His hands closed tightly around the heavy coffee mug.

"Over to the east we have our only other nuclear submarine base, at Petropavlovsk. There again, we know that as soon as one of our submarines heads for the open Pacific it must run the guantlet of your listening devices and mines.

"You can understand, I think, that this has made our admirals paranoiac. Your nuclear missile submarines can roam the seas of the world without our knowledge of where they are. Ours cannot."

"The weak point in that argument, Igor, is that you know damned well that we are never going to launch a nuclear attack against anyone."

Shevenko shrugged. "I know that. I even believe it. But that is not the only thing that concerns our military leaders and our Politburo.

"Your president has started on a course that will lead to friendship between the United States and Mainland China."

"Communist China," Wilson interrupted.

"Mainland China. Those bastards are not Communists. But let's not argue about semantics. Mainland China is not only dangerous to us but also to the rest of the world, a point that your president cannot seem to recognize.

"Some of the fools in our Navy developed a new torpedo. If you don't know all about it I am sure our friends here do and will tell you if you ask. Like too many military men, yours and ours, they could not rest until they had tested this new torpedo under actual conditions.

"That is the truth of this madness, the only truth. I give you my word, which is good no matter what you happen to think."

"Why did you argue against the operation. Don't you share the same fears?"

"I am a realist, Bob. You know that. I argued against it because I can see the long range consequences. You might attack in retaliation. One for one and then two for two and then the nuclear holocaust we all fear if we are sane. We, you, would be burnt toast with no marmalade because if you strike first you cannot stop our counterstrike any more than we can stop your counterstrike if we were to attack first." The eyelids over the hard blue eyes opened wide as Shevenko stared at Wilson.

"Our admirals have gambled that you would not respond. I am not so sure. Not even now, although when our good friend the doctor asked me to come here at once I reasoned that you wanted to talk instead of starting a war."

"Don't be too confident," Wilson said.

"If you are foolish," Shevenko said, "if a nuclear war does start who stands to gain? Peking. Only Peking. They would love to see us at each other's throats with nuclear weapons. They would rule the world when the fires were out, as they will anyway in fifty years or less.

"So how do we avoid this? You would not have asked to meet me if you did not have some plan."

"The people I am speaking for want Brezhnev to get on the hot line to the President," Wilson said. "If he will do that and tell the President that a horrible tragedy has happened and that it was a terrible mistake maybe we can get out of this mess by covering up the cause of our submarine's loss."

"Does your president want Brezhnev to do this?"

"He doesn't know anything about this, yet."

"Leonid Brezhnev is a proud man, Bob. Your people are asking for a lot. I don't know if I can do what you ask. You must have considered this angle and you must have an alternative."

"Your submarine will be destroyed," Wilson said.

"Tit for tat," Shevenko murmured. "Once that happens there will be no easy way to stop it. I can try. But I may not be able to even see Leonid let alone sit down and talk about this matter."

"You were able to talk to Khrushchev in Sixty-two," Wilson said. "If I recall you had more to do with stopping that Cuban missile crisis than anyone."

"Nikita was a shrewd peasant, a poker player. He knew when to throw in his hand. I don't think Brezhnev plays poker. He is stubborn, very proud. You are asking him to humble himself."

"Better to be humble than to be burnt toast."

"And if he does listen to me, what sort of reparations will your president demand?"

"I don't know if he will demand anything. Let them work that out."

Shevenko sighed. "I will try, old friend. I will do my best. I will give you my word on that on the grave of my mother whose soul is now with God."

"You toss His name around pretty loosely for a Communist, don't you think? Isser almost choked when you said that."

"My mother taught me well. She taught me that God forgives all sins. In my work I have had to do some things that even our hosts might consider sinful." Isser Bernstein rolled his eyes upward and shook his head. Shevenko saw the gesture and smiled.

"The package your people took from me when I got into

your car, Isser, could I have it now? Your bomb people have had time to open it and see what is inside."

Moise Shemanski left the room and returned with a brown paper package tied with cord.

"Cuban cigars," Shevenko said to Wilson. "We know that your new boss likes a good cigar after dinner. These are the best. The paper and string are from New York. You could maybe tell him that a friend in the United Nations gave you the cigars. He would probably faint if he knew you got them from a KGB man." He sat back in his chair and grinned at the other men.

"I can give you four or five days, no more," Wilson said. "My people have to know by then if Brezhnev will make the phone call."

"Of course," Shevenko said. "Isser, could you do me a small favor in return for my coming here on such short notice? If I sent you a bottle of the water in our building could you have your chemists analyze it? Our chemists know nothing about coffee, they only know about tea. If it's the water ruining my coffee I may have to get bottled water from West Germany." He turned back to Wilson.

"One more thing, I was going to notify you through Dobrynin that I have asked Fidel to get me tickets to the Super Bowl game in Miami. I asked him to route me from Havana through Mexico City. I'll keep you advised of my itinerary through the diplomatic pouch, if that's all right with you."

Wilson shrugged.

"I'll call Isser every day; it's easier for me to contact him than to get in touch with you."

The door opened and two Mossad agents came in. Shevenko stood up and shook hands with the three men and left. Bernstein led Wilson into the living room and Naomi came in with a plate of sandwiches, crisp slices of cucumber between thin slices of whole wheat bread that had been spread with sour cream.

"You should have served him some of these sandwiches,"

Wilson said. "He might have offered to buy up your whole cucumber crop."

"I will watch him drink coffee but I will not eat with him," Bernstein said. "You shook him badly with those pictures. He caved in, admitted the crime. I have known him a long time. I have never seen him so upset."

"I didn't see any sign of that," Wilson said. He finished his sandwich and reached for a second one as Naomi poured fresh coffee.

"People in our business are schooled to show no emotion in their face or their hands," Bernstein said. "I was watching his feet under the table. He was upset."

"The important thing is that he got the message," Wilson said. "All I have to worry about is whether he will contact Brezhnev and if he does, if Brezhnev will call the President."

Bernstein chewed slowly. "I would say that Shevenko will try to carry out his part of the bargain. But there is a manic atmosphere in the Politburo. Brezhnev might not be able to take the political risk of backing down from a Politburo decision."

"How much do you know about that?" Wilson eyed the Mossad chief.

"I know the vote to test the torpedo was five to four. One member of the Politburo was sick and did not vote. Brezhnev could have cast the tie vote and that would have ended the matter for some time but he did not vote. So he might not feel strong enough to risk calling the President." He looked at his wrist watch. "Time for you to go, my friend. Pray tonight, as I will, that this madness will go no further. I will be in touch with you after each of Shevenko's calls to me."

Sitting in the living room with Schemanski, who was finishing the last of the sandwiches, Bernstein turned to his aide. "Did you catch that reference Shevenko made to Bob, telling him to tell his boss that he got the cigars at the United Nations? Leah told us that his cover for being away from his office was an inter-office memo ordering him to go to New York to see some people at the UN. You'd better get word to Leah at once and warn her that Shevenko may have an agent inside the CIA who also reads inter-office memos."

"I think you'd better warn Mr. Wilson, too," Shemanski said.

"How can I do that? If we do he'd start searching for Leah. I don't want her cover blown. It took a long while to get her in place."

"We should find some way to tell him," Shemanski insisted. "It's not nice to keep that sort of thing from a friend who once saved the lives of your wife and daughter."

"He saved my life too, more than once," Bernstein said. "I owe him debts I can never repay. Let me think about it. I want you to take the tape reel off the recorder and get the film from the camera upstairs. I wonder if there was enough light in the kitchen to get good pictures of those photos Bob spread out on the table?"

"I'm sure there was," Shemanski said.

"We'll know soon enough," Bernstein said. "Get the tape and the film and then we'll go back to the office."

CHAPTER 6

Igor Shevenko retraced the route he had taken to get to Israel. By plane from Lydda Airport to Rome and then on to West Berlin. He was met at the airport there by a nervous agent who was not worried at the prospect of easing his Director back through the Iron Curtain but concerned that Shevenko would think him nervous and thus not trustworthy. He boarded a Soviet airliner with a malfunctioning heater system and spent the trip to Moscow shivering in the cold. In his office he rubbed at eyes that were scratchy from lack of sleep. Stefan Lubutkin rushed in with hot coffee and a plate of caraway seed cookies.

"You are tired, Comrade Director," Lubutkin said solicitously. "The meeting in East Berlin was difficult?"

"All meetings are a waste of time, you know that," Shevenko growled. "East Berlin is a dead city, I hate it. Not even Lenin could have revived it." He looked at his aide out of the corner of his eye, wondering if Lubutkin suspected that he had gone far south of East Berlin.

"It is not a frivolous city, that is true," Lubutkin said solemnly. "But in time, when Germany is reunited under our rule, it will change."

"Get me Admiral Zurahv on the phone," Shevenko said. He chewed a cookie, savoring the delicate taste of the caraway seeds.

An hour later Shevenko met the Admiral in a park. The two men, the Admiral, bearlike in his uniform greatcoat, Shevenko in a heavy sheepskin-lined coat and a warm muffler, walked along a pathway.

"It is safe to talk here, Admiral," Shevenko began. "What I have to tell you is for your ears alone." He stopped and flicked a heavy gobbet of snow from the winter-nude branches of a bush.

"The Americans have found their submarine, Admiral."

"Impossible," the Admiral grunted. He kicked at a clump of ice on the pathway and sent it skittering. "You cannot put a diver down two thousand fathoms and the only deep submergence vessel that could go that deep is in Hawaii."

Shevenko reached inside his coat and pulled out a brown manila envelope. He opened it and handed one of the two photographs Wilson had given him to the Admiral.

Zurahv studied the picture for a long moment and then stared at Shevenko, who handed him the envelope. "I got this from one of my people who was afraid to trust it to the diplomatic pouch, Admiral. I had to go to East Berlin to meet him. I brought the picture back to give to you. I assure you it is genuine."

Zurahv held the photograph up and looked at it closely. He put it in the envelope and smiled at Shevenko. "I know it is genuine, Comrade," he said jovially. "It bears out exactly what the research people said would happen when the weapon hit the screw of a ballistic submarine and that research report is known by only a very few people. So now we must go to full production of the weapon."

"That is your decision to make of course, Admiral. But now that you are convinced that the information I learned is genuine I must offer you the rest of the package. I assure you it is also genuine.

"The Americans have not announced the loss of their submarine. They will do so, of course, and attribute the loss to an unknown mechanical failure. But not until after they have destroyed one of our submarines, Admiral. The obvious target of them is the submarine that carried out the weapons test. If I may, sir, I would suggest you move that submarine to a safe area."

"Bull's balls!" the Admiral snorted. "The Americans would not dare take such an action. They don't have the political freedom to act in that way. They don't have the will to do such a thing."

"If the cow had the balls she would be the bull," Shevenko said softly. "Never underestimate what an enemy might do."

"How certain is your man that they intend to retaliate in this manner?" Admiral Zurahv asked.

"He is as certain as that photograph, Admiral. What gives his story greater credence is the fact that the President has not yet been informed of the loss of their submarine. Only a very few top naval officers know about it. They have decided on retaliation on their own."

"Igor, old friend," the Admiral said, "We both know the Americans would not dare to do such a thing. They never have. History proves that."

"Don't depend on history, Admiral. A small group of dedicated naval officers, let us say almost as dedicated to their cause as you are to ours, such a small group can insure secrecy of their actions and can act. They will retaliate."

"No," Zurahv said. "I do not agree. They know what we would do if they did that. We would put all our important people and most of our population into the air raid shelters and do what we should have done long ago, burn every major city in America, destroy every military installation. They have no civil defense, your own reports have proved that, no way of protecting their population as we have." He filled his great chest with the cold air and let it out with a mightly whoosh. "And then, my friend, we will do the same thing to Mainland China!"

"I don't disagree with your thesis, Admiral, but I would

point out that we cannot keep our people in the shelters for very long. The psychiatrists and psychologists say that two weeks is the maximum before severe strain sets in. The American missile submarines, knowing their homeland is a charred waste, could wait longer than that before they loose their nuclear devastation on us."

"You make a good point," Zurahv said. "But I still cannot accept the idea that a small group of naval officers will act this way. It is not the way they are trained, not the way they think."

"The man who commands their submarines in the Atlantic is named Brannon. He is a ranking Admiral. Do you know him?"

"I have never met him, of course," Zurahv said. "I know his record. A courageous and aggressive submarine commander in the Great War. A very good administrator since the war. A professional."

"Aggressive, you say," Shevenko murmured. He stooped and picked up a chunk of ice and tossed it into the middle of a bush heavy with wet snow. The ice chunk sent a cascade of snow tumbling to the ground.

"From small disturbances much downfall," Shevenko said in a soft voice. "I must be getting back to my office, Comrade. *Blagodar'yoo.*" He used the colloquial "thank you" and smiled. "I trust that what I have told you, the picture I have given to you, will remain only with you?"

"You have my word, Igor, and my deepest thanks," Zurahv said.

As soon as he returned to his office Admiral Zurahv called for the file on Vice Admiral Michael P. Brannon. He read it through slowly and then rang for his aide.

"Send a priority message to Captain Kovitz. Order him to clear his patrol area at once and proceed, submerged, to Tripoli. No shore leave for officers or crew. Further orders will follow. Tell my staff I want to see them here within the hour."

Stefan Lubutkin laid Admiral Zurahv's decoded message

on Shevenko's desk. "The Admiral has switched over to his new code, sir."

"As long as he doesn't know we can read it," Shevenko said. He picked up the message, read it, and smiled.

Bob Wilson slept soundly on the flight to New York and dozed fitfully on the short flight to Washington. The Agency limousine was waiting for him at Washington's National Airport. Carrying the wrapped box of cigars he went directly to Admiral Benson's office.

"Cuban cigars," he said. "Friend of mine at the UN gave them to me. I stopped there to cover the memo you sent."

"How nice of him," Benson said. He looked at Wilson. "How do they get Cuban cigars at the UN?"

"I think they come in through Switzerland. You want me to give you a debriefing now or wait?"

"Now," Benson said. He uncapped a gold pen.

"I was met at the Lydda Airport and taken to Dr. Saul's country place. He knew about the loss of the *Sharkfin*. There's been too much radio traffic and they can read most of our codes, just as we can read theirs. Dr. Saul knew why the Soviets sank the *Sharkfin*."

"That's incredible!" Benson said. "I know the Mossad are good but to know something like that?"

Wilson shrugged. "Look at it this way, sir. The Mossad has an advantage no one else has. The Soviet Union is full of dissident Jews who want to emigrate to Israel and the Russians won't let them go. Every once in a while the Mossad smuggles some of them out of Russia. Nearly all the Jews in the Soviet Union are sponges. They soak up all sorts of information and some of them feed it to Mossad agents in the hope they'll be taken out of Russia. You get enough pieces in place and you can solve any jigsaw puzzle."

"Did Dr. Saul know why the Soviets did this?"

Wilson repeated what Shevenko had told him. When he finished, Benson asked what his response had been.

"Dr. Saul has a top agent in Cairo. That guy knows the top KGB man in Cairo so word is going to get back to the KGB inside a day. I told Dr. Saul to tell the KGB that the only way out of this mess is to have Brezhnev call the President and tell him a terrible mistake has been made and that it won't happen again."

"What makes you think Brezhnev would do that?"

"I don't know if he will," Wilson said slowly. "But it's worth a try. If he does then the whole mess stops right there. I think that the Kremlin will read the message pretty clearly. They play hard ball all the time. This is the sort of language they understand and pay attention to."

Admiral Benson capped his pen. "I think we'd better go see Admiral Brannon. But I don't think we should tell him that you passed the word that we might sink the Soviet submarine. No sense in getting his Irish up. I just thought of something. Suppose that Brezhnev does call the President? The whole overhead will fall on Admiral Brannon for not reporting the loss of the *Sharkfin.*"

Wilson ground out his cigaret in an ashtray. "That's his worry, sir. He was the one who decided to keep this quiet, not us."

Admiral Olsen reached for the coffee carafe and poured for himself and Mike Brannon. "What do you think, Mike? I don't much like Wilson going off like that without telling us but it's done now and we can't undo it. Do you think Brezhnev will call? And if he does what the hell are you going to tell the President when he wants to know why he wasn't told about the *Sharkfin?*"

"I don't think he'll call," Brannon said. "If he does I can take the heat. I've got a hunch there's a lot we're not being told. That damned Soviet submarine was picked up on SOSUS heading back into the Mediterranean. God knows where she'll end up, maybe in the Black Sea." He drained his coffee cup.

"Get off a message to Dick Reinauer on the *Orca.* I want him to proceed at all possible speed and rendezvous with the *Devilfish.* Tell the Black Room I want an ID on every ship that goes through the Strait of Gibraltar, I want to be told that information no matter what the time of day or night. I'll blockade that damned Strait and if that murdering bastard of a submarine comes out I'll sink the son of a bitch!"

Admiral Zurahv finished telling his staff what Shevenko had told him an hour or so earlier and passed the photograph Shevenko had given him down the table.

"Give me your thoughts, gentlemen," he said in his heavy voice.

"Comrade Admiral," a heavy set naval captain sitting down near the end of the table said. "The evidence is clear from this photograph. The Americans have found their submarine and any naval officer of experience can tell what happened to it.

"What we must do now is reason how they found their ship. I would say they used a bottom-charting sonar ship. They are very good at charting the ocean bottoms with sonar. We are sent their bottom charts from the United Nations and I have found them to be most accurate.

"If they used a sonar search to find the submarine then they would mark the submarine on the bottom with sonar buoys. We use sonar buoys in the same way, when we have lost a practice torpedo, for example. Sonar buoy batteries operate for a month before they run down."

"So?" Admiral Zurahv rumbled.

"When I was reading the daily ship movement report this morning I noticed that we have a freighter loading citrus fruits and tobacco in the port of Bengasi. We used that same freighter last year in submarine maneuvers off the Aleutians. She has simple but effective sonar equipment on board. I suggest we send that ship along the course of the American submarine to listen for sonar buoys."

"A good idea," Zurahv said. "What's her next port of call, do you remember?"

"Odessa, sir."

"Change it," Zurahv ordered. "Get those assholes in the commercial departments moving to sell her cargo in France or the Netherlands so we'll have a reason for changing her next port of call. Notify Lloyds of the change of ports, we want this to look normal." He looked down the table.

"How many of the new torpedoes do we have on hand?"

"Eleven, sir," a Commander answered.

"Send them to attack submarines. Order a crash production schedule at once. As soon as the new torpedoes come out of the factory I want them tested and sent to operating submarines. Dismissed."

CHAPTER 7

The U.S.S. *Orca*, sister ship of the U.S.S. *Devilfish*, raced southward at 500 feet, her nuclear reactor plant turning out 75 percent of its rated capacity. There was an air of quiet satisfaction, of competence proved, aboard the *Orca*. The chase of a Soviet missile submarine that had been detected by the sensor network as it left the Atlantic and headed northeast between the British Isles and Greenland had been successful.

The *Orca* had taken up the chase, traveling at high speed until the computer charting of the Soviet submarine's course and position indicated that *Orca* was within extreme sonar range. The *Orca*'s crew went to Battle Stations and Captain Dick Reinauer began the delicate process of closing on the Soviet submarine without being detected. Periodically, the *Orca* turned to port or starboard to allow the lateral sensors along its hull to focus on the noise made by the other submarine as it moved through the sea. Gradually, steadily, the *Orca* closed the range.

The Soviet submarine, apparently unaware it was being followed, continued steadily on course. The *Orca* crept closer, running silent with all unnecessary machinery shut down to avoid detection. The crew talked in whispers. Captain Reinauer spoke softly into a telephone to the Battle Stations sonar operator.

"How do you read him?"

"He's noisy as hell," the sonar operator answered in a whisper. "He's got a cooling water pump that must have worn out its bearings. He's got a chip on one blade of his screw or else the screw is warped a little, he's making a hell of a lot of screw noise."

"Start computer constant ranging," Reinauer ordered. He watched the video screen in front of him in the Attack Center as white figures began to appear on the screen.

"Twenty-one hundred yards," Reinauer whispered to Arnold Eckert, his Executive Officer. "I think this is close enough. We'll take him now." He picked up the telephone.

"Sonar, stand by for a transmission." He turned to Eckert. "Come left to course three three five. Sonar, send the following message. 'Tag, you're it. Sorry we can't invite you aboard for a cup of coffee.' End of message. I want you to hit him with every decibel we've got in the transmitters. XO, come to all ahead full as soon as the transmission starts. Sonar, transmit!"

The sonar operator on the Soviet submarine screamed in agony and tore his earphones off as the *Orca*'s powerful sonar transmitters blasted their sound into the Russian submarine's sonar ears. There was silence for a few moments and then the Soviet submarine's answer came back.

"We would prefer tea, thank you. You are very good at this game, my friend. I may send my sonar crew for a long walk on the ice the next time we go to the Pole. End transmission."

The *Orca* swung away in a long curving arc, slowing to her usual twenty-knot cruising speed. "We can chalk up a solid hit on that one," Reinauer said with a grin, his white teeth gleaming in his curly black beard. "We nailed that rascal fair and square. He never heard us at all. That's the third one of those bastards we've sneaked up on without them knowing it. Let's go home, Arnie. Set a course for Holy Loch." He turned to the Officer of the Deck.

"Take her up to periscope depth and send an exercise concluded message. Tell them the score is three to nothing, our favor. We'll advise ETA at Holy Loch later."

The *Orca*'s radioman sent the transmission and then punched a button on a tape cassette as a light showed on his console. He picked up the telephone and dialed the Attack Center.

"Incoming radio traffic, sir. Routine message indicated."

Sitting in his small cabin Captain Reinauer read through the message. Lieutenant Eckert, who functioned as the ship's Navigator as well as Executive Officer, came into the cabin.

"You wanted me, sir?"

"We aren't going home," Reinauer said. "We're ordered to rendezvous with the *Devilfish* down off the Strait of Gibraltar. ComSubLant's orders. He'll advise us further."

"I wondered where the *Devilfish* was going when she left Holy Loch in such a hurry," Eckert said. "Gibraltar? I'd guess some of the Sixth Fleet is going home and we're going to make dummy attacks. When it's over maybe we'll get liberty in some good port in Portugal or Spain."

"Lay down a course and advise me of our ETA on station," Reinauer said. "We're supposed to make all possible speed. Put that in the log book."

"Will do," Eckert said. "Bet you a beer that Iron Mike has got something planned to shake up the surface ship boys. And we can do that, provided the *Devilfish* doesn't foul things up."

"Bob Miller doesn't make mistakes," Reinauer said. "He's a damned good submariner and the *Devilfish* is a good ship."

"Nobody's as good as we are, Skipper. Oh, almost forgot, sir. Turk Raynor wants to see you on personal business. You want me to notify him he can see you now?"

Reinauer nodded. "Better notify the crew we're not going back to Holy Loch, that we're on a special training exercise with *Devilfish*. I want everyone on their toes. I don't want *Devilfish* to outdo us, no matter what the exercise is."

Wilbur "Turk" Raynor, TM1/c, rapped softly on the bulkhead of the Captain's cabin and entered when he heard the command to do so. He stood at attention in the center of the small cabin.

"At ease, Turk," Captain Reinauer said. "Sit down in that chair. What's on your mind?"

"I want off, Captain," Raynor said. His large, seamed face was set and hard.

"Off? What do you mean?"

"I want a transfer back to the diesel boats when we get back to port, sir."

Captain Reinauer took a pack of cigarets out of his pocket and offered one to the torpedoman, who shook his head. "Now wait a minute, Turk. You know what you're asking for? You're asking for the worst mark that could ever be put in your record, you realize that?"

"Yes, sir, I know that. I still want off, sir."

"Let's make it man to man," Reinauer said quietly. "Word of honor, Turk. What you say to me is like saying it to one of your gang. What's wrong? This is a happy ship, isn't it?"

"It's a good ship, Captain, and you're a good skipper. The best. But I'm just tired of being a second class citizen in this submarine Navy. I want back on the diesel boats where I don't have those damned nuke people to contend with."

"Second class citizen is a pretty harsh phrase," Reinauer said slowly. "You're the leading torpedoman aboard. I've given you as high a quarterly marks as I could give, four-oh on deportment and everything else except three nine on proficiency in rate and no one is four-oh in proficiency. Not even the captain of a submarine."

"That's one of the things I want away from, sir. All the nuke people get an automatic four-oh on everything, direct order from Captain Steel. It isn't fair, sir."

"That's something I can't change," Reinauer said. "Okay, we're talking man to man, what I say stays with you. What you say stays with me. Let me tell you a few things you might not know.

"I've given you the quarterly marks you deserve and those

marks are damned high. That makes you a good man in the Navy's eyes. If you ask for a transfer out of nuclear submarines that's a black eye for Captain Steel, if you see what I mean. He doesn't want good men asking to get out of nuclear submarines.

"What they'll do when we get back to port and I submit your request is haul you up in front of a special board. The only way that board can justify the transfer of a good man is to find him unreliable to serve in any area where there is nuclear power or nuclear weapons.

"You know what that means? It means the end of your career. You'll never make Chief. I doubt you'll get diesel submarine duty. They'll put you on some yard tug or as a Master at Arms in some recruit training camp until you get your twenty years in. How long will that be, three more years? Or they could send you to a weather station up on the deep frost line in Alaska. You'll never make Chief, never."

"I'm never going to make Chief anyway," Raynor said stubbornly. "I've taken the Chief's exam every six months for the past four years, sir. Never scored less than three nine. They don't make very many Chief Torpedomen, you know that. Those they do make are all nuke dudes, that four-oh across the board on their quarterly marks gives them the edge they need to beat the non-nuke types. It's a losing game, Captain."

"It might change, you know that. A lot of things have changed since Vice Admiral Brannon took over as ComSubLant. The word I've been given is that he isn't through making changes in some of Captain Steel's directives."

"That won't change things much, Captain. This whole submarine Navy has to be changed, sir. We're talking man to man, okay, let me lay it on you.

"I've been in the Navy for seventeen years. I've got a clean record, never been in trouble, always did my job. I've been First Class for nine years, sir. You've got Chiefs in this nuclear Navy who've only been in the Navy for five, six years! They ship in for nukes under that damned Ninety-Nine Zero

One program, they go to school for two, three years, and they come out of school as Second Class Petty Officers. A year later they're made First Class. A year after that they're Chiefs.

"I know that Admiral Brannon has made changes. He's a good man, I had him as a Squadron Commander when I first went to diesel submarines, when I got out of boot camp and sub school. When I went into the nukes the damned nuke sailors didn't even have to carry stores and that was Captain Steel's direct order. His nuke people didn't even have to keep their living spaces clean! We guys, the second class citizens who hadn't qualified for his nuclear schools had to do the dirty work aboard submarines. Sure, I know Admiral Brannon has changed a lot of that stuff but I'm still a second class citizen in this Navy, Captain.

"Look at this ship. It's a damned good submarine and you're a damned good Captain. But when we're in port, which isn't very damned much, we have two Officers of the Watch, one senior officer in charge of the reactor end of the ship, one junior officer in charge of the rest of us. We have two Chiefs of the Watch, two Watch sections. Last time we were in port I was Acting Chief of the Watch and the Senior Chief of the Watch was a nuke Chief Electronics Technician who's been in the Navy six years and he never smelled salt water until he came aboard here six months ago. And he's giving me orders! I've had it up to here, Captain. I want off, sir. And if they don't like it they can give me my discharge."

"You feel that strongly, Raynor? You'd throw away seventeen years of good service?"

Turk Raynor stood up. "Yes, sir, I do."

"Think it over," Captain Reinauer said. "We're probably going to be on this exercise for a week or more. See me before we get back into port and let's talk again." He smiled. "And thanks for leveling with me, Turk. I appreciate it."

Eckert knocked at the cabin bulkhead and came in and found Captain Reinauer sitting at his desk.

"Here's our ETA on station, sir, and our course. What did the Turk want, Skipper, anything important?"

"He wants out of nukes," Reinauer said.

"My God, another one? The Chief Quartermaster put the same request to me earlier today. Two people in the radio gang feel the same way. It's almost like a disease."

"Call it the 'Captain Steel disease,'" Captain Reinauer said. "What the hell can you do about it?"

"Not much except what I'm doing," Reinauer said. "Write another confidential letter to Admiral Brannon and fill him in on the way things are."

The buzzer on Mike Brannon's telephone console sounded. "Commander Fencer of Operations on the line, sir," Brannon's Chief Yeoman said. Brannon picked up the phone and punched the lighted button on the console.

"Commander Fencer, sir. We have a SOSUS report on a surface ship that cleared the Strait of Gibraltar. That ship then proceeded on an identical course followed by the *Sharkfin* and held to that course until it passed out of sensor range, sir."

"You wouldn't have an ID on that ship, would you, John?"

"So happens we do, Admiral. We footprinted her a year or so ago off the Aleutians. She was working as a target for Soviet submarines and she got over the SOSUS network there. We got her footprint and an aircraft visual on her, sir. She's a Soviet general cargo freighter, ten thousand tons, cargo booms fore and aft. She's got some sonar gear aboard. We heard her working the Soviet submarines."

"Thank you," Brannon said. "Please keep me informed." He turned to John Olsen who had walked in with a thick stack of papers.

"Manpower reports on re-enlistments, Mike." Brannon filled Olsen in on the report from the Black Room.

"What the hell is she doing running down the *Sharkfin*'s course line?" Brannon said. "How many Soviet freighters clear the Med and head out on that course? She'd be on a more southerly heading if she was going to Cuba."

"We could find out," Olsen said. "If Fencer has her foot-printed then he knows her name and registry. We could check with Lloyds. Where's the *Medusa?*"

"I moved her fifty miles to the north. *Devilfish* is near her. I didn't want *Medusa* too close to the *Sharkfin* in case that rogue submarine came back. The captain of that damned submarine might be off his rocker. If he came back and saw *Medusa* there he might take a crack at her.

"Let me know what Lloyds says about that freighter's next port of call," Brannon walked to the chart on his wall and studied it as Olsen left.

B ob Wilson's secretary stepped out of her office. "Marjorie just rang me. Admiral Benson is on his way down the hall to see you. Button your shirt collar and get your tie back up where it belongs. I'll get some coffee. Do all sailors drink coffee all the time?"

"Yup," Wilson said. He cinched up his tie and straightened up the mass of paper on his desk. Admiral Benson walked in the door as Wilson's secretary put two cups of coffee on his desk. The Admiral smiled his thanks and sat down in a chair beside the desk.

"You hear anything from the Mossad as yet?"

"Just conversation," Wilson said. "Dr. Saul calls every day. Their reports confirm what we're hearing. A lot of in-fighting going on in the Politburo. We can make a good guess what it's all about."

"No indication of whether Brezhnev will call the President?"

"We'll know the minute he does," Wilson said. "We've got a tap on the hot line so we'll know as soon as he calls."

Admiral Benson's face went white. "My God!" he said in a half whisper. "You can't be serious! The Agency hasn't tapped the President's hot line to the Soviet Union!"

"We did that the day it was installed," Wilson said. "It would surprise you to know how mealy-mouthed some of our big, bold Presidents really are. I think what this country needs is a President who knows all the four-letter words and who'd say them out loud to the Russians." He grinned at Admiral Benson.

"I'd love to have a camera in place in the Kremlin if we had a President like that and watch the interpreter's face when he had to tell Brezhnev that the President of the United States just told him to go fuck himself."

Admiral Benson shook his head like a prize fighter who had just been hit with a hard left hook. "When is the deadline for that phone call?"

"Tomorrow evening, sir. But we shouldn't be too rigid on that. You've got a seven hour time difference between Moscow and here. The Politburo likes to meet in the evening, which makes it early afternoon here, but sometimes they meet until late at night. Which means they might not take any action until the following day, Moscow time."

"So we wait," Benson said.

"Yup," Wilson said. "And for your information, sir, Admiral Brannon has ordered another attack submarine to join up with that one he sent to where the *Sharkfin* was sunk."

CHAPTER 8

Admiral Brannon stopped at the desk of his Chief Yeoman and took off his muffler and his heavy uniform overcoat. The Chief looked at his desk notepad.

"You've got a meeting with the Joint Chiefs of Staff at lunch, sir. One call this morning from the Sub Base at New London. They want to know when *Sharkfin* will arrive. I told them you'd get back to them sometime today. Admiral Olsen is in your office, sir." Brannon nodded his thanks and went in to his office.

"Morning, John," he said to Olsen. "You get any information on that Soviet freighter from Lloyds?"

"Her original port of call was Odessa with tobacco and citrus fruits from Libya, Mike. Her skipper notified Lloyds that his owners had diverted him to France, to Brest."

"Doesn't figure," Brannon said. "He could have gone across the Mediterranean and offloaded in Marseilles. Saved a lot of sea time and fuel. Fencer said that freighter had worked with Soviet subs off the Aleutians, that's where they got her footprint. He said the freighter was working Soviet submarines with sonar. My guess is that the Russians have sent her down *Sharkfin*'s course to find out if the *Medusa* put down sonar buoys around the *Sharkfin*."

"Might be that they didn't believe what Wilson told to his contact in Israel," Olsen said slowly. "They want to run a check for themselves." He looked at Brannon.

"The deadline for that phone call from Brezhnev is tonight, Mike."

The red light on Bob Wilson's scrambler telephone flashed and then began to blink. Wilson picked up the telephone handset and heard Isser Bernstein's voice.

"I don't have good news, Bob," Bernstein said. "We have learned that the person who is supposed to make that telephone call has been sick in bed for the past week. He has a bad case of Asian Flu." Bernstein chuckled. "I think that's a sort of poetic justice, Asian Flu. He has seen no one but his doctors, taken no phone calls since he got sick."

"You're sure?" Wilson asked.

"He has been under the care of the best chest man in his country. The doctor is of my faith and is an old friend of mine. I am sure. What I think you should do, old friend, is to put everything on the back burner, as you people say. Delay events as long as you can."

"I agree," Wilson said. "Shalom." He put the handset back on its cradle and sat staring at the wall of his office, debating in his mind if he should tell Admiral Benson what Bernstein had told him or to let events take their course.

A few minutes after Wilson had talked with Isser Bernstein, Stefan Lubutkin stuck his head around the door into Shevenko's office. "If there is nothing more, Comrade Director?"

"No, nothing. It's the ballet tonight, isn't it?"

"Yes, sir. And thank you. Until tomorrow, Comrade Director."

"Have you got a pretty girl to take to the ballet, Stefan?" Shevenko called out. "I understand that girls are quicker to yield after they have watched the male ballet dancers perform." Lubutkin blushed and withdrew his head.

Later that evening, during the second act of the ballet, Lubutkin left his seat and went through a heavily brocaded curtain that concealed an exit door. He slipped through the door and stood in the dark alleyway outside the theatre. He saw the black limousine and walked to it and opened the door and got into the back seat. Admiral Zurahv smiled at him.

"Your boss lied to us, Stefan," the Admiral said. "The Americans did not find their submarine. If they had done so they would have marked the spot with sonar buoys. There are no such buoys."

"The picture?" Lubutkin said. "It looked genuine."

"It did," the Admiral said. "But it could have been faked. I am having it analyzed now by one of our photo experts."

"He lies to everyone," Lubutkin said. "And he lies about everyone. He lied to me. He told me he went to East Berlin and that is where he got the picture and the information. Our man in East Berlin never saw him."

"He did leave Moscow," Zurahv said. "One of my people saw him board the airliner, saw him return. Where did he go?"

"I think to West Berlin," Lubutkin said. "I think he went there to see a woman. He is a notorious one for women."

"A woman?" Admiral Zurahv said genially. "He doesn't know what a treasure he has in his own office. You'll stop by my apartment after the ballet, little one?"

"Now, if you like, darling," Lubutkin said. "The ballet is boring." His slim hand found its way under the flap of the Admiral's greatcoat. "You're such a big bear of a man," he murmured. The Admiral grinned and picked up the car's telephone and dialed a number. "Let me talk, you naughty boy," he murmured.

"Zurahv here," he growled into the telephone. "Issue orders at once to Captain Kovitz to leave Tripoli and to proceed down the course line of his target and listen for sonar buoys. Yes, I know what the freighter Captain said. He's a merchant marine captain and he knows little about sonar. I want a reliable check. Yes. Send those orders at once." He hung up the telephone and spoke into the car's intercom system to the driver.

"My apartment." As the car moved out of the alleyway he unbottoned his greatcoat to give Lubutkin greater freedom.

Captain Nikita Kovitz watched from the bridge of his submarine as the crew of a Libyan motor launch struggled to unshackle a cable that held his ship's bow to a mooring buoy in the outer reaches of Tripoli harbor. There was a splash in the water and a bellow of criticism from the coxswain of the motor launch. Captain Kovitz grinned at the Officer of the Deck.

"Clumsy bastards probably dropped the shackle in the water. Those monkey men can't do anything right. Wait until they get well clear with that motor launch before we get underway. We'll be on the surface for an hour before submerging. Keep a sharp lookout for fishing boats. The bastards don't usually carry running lights and if we hit one of them we'll be tied up in court here for six months. I'm going below, notify me fifteen minutes before we dive." He dropped down the ladders to the Command Center where he checked the log book and then he went to his cabin. His Navigator came in response to his summons.

"I want to traverse the Strait of Gibraltar at night, submerged, Navigator. Make sure that our speeds are right for that timing. When we leave the Strait we'll go to four hundred feet and proceed at fifteen knots. We'll slow to ten knots when we reach the target area. I want a Battle Condition One sonar watch set at that time."

"The earlier message said that a freighter equipped with

sonar made that run and got a negative result," the Navigator said. "If we're listening for sonar buoys it must mean the Americans have found their submarine and have marked it. I can't believe that, not in that depth of water."

"Nothing is impossible," Kovitz said. "If Admiral Zurahv sent a freighter to search out the possibility of sonar buoys around our target it means that someone has told him the Americans found their submarine. I don't think the Admiral would come up with that idea by himself. He's not one of our more innovative thinkers.

"Apparently he wants us to double-check on the freighter's results. That figures, our sonar is much better than what they'd have on some freighter."

"Yes, sir," the Navigator said. "I've been wondering why they ordered us here to port in such a hurry. Do you know?"

"No," Kovitz said. He got up from his chair and went to a chart on the bulkhead above his desk. "Once we begin the sonar search I want everyone to be alert. If we don't find anything on the first run down the course line we'll make runs back and forth on either side of the course line. The target may have skewed well off the course line after she was hit."

"Yes, sir," the Navigator said. He cleared his throat. "Comrade Captain, we are not at war so one must assume that some very complicated political events are taking place. The summons you received to fly to Moscow, you didn't mention anything about that trip to me, Comrade."

"No, I didn't," Captain Kovitz said. "You'd better take care of laying down the courses and speeds, we'll be submerging in a half hour or so."

Admiral Brannon was finishing his second cup of coffee when the telephone rang at 2000 hours, eight o'clock in the evening. His wife rose from the dinner table and went into the kitchen to answer the phone. She came back, smiling and nodding her head at Brannon, who went into the kitchen and picked up the phone.

"Commander Fencer, Admiral. The Watch Officer in the Black Room just informed me that the submarine that had been patrolling off Morocco and then left that area and went into the Mediterranean has been footprinted clearing the Strait of Gibraltar. She's running on the same course as *Sharkfin* was on, sir."

"Thank you, Commander. Are you at home? Could you meet me in the Black Room in, oh, half an hour or so? Good." He put the phone in its cradle and then picked it up again and dialed the Officer of the Day at the Pentagon and ordered a car and driver to pick him up and another car and driver to get Admiral Olsen. Twenty minutes later he walked into the Black Room.

"You got here in a hurry, John," he said to Olsen. "Your Swedish ESP working or something?"

"No, sir. This is Joan's bowling night and I stayed in the office to catch up with some of the paperwork. The OOD checked the Out Log and found I was still in the building." He nodded at the lighted glass wall of the Black Room where a black line was barely moving on a course slightly to the north and west out of the Strait of Gibraltar.

"Our boy is back. He sure as hell isn't on his way to his regular patrol area off Morocco. If he were he would have turned south by now."

Brannon turned to Commander Fencer. "You people do a damned good job, John. I want you to tell your watch standers that, if you will.

"Could you have them lay down *Sharkfin*'s course from her last position report on out to where we found her?"

Fencer spoke into the microphone and a red line appeared on the glass wall and overlaid the creeping black line.

"I wonder where that murdering son of a bitch is going, what he's up to?" Brannon growled. "Is he going back out to the scene of the crime to gloat?"

"Might be something else," Olsen said. "Wilson told his contact to tell the Russians that we had found *Sharkfin* and taken pictures of her on the bottom. The Russians are pretty damned good sailors. If I were in their shoes right now I'd figure that if we found the *Sharkfin* we'd put down sonar buoys to mark her on the bottom. Maybe they're trying to listen for those buoys, see if we were running a bluff."

"*Medusa* would drop sonar buoys, wouldn't she, when she found *Sharkfin* on the bottom?" Brannon looked at Commander Fencer.

"Yes, sir, that's standard operating procedure. When the *Medusa* picks up an ocean bottom formation that looks odd or unusual and needs detailed charting, she drops sonar buoys to mark the area so she can home in on the buoys and make as many runs over the area as she has to get a good bottom charting or to take pictures."

"Then he'll hear the buoys and they'll know we're not bluffing," Brannon said.

"I don't think so, sir," Fencer said. "*Medusa* is an oceanographic ship, sir. The sonar buoys she uses are Title C, disposable. They beep for just twenty-four hours, as a rule. Long enough for the ship to make its runs. The buoys are rigged with an anchor and fifty fathoms of line. After twenty-four hours they automatically flood, go dead and sink to the bottom."

"Then the bastards won't know," Brannon said slowly. "They'll think that Wilson was running a bluff. Damn it!" He turned to Commander Fencer.

"I'll be in my office. Please have your Watch Officer keep me informed."

John Olsen found the coffee gear in the Yeoman's office and made a pot of coffee. When he walked into Brannon's office he found the Admiral standing at his wall chart, a pair of dividers and a parallel ruler in his hands.

"*Orca*'s last position report puts her here, at this point," Brannon said. "I figure she's here by now, at this mark. *Devilfish* is to the north, near the *Medusa.*"

"Let's get a maneuvering board and work this out," Olsen said. "We want to give *Orca* and *Devilfish* the advantage of position, every advantage we can so they don't join *Sharkfin* on the bottom."

Brannon turned from the chart. "You're assuming that I'm going to order them to go after the Soviet sub?"

"What else?" Olsen grunted.

CHAPTER 9

The surface of the sea was wine dark in the last minutes before the dawn. A sparkling crest of foam on an occasional wave made a small spot of light here and there as the slender communications array of the U.S.S. *Orca* rose above the water and extended upward. In the submarine's Communications Center the radioman on watch acknowledged the Attack Center's report that the antennas were clear of the water. He punched a button and a tape with *Orca*'s latitude and longitude entered on it transmitted the information in a burst of high-speed sounds. Twenty-three thousand miles overhead a Navy Communications satellite picked up the three-second-long transmission and entered it in its computer for rebroadcast to Washington. The satellite computer, alerted by the *Orca*'s coded identification signal, energized its storage bank and transmitter and an answering stream of signals transmitted at high speed went arrowing downward through space to the *Orca*'s antennas.

"Incoming traffic," the senior radioman said to his watch mate. The two men watched a tape whir through its guides as it absorbed the message from the satellite. When the tape had stopped the radioman notified the Attack Center that the position report had been transmitted and incoming traffic received. The *Orca* planed downward to its normal operating depth of 400 feet. The senior man on watch removed the tape cassette from the receiving machine and put it into a decoding machine.

"Wonder what they got for us now," he said to the other man. "Maybe it's orders to go to some good liberty port. We ain't doing anything out here but stooge around on some fucking exercise that even the Old Man don't seem to know anything about." He pushed the On button on the decoding machine and the tape began to move slowly through the machine's printing heads. The tape stopped and a red light showed on the decoding machine as a buzzer began to sound.

"Oh, oh," the radioman said. He punched the Off button on the decoding machine and picked up a telephone and dialed the Attack Center.

"This is Communications for the OOD," he said. "Notify the Captain that we've got a Red Alert on the incoming traffic tape, sir."

Captain Dick Reinauer came into the Communications Center, reaching for the small key that hung on a thong around his neck twenty-four hours a day. He slipped the thong over his head and nodded at the two radiomen, who stepped outside of the compartment into the passageway. Reinauer inserted the key into the decoding machine and turned it slowly to the left and then back to the right. He punched the On button on the machine and watched as a long strip of paper tape began to come out of the machine. He gathered the tape up when the machine stopped printing and nodded genially to the two radiomen as he left the compartment.

Sitting in his cabin, the *Orca*'s Commanding Officer smoothed the tape out on his desk and began to read the message.

"This is a combat order. Repeat. This is a combat order. It is not repeat and underline not a drill.

"A Soviet late-model attack submarine made an unprovoked attack on the U.S.S. *Sharkfin* as that ship was en route to its home port. Site of the attack was 252 miles west of the Strait of Gibraltar on *Sharkfin's* base course of 278 degrees true.

"U.S.S. *Medusa* has located *Sharkfin's* wreckage and obtained clear pictures of the fatal damage inflicted by a torpedo hit in *Sharkfin's* stern.

"There is no repeat no doubt that a Soviet submarine made the attack that sank *Sharkfin* with all hands. The Soviet was footprinted on SOSUS as it followed *Sharkfin* and when it returned from the attack.

"The Soviet government has been informed of the attack and the photographing of *Sharkfin's* wreckage. The Soviet government has been given ample opportunity to respond and explain this unwarranted and heinous attack and has refused to comment.

"The Soviet submarine that attacked *Sharkfin* is now back in the area. It is westbound out of Gibraltar on course 278 degrees true. It crossed the western boundary of the SOSUS array at 1800 hours last at a reported speed of 15 knots.

"You are ordered to find and sink the Soviet submarine. Repeat. Find and sink the Soviet submarine. Similar orders are issued to *Devilfish*. Co-ordinate your attack as you see fit.

"You will not divulge this message to anyone other than your XO. You will inform your Wardroom and crew that *Orca* and *Devilfish* are engaged in a tactical weapons exercise to find and destroy a sophisticated new target which simulates the sounds of an enemy submarine. God be with you. Signed Vice Admiral Michael P. Brannon, ComSubLant."

Captain Reinauer cut the tape into six-inch-long strips and carefully peeled the backing from each strip and pressed the tape's gummed backing onto a sheet of paper. He tugged at his black beard as he read through the message for the second time and then he buzzed for his Executive Officer. Lieutenant Commander Eckert came into his cabin and Reinauer handed him the message. Eckert read it and looked up, his face pale.

"My God, Skipper, this means we're at war!"

"I don't think so," Reinauer said slowly. "This message went only to us and to the *Devilfish*. If we were at war it would go to all ships. It could be one of Iron Mike's exercises to make us think we're in a combat situation so he can evaluate our readiness. There just might be a new type of target out there that we have to find and destroy."

"There might be but you don't really believe that," Eckert said. "Mike Brannon's a tough man and he's hell on readiness but I don't think he'd do something this far out, do you?"

"No," Reinauer said quietly. "I have to believe what this message says, that some Russian submarine sank the *Sharkfin*. I think it might have happened when *Devilfish* left Holy Loch so suddenly a while back. Then when Moscow clammed up he sent us down here to get the Russian." He reached in his desk drawer and pulled out a chart of the area, a pair of dividers and a set of parallel rulers.

"Get me the computer readout of our position and where *Devilfish* is." He positioned the parallel rulers over the compass rose on the chart and carefully moved the rulers until he could draw a course line of 278 degrees true out of the Strait of Gibraltar. Using the dividers he measured off 252 miles along the course line and placed a small "S" on the line. Eckert came back into the cabin with the information Reinauer had requested and then Reinauer marked in the position of the *Orca* and *Devilfish*. He marked in a small "R" on the course line.

"We're almost dead ahead of the Russian if he keeps coming along that course line," he said slowly. "We're closer to him than *Devilfish*. He's coming right down our throat." He used the dividers. "*Devilfish* is a good thirty miles away from the target." He sat back in his chair and rubbed his bearded chin.

"Damn it, we're too close together to talk to *Devilfish*. The other guy will hear us. We'll have to play it by ear, try to figure out what Bob Miller in *Devilfish* will do."

Eckert studied the chart. "You know," he said, his voice rising slightly, "this set-up isn't that much different than the last time we worked with *Devilfish* off Iceland, when we made a dummy attack on that missile sub, what was her name? *Saint Louis,* that was it.

"In that exercise *Devilfish* was out ahead of the target and she went to full speed. The *Saint Louis* heard her and turned to starboard, toward us, and we went to full bore and the skipper in the *Saint Louis* had to turn away from us. While we were doing that *Devilfish* closed the range and fired the rocket grenades and got two simulated hits." His forefinger traced a line on the chart.

"Now it's us ahead of the target and *Devilfish* off on his starboard side. If we go to full bore and close the range he'll sure as hell hear us and the odds are he'll turn away to starboard. He doesn't know *Devilfish* is out there, and he'll make a run for the coast of Portugal, to get into their territorial water. If he does that and *Devilfish* goes after him he'll have to turn away, just as we made the *Saint Louis* turn away."

Reinauer sat, absorbing what Eckert had said. "Yeah. If he sank *Sharkfin* and if he hears us closing on him at full speed he's going to be nervous. If I were in his shoes I'd run for Portugal at high speed. Then if *Devilfish* picks up the cue and goes after him he's boxed, he's got to turn away. If *Devilfish* reads this as we do."

"I think Captain Miller will read it that way," Eckert said. "If he doesn't, Carmichael sure as hell will. He's as sharp as a damned tack." He looked at Reinauer. "What weapon will you use, sir?"

"SUBROCS," Reinauer said. "I don't want to get too close to that bastard. If he sank the *Sharkfin* he might have some long range torpedoes aboard. *Sharkfin* was a good ship, good crew. If we can hit him I don't want to leave anything the Russians can find." He pushed back his chair and stood up.

"Let's get started. Get off a receipt for the message. Just say 'Message received. Orders will be followed.' Pass the word to the crew that we're on a special tactical weapons firing exercise with the *Devilfish* and we've got to beat her so everyone sharpen up."

"Supposing Iron Mike has blown his ballast, gone crazy?"

Eckert's saturnine face was dark. "If we sink a Russian submarine God only knows what will happen to us, to you and me."

"I've thought of that," Reinauer said. "We're trained to fight a war if it ever comes. We're trained to obey orders. That's all we have to think about, all we have to do, obey orders, Mister." He picked up an eraser and rubbed out the "R" he had pencilled in to show the Soviet submarine's position and wrote in a "T."

" 'T' for target," he said. "Send the crew to Battle Stations."

The sonar operator on watch on the Soviet submarine stared at his video screen and reached for his telephone.

"Contact! Bearing three five five. Contact sounds like a submarine. Closing fast!"

Captain Nikita Kovitz threw a switch that energized the sonar display screen in the Command Center. He looked at the small white dot on the face of the screen and turned to his Navigator.

"I don't know who that is but I'll bet he's not a friend. Right rudder, fifteen degrees. Increase speed to thirty knots." He pulled the Navigator's chart over in front of him and studied it.

"Give me a course and distance to the coast. Set Battle Condition One."

The Soviet submarine heeled hard to starboard as her helmsman put the rudder over fifteen degrees and the ship picked up speed. The crew, stumbling and reaching for the handholds built into the ship's hull for such purpose, scrambled to their battle stations. Captain Kovitz acknowledged the Navigator's course change to head for the coast of Portugal and watched the white dot on the video screen.

"Let me know if the contact changes speed or course to follow us," he said. The Navigator picked up the telephone and spoke quietly to the sonar operators.

"Sonar reports the contact is definitely a submarine and

closing range rapidly, sir," he said to Captain Kovitz. "Sonar requests permission to echo-range on the target to get a precise range, sir."

"Permission not granted," Kovitz snapped. He watched the relative bearing of the contact gradually open. "Ah, he's not turning to chase us," Kovitz said. He raised his head slightly as a voice came out of the loudspeaker in the overhead.

"Sonar reports that the contact is steady on course."

"Maintain a sonar watch all around," Captain Kovitz said. "Increase speed to eighty percent of maximum reactor output." He bent his head and looked at the course the Navigator had pencilled in on the chart. "Good," he said. "The contact is running at high speed, he probably didn't hear us. We'll head for Portuguese territorial waters and wait this out and see what happens. Once the contact has cleared the area we'll get back on course and find out about those sonar buoys."

"Contact! Second contact!" the loudspeaker bellowed. "Bearing zero two zero. Second contact appears to be a submarine that is now coming to high speed!"

"Damn!" Kovitz snapped. "Another one out there! Right full rudder. Maintain emergency speed. Make depth five hundred feet. Make course one six zero."

The Soviet submarine commander stood at the table in the Command Center, watching the Navigator draw in the relative positions of the two contacts and his own ship.

"I don't like the looks of this," he said in a low voice to the Navigator. "Two submarines. It looks as if they were waiting for us. Get me as accurate a bearing as you can on the first contact. Let's see what we can do to outfox those people out there."

"Americans, I'd guess," the Navigator said glumly. "Waiting for us to come back to where we fired at the target. That was a mistake, to order us back here, Comrade Captain."

Captain Kovitz ignored the remark. He studied the sonar display screen. Both contacts were clearly visible on the screen. The first contact was out on his starboard bow, the second almost directly astern.

"Cat and mouse," he said in a low voice to the Navigator. "If we could outmaneuver this second contact astern we could get to Portuguese water. But how do we get past him? As they used to say in the old sailing ships, he has the weather helm on us. He can cut us off before we reach the coast." He looked again at the video screen.

"Get me one echo-range reading on the first contact. Once we know how far away he is we'll go to one hundred percent of the reactor output. If our engineers are right we will be faster than he is and we can outrun the bastard."

"Range to the first contact is fifty thousand yards, five and four zeros, sir. Bearing to the first contact is now zero nine zero, sir."

"Come left to course one nine eight, hard left rudder, all ahead, full output," Captain Kovitz snapped. "We can outrun this hunting dog and get back to the Strait of Gibraltar. This second contact," he put his finger on the chart, "the second one is too far off to close with us." He clutched at the table as the submarine heeled sharply to port and he felt the vibration in his feet and legs as the nuclear reactor went to full emergency power.

"Bearing on the second contact is now two five five, sir. Lateral display triangulation indicates range to the second contact is sixty thousand yards, six and four zeros, sir." The loudspeaker vibrated slightly as the sonar operator stopped talking.

"Thank you," Kovitz said. "I think we can do this," he said to his Navigator. "I don't like running from anyone but the odds of two to one are not to my liking. Too bad we don't have any long-range torpedoes aboard or we could make those two bastards think twice."

"Range to the first contact is opening slightly," the loudspeaker said. "Range to the second contact is holding steady, sir. It is very hard to get accurate ranges at this speed, sir."

"Understood," Kovitz said. He smiled at the Navigator. "We are faster than they are. It will be all right."

"Torpedoes! Second contact has fired two torpedoes! The torpedoes are coming this way!"

"Left rudder, left full rudder, make course one one eight!" Kovitz ordered. "He's a fool. The Americans don't have torpedoes that will reach out that far. We'll show our ass to him and let his torpedoes run out of fuel and sink. Sonar! Keep one ear on those torpedoes. Let me know the second they stop running." He turned to the Navigator, who was noting the change of course on the chart.

"This delays us a little but as soon as his torpedoes stop running we'll get back on course." His Navigator forced a smile.

"The stag and two wolves and the stag is the cleverer of the three," he said in a low voice.

In the *Orca's* Attack Center Captain Reinauer was studying the plot on the computer video screen. He traced the line of the Soviet submarine's course with a forefinger.

"Like we figured. Miller turned him away from a run toward Portugal. Now it looks as if he's trying to get back to the Strait. Bastard might make it, too, he's damned fast. Faster than we are, I think. We aren't closing range at all." He spoke into the battle telephone that hung around his neck.

"Sonar, can you get me anything on the lateral at this speed, can you pick up the *Devilfish?*"

"Affirmative, sir. We have the *Devilfish* now. He's way out there on our port side, bearing is three one seven, sir." Reinauer watched as Lieutenant Bill Reiss, the Weapons Officer, typed in the bearing of the *Devilfish* on the computer keyboard. A small white dot appeared on the video screen indicating the position of the *Devilfish.*

"Very well," Reinauer said. He unsnapped the tape that held the telephone set around his neck and laid it on the table. "I'm going down to the torpedo room, XO. Be back in a minute or two."

Turk Raynor turned as Captain Reinauer walked into the torpedo room.

"I think we'll be firing in ten minutes or less," Reinauer

said. "I want to use two SUBROCS, one from each side of the room. What burn separation do you have cranked into the missiles, Turk?"

"Max range, Captain," Raynor said. "We've got one SUBROC and one Mark Thirty-Seven, Mod Two in the tubes starboard. Same on the port side, sir."

"Shift from manual burn time separation to computer separation," Reinauer ordered.

"Aye, aye, sir," Raynor said. "Gonna take the target out before *Devilfish* gets into torpedo range, sir?"

"That's what we're going to try," Reinauer said. "That is, if the missiles work. *Stingray* fired two SUBROCS a couple of weeks ago and they came out of the tubes and sank."

"That's *Stingray*," Raynor growled. "Every missile, every fish I'm responsible for on *Orca* will work, Captain."

"That's all anyone can ask for," Reinauer said, his voice mild. He climbed the stairs to the Attack Center and heard the loudspeaker.

"*Devilfish* has fired two torpedoes!"

"All ahead one-third," Reinauer snapped. "Sonar, nail down that target for me! Engine Room, stand by to give me every pound of steam that plant will put out. Right ten degrees rudder." He waited, looking at the computer video screens, watching the white circle on the screen shifting, trying to put himself inside the mind of the Soviet submarine captain, trying to reason out what the other man would do when he heard the torpedoes running toward him.

"Rudder amidships," he ordered.

"Captain Miller fired from too far out," Eckert, standing at his shoulder, spoke in a whisper. "If the target turns and runs away from the fish he'll be able to outrun them." He nudged Reinauer's shoulder. "That's what he's doing now!" Captain Reinauer looked at the changing circles on the video screen, his teeth showing in a smile in his black beard.

"Precisely!" he whispered to Eckert. He raised his voice. "Damn it, Sonar, lock in on that target!"

"Target is changing course to starboard. He's making lots

of knots, we're getting a turn count a lot higher than he ran at before. He's going fast!''

"All ahead emergency!" Reinauer ordered. "Come to course one nine eight. Bill, I want a computer solution of the attack problem." He watched as the computer video screens changed radically and then showed the three ships.

"Firing range, sir?" Reiss said calmly, his fingers poised above the computer keyboards.

"Forty thousand yards. Co-ordinate sonar and fire control computers. I want to fire two SUBROCS, shallow parabola. I want one missile on each side of the target." Reiss's fingers flew over the computer keyboards.

"Burn separation of rocket and missile warheads will be at thirty-eight thousand yards, Captain," Reiss said. "Computer indicates a free fall arc of two thousand yards for the warheads. Burn separation times have been cranked into the missiles, sir.''

"Very well," Reinauer answered.

"Target is turning to its port," the loudspeaker said. "Torpedoes fired by *Devilfish* ran down just before he made his turn. Bearing on the target is now zero two zero, sir.''

"Very well," Reinauer said. "All hands stand by. This will be a firing run." He studied the main video display screen. Two dotted white lines ran from the *Orca's* position to each side of the target on the screen. A figure appeared beside the target's position: range 39,000 yards.

"One hundred feet," Reinauer ordered. "Make turns for one-third speed at one hundred and fifty feet. Open tube doors at one hundred twenty-five feet. Stand by in the torpedo rooms for manual firing if automatic fails.''

The firing problem was now committed to the computers. The sonar transmitters were sending out a steady barrage of sonar beams. The receivers picked up the return echoes and the computers analyzed the time interval and changed it into yards from the target and then fed the bearings and the distance to the target into the fire control computers which in turn sent commands to the electronics within the SUBROC missiles. The main display screen showed the target beginning to turn to starboard and then coming back to port. The two dotted white lines that straddled the target shifted with the target's movements.

"That's one hell of a sophisticated device out there," Lieutenant Reiss said. "It's jinking from one side to the other, just like a submarine would if it were being hit with a ranging sonar beam."

"You can't tell what those electronic people will come up with," Reinauer said.

"One hundred feet, steady platform," the helmsman said.

The figure beside the target on the display screen began to change to reflect the *Orca's* decreased speed. Lieutenant Reiss punched two keys on the firing console.

"Weapons are on automatic firing mode, sir," he said.

"Very well," Reinauer answered. As the figure on the screen changed to 40,000 yards Reinauer felt the slight jar under his feet as the air and water rams hurled the SUBROC missiles out of the torpedo tubes. He waited, feeling strangely at peace. The worry he had felt during the chase had fallen away. The doubts that had crowded his mind were gone.

"Missiles away, sir." Reiss said.

The two SUBROC missiles surged upward through the water and shot through the surface of the sea into the air. The rocket motors ignited with loud bangs and the missiles began racing above the surface of the sea in a shallow arc at just under the speed of sound. Nineteen miles from the *Orca* the rocket motor mounts that fastened the rockets to the nuclear warheads separated in a series of small explosions and dropped toward the sea. The warheads continued on in the shallow arc for another mile and then splashed into the sea and began to spiral downward.

The sonar operators aboard the Soviet submarine heard the two missiles hit the water on either side of their ship, heard the turbulence as the missiles corkscrewed down through the water. In the ship's Command Center the slamming sound of the missiles hitting the water echoed throughout the compartment and the display screen suddenly showed two white blips, one on each side of the submarine.

"Deep! Take me deep!" Captain Kovitz screamed. "Forty-five degree down angle! Full power!" The Soviet submarine tilted sharply downward and in the few seconds of life that he knew he had left Captain Kovitz stared at his Navigator.

The mass of hydrogen atoms in each of the SUBROC missile warheads fused and the warheads exploded with a burst of energy equal to the energy of the atomic bomb that had exploded in the air above Hiroshima. The Soviet submarine, caught between the two bursting warheads, disintegrated. A cloud of fragments of what had once been an attack submarine and the 110 men who had manned it, drifted slowly downward. The metal and plastic fragments in the cloud were indistinguishable from the tiny fragments of unincinerated bone that sank into the dark depths of the sea. Caught by a slow and vagrant current a part of the cloud of particles moved in the direction of the dead hull of the U.S.S. *Sharkfin.*

"Sonar reports it cannot find the target," the loudspeaker said.

"Very well," Reinauer said. "Continue to search." He gripped the edge of the table he stood against, wondering if the Russian captain had known that the missiles had been fired at him, whether he had realized that his life was over. He shook his head, suddenly conscious of fatigue.

"Sonar reports no target. *Devilfish* wants to talk, sir."

"Tell him to go ahead," Reinauer said.

"*Devilfish* says tallyho and well done and expects credit for assistance," the sonar operator reported.

"Tell him he deserves all the credit we can give him," Reinauer said. He turned to Eckert.

"Secure from General Quarters. Put me back on our regular station. Depth four hundred feet. I want to see you in my cabin as soon as you get things squared away."

Eckert walked into the Captain's cabin and dropped into a chair. "God, I feel tired," he said. "Like I'd been put through a wringer. After we fired I felt like I wanted to throw up."

"Don't think about it," Reinauer said harshly. "Think about the fact that the target we hit sank the *Sharkfin* with all hands and from what the message said the *Sharkfin* never had a chance. Think about that!"

"Sorry," Eckert said. "Should have kept my big mouth shut."

"Forget it," Reinauer said. "I'll draft a message to ComSub-Lant. The SOSUS array must have picked up those explosions and he'll be sweating his balls off until he finds out it was our missiles."

"He'd better sweat about something else, Skipper," Eckert said. "The people in the sonar gang aren't buying that crap about the target being an electronic gadget. They know it was another submarine."

Vice Admiral Mike Brannon's face showed the exhaustion he felt as he paced the length of his office. John Olsen dozed quietly on a sofa, his short collar open. The telephone rang loudly in the stillness and Olsen came bolt upright on the couch as Brannon leaped for the phone. Olsen saw the relief flood over his face as Brannon carefully put the telephone back in its cradle.

"Good news?" Olsen said quietly.

"That was John Fencer in Operations," Brannon said. "He just ran a message from *Orca* through the decoders. *Orca* and *Devilfish* trapped that murdering bastard. *Orca* fired two SUBROCS, one on each beam of the target. The target disappeared. *Orca* will send more information later." He stretched his arms over his head, his big shoulder muscles creaking.

"So what comes next?" John Olsen said. He turned as a soft knock sounded at the door and the Chief Yeoman came in with a tray holding a carafe of coffee and some sandwiches. Commander John Fencer followed the Chief into Brannon's office.

"Figured you'd be hungry about now," the Chief said. "The Commander here sure as hell is. He told me so. I drew night rations." He put the tray down on a coffee table.

"You been here all night?" Olsen asked as he reached for the coffee carafe.

"Here and in Operations," the Chief Yeoman said. "When the Boss works, I work, sir." He looked at Admiral Brannon. "Hell of an operation, sir. Like the old days."

"Yes," Mike Brannon said. "Keep it under your hat, Chief. As long as you're here, stand by in your office." He turned to Commander Fencer as the Chief closed the door behind him.

"I appreciate your taking care of the decoding. When you called me a couple of hours or so ago and said you had evidence on the SOSUS of a tremendous explosion, well, time passed damned slowly after that. Help yourself to chow and coffee."

"Thank you, Admiral," Fencer said. He picked up a bologna sandwich and nodded his thanks as John Olsen filled a coffee cup for him.

"I don't know how far away the combat scene was, Admiral," Fencer said, "but the SOSUS array picked up the explosions. They're pretty damned sensitive."

Brannon nodded and reached for his telephone. He buzzed the Chief's office outside of his door. "Please call Admiral Benson at once. He'll be asleep but get him up if you have to send a courier over to his house. I want to talk to him. Right now."

Admiral Benson called within ten minutes. Mike Brannon filled him in on the information that had come from Reinauer in the *Orca* and hung up the phone.

"Benson will call Bob Wilson and get him on the horn

right away to his contact in Israel. In a few hours they should know about this in Moscow."

"And then the shit will hit the fan," Olsen said.

Igor Shevenko put down his telephone and stared at the wall on the far side of his office where a long shred of paint had peeled away and was swaying in the hot air rising from the radiator beneath it. Wilson had not been bluffing, he thought. The American admirals had retaliated. He put his powerful hands on the sides of his head and squeezed. Admiral Zurahv would be in his office. He reached for the telephone and started to dial the number and then stopped.

"No," he whispered to himself. "No. The wolves will be among the sheep soon enough when Kovitz fails to report on the sonar buoys. I've got a day, maybe a day and a half before the word will be out." He reached for the phone again and dialed the private number of Leonid Plotovsky. Maybe Plotovsky could get through the privacy the doctors had thrown up around Brezhnev's hospital room. The man was reportedly on the mend. He waited as the telephone began to ring on the other end.

"Tit for tat," he murmured, "and where do we go from here?"

CHAPTER 10

Captain Herman Steel arrived at Admiral Brannon's office five minutes early for the meeting Brannon had called. He looked at the ancient Timex wrist watch he wore, an irritable expression on his face as he watched Brannon's Chief Yeoman making a pot of coffee.

"How many man-hours a year do you waste preparing that poison, Chief?" he asked in his rasping voice.

"I don't rightly know, sir," the Chief said. "I'd assign the job to a lower rating but the Admiral is particular about his coffee so I do it myself." He smiled and raised a hand in greeting and Steel turned and saw Admiral Benson and Bob Wilson approaching. He turned his back on the CIA Director and his aide.

When the three men walked into Admiral Brannon's office they found Admiral John Olsen there, sitting on one of the sofas with his long legs stretched out in front of him. Admiral Benson and Wilson took seats on the other sofa and Captain Steel chose a comfortable upholstered chair next to a coffee table.

"You'll excuse the appearance of John and myself," Brannon said. He rubbed a big hand over his unshaven chin. "We've been keeping an all-night watch here in the office. I asked you to come by because we have some information to report." He settled back in his swivel chair. "Mr. Benson and Mr. Wilson know about some of the information but we have since learned more." He paused.

"The Soviet submarine that attacked and sank the *Sharkfin* has been destroyed." Brannon's voice was flat, without intonation or inflection.

"The operation was carried out early this morning, local time. As soon as we received that information I called Admiral Benson and requested that he get Mr. Wilson to call his contact in Israel and have that contact inform the KGB of the action we took." He looked at Admiral Benson, who cleared his throat.

"Mr. Wilson made contact," Benson said. "By now the KGB knows that the Soviet submarine has been destroyed."

"The Plain of Megiddo!" Captain Steel said in a low voice. "Armageddon!" He lunged up out of his chair, his eyes blazing.

"Knock the chip off my shoulder and I'll smash your face in turn!" Captain Steel's thin nostrils flared. "Do you think the Soviets will take this lying down? My God, you even used nuclear missiles! Do you think those missiles are toys to play with?"

"No." Admiral Brannon said.

"What do we do now?" Steel said. "Do we sit here until the Soviets decide to launch a nuclear strike at us?" He raised his arms and then lowered them and turned to stare at Admiral Benson and Bob Wilson.

"And you two, what are you, puppets? You play at charades in the international theatre of nations. You cause the murder of heads of state in the name of our national security, you suborn foreign governments. My God, you're so incompetent that you couldn't even invade Cuba successfully!"

"That's enough! Sit down!" Admiral Brannon's voice, honed by years of command, cracked like a whip in the office.

Captain Steel half turned, stared at Brannon and then sat down, his back rigid, his face white. Mike Brannon studied the lean, quivering figure in the chair.

"Your concern interests me," Brannon said in a soft voice. "We are all concerned about the Soviet reaction but your concern seems to me to be something more than ours, sir." He leaned back in his chair, his blue eyes fixed on Steel.

"We all know that if the Soviets launch a first strike nuclear attack against the United States most of our land-based nuclear missile sites will be wiped out in the first phase of the attack.

"The Navy's ballistic missile submarines then become our major counterstrike force. We can destroy the entire Soviet Union from the sea. That's what we have always said, what we have led our people, our allies, and the Soviet Union to believe." Brannon came up out of his chair, his big hands resting on his desk top, his head thrust forward belligerently.

"But we know differently, don't we, Captain Steel? We know that when I came aboard in this job three years ago morale in the nuclear submarine Navy was at point zero! We know, don't we, you and I, that maintenance of ships and equipment was shameful, so shameful, sir, that I'd bet that half of the nuclear missiles on our submarines would not have launched! Torpedoes, Captain, torpedoes were so poorly maintained that many of them were literally frozen in their tubes, frozen there with dirt and crud!

"Your damned coddling of your nuclear school graduates split nuclear submarine crews into two camps, the nukes and the operating sailors. Morale went down to point zero. Your orders accomplished that and did even more, your orders destroyed the fundamental concepts of military discipline." Brannon shook a thick finger at Captain Steel as Steel started to rise from his chair.

"You will hear me out, Captain. It's taken me three years to right a good many of the wrongs you have done, wittingly or unwittingly. You fought me every step of the way,   went behind my back. I have never made an issue of your opposition but I am sick of that opposition and I will have no more of it.

"There's still a hell of a lot more work to be done before this nuclear submarine Navy of ours—ours, Captain, not yours—before it is the force it must be to be an effective deterrent." He pushed back from his desk and sat down in his chair.

"If you want to know, Captain, one of the major factors in my decision to destroy the Soviet submarine that killed *Shark-fin* was the knowledge that we are not fully able to conduct an all-out nuclear war on the Soviet Union. I reasoned that by taking strong action we would convince the Soviets that we are ready. I don't think they know the miserable condition of many of our nuclear ballistic missile submarines. I don't think very many people know those conditions, other than the officers who command and serve on them and I issue you fair warning right now that what is said in this office in this meeting will not be told outside of this office. If it is I will destroy you without a second thought!"

Captain Steel shrank back into his chair. "Did you bring me here in front of these people to threaten me? Did you bring this nation to the brink of nuclear holocaust to get rid of me? If so, Admiral, you have made the biggest mistake of your life!"

Brannon's eyes held Steel. "If you think that, Captain," he said softly, "if you think that then your ego is beyond my comprehension, sir. And if you think that I cannot destroy you then you are mistaken. If the *New York Times* or the *Washington Post* were to be given documented evidence of the deplorable state of our nuclear submarine Navy when I came aboard I can assure you that the Chief of Naval Operations and you and I, would all be out on our collective asses.

"I am prepared to take the consequences for my actions. Just as you had better be prepared to take the consequences if you choose to go running to your friends in the Congress.

"To set your mind at rest, sir, I intend to wait three days for a Soviet response through Mr. Wilson's contacts. If there is no response I intend to go to the President and the head of the National Security Council and inform them fully of what has happened. If the President agrees we will then announce the loss of the *Sharkfin* due to unknown causes."

Captain Steel sat in his chair, his body huddled in on itself. Then he began to straighten up. His eyes stared at Mike Brannon.

"You have reminded me twice in recent days that you are a Vice Admiral and I am a Captain, sir, that I have no choice but to obey your lawful orders. Very well. But remember this, sir; if there is no response from the Soviets to this maniacal action on your part I will appear with you when you make your explanation to the President and I will destroy whatever warped line of reasoning you present. That is not a threat, it is a plain statement of fact. Sir!" He rose and left the office, slamming the door behind him.

Admiral Olsen uncoiled his long frame from the sofa and poured coffee for the others. "He means that, Mike. He'll be there and he'll have the chairmen of the House and Senate Armed Services Committees in tow and they'll be loaded for bear. Or for Mike Brannon."

"I'll face that problem if and when it comes," Brannon said. He sipped at his coffee. "Bob, you're the ranking expert on the Soviet mind. What do you think they'll do when they know they've lost one of their submarines?"

"They could begin a nuclear war," Wilson said slowly. "But I'd rule that out. When you hit back at them you sent a message they understand. You're playing hard ball in the Big Leagues and they understand that, they do it all the time. I don't think they'll do anything. If it's any use to you, Admiral, I'd be willing to testify that it's my opinion that if you hadn't taken the action you did the Soviets would have gone a hell of a lot farther in their next try."

"Thank you," Brannon said. He turned toward Admiral Benson. "I expect to be kept fully informed of any information you get, anything." He stood up and walked around in front of his desk.

"Will do, sir," Admiral Benson said. "My God, that must have been something, that action! Submarines fighting submarines underwater! I know a lot about combat in the air, one on one with the other guy, but submarines and underwater where no one can see anything, that's something I can't even imagine. Two SUBROC missiles, you said? What happens when those things go off near a submarine?"

"Ideally," Mike Brannon's words came slowly, "you try to land one missile on each beam of the submarine. The explosions are simultaneous. The target is completely destroyed. Nothing is left." He stared at the rug on the floor of his office. "A lot of men die, that's what happens." He walked to the door and Admiral Benson and Bob Wilson left his office.

Igor Shevenko stopped at the door of his office and turned as Stefan Lubutkin came out of his office with an envelope in his hand.

"Genuine?" Shevenko asked.

"Yes, Comrade. I had a friend get these from a naval supply depot. Without a requisition, of course, a friend doing a favor for a friend." Shevenko nodded and put the envelope in the inside pocket of his jacket. He left the KGB building and walked a block and got into a limousine that slowed and moved in to the curb for him. He settled in the rear seat beside Leonid Plotovsky.

"I am sorry to have insisted on privacy, Comrade," Shevenko said. "I took the liberty last night of having one of my experts look at your car while it was parked. He found these." He reached in his pocket and handed the envelope to Plotovsky, who opened it and let two tiny electronic devices spill out into his seamed, clawlike hand.

"Electronic bugs, Comrade," Shevenko said softly. "Manufactured, I am afraid, by the electronics division of our Navy."

"Zurahv!" The old man spat out the word.

"I don't know, sir," Shevenko said. "I could find out, perhaps. But that is not the real reason I asked to meet you privately." He took a deep breath as Plotovsky put the electronic bugs back in the envelope.

"What is the reason for wanting to meet this way?"

"I have been given information that I do not doubt, sir." Shevenko quickly and concisely detailed the retaliation that the Americans had taken against the Soviet submarine.

Plotovsky turned his lizardlike eyes on Shevenko. "How long will it be before Zurahv knows he has lost a submarine?"

"I would say within three days, sir. It is not too unusual for one of our submarines to fail to report its daily position. It is quite unusual if one goes for two days without reporting its position. One other factor. Our submarine was checking to see if the Americans had put down sonar buoys around the wreckage of their submarine. Admiral Zurahv is anxious to get that report. When it fails to come he will know something is wrong."

"But you came to me first," Plotovsky said in a soft voice. "You have the position, the authority to ask for a hearing before the Politburo where you could put this on the table for everyone to consider. Why didn't you?"

"You led the minority vote to oppose the test of the new torpedo, sir. You are the logical one to prevent Admiral Zurahv's genie from escaping from the bottle, Comrade."

"You talk in riddles," the old man said irritably. "Bottles and genies. Educating you in the West might have been a mistake, Igor."

"I trust not, sir. I know the American mind. It tends to relate crises to sports, that is, in American football a favorite offensive play is to fake a smash into the line and then throw a long pass. They even call such a pass a bomb."

"I don't know anything about American football and I don't want to," Plotovsky grunted. "Put it in terms I am familiar with."

"Chess," Shevenko said with a slight smile. "We have taken out one of their bishops. They have retaliated by exposing their queen to take a knight in return but if we move for their queen we risk an exchange of all the major pieces. The board will be dominated by pawns."

"I understand," Plotovsky said. "Keep in touch with me. I'll take you back near to your office."

Vice Admiral Brannon stood in front of the chart on his office wall. Admiral Olsen stood beside him, holding a pad and pen.

"I want a Quiet Alert," Brannon said. He put his finger on the area between the northern tip of Norway and Bear Island, in the Barents Sea. "If the Soviets come out of Polyarnyy with their missile subs they have to come through here." His finger moved across the chart to the areas between Britain and Greenland and between Greenland and Iceland.

"If any of them are already west of Bear Island they've got to move down through this area to get to the Atlantic. We've got the passes covered with the SOSUS arrays and passive mines. Same over on the east coast, the Sea of Okhotsk. If they move I want to know it. I want all attack submarines at sea. Deploy them in Quiet Alert positions to intercept anything that manages to get through the passive mine defenses." He walked over to his desk and sat down.

"I don't think they'll move anything by sea," Olsen said. "If they're going to attack they'd do it with land-based missiles. They have to figure that if they move by sea we'll react as we did to the sinking of the *Sharkfin*." He stopped as Brannon's phone buzzer sounded. Brannon picked up the telephone and listened. He put down the phone and turned to Olsen.

"Admiral Benson. He says they have reports of wide scale Chinese actions against Soviet units along their borders."

"Which means?" Olsen said.

"It probably means that Peking is reading our radio traffic. Benson says there's no reason for these flare-ups along the border. The border's been quiet for months. He thinks they know what's happened."

"Works in our favor, doesn't it?" Olsen said. "The Soviets might think twice about taking on us and the Chinese at the same time."

"Or they might welcome the chance," Brannon said.

CHAPTER 11

By any normal standard Captain Herman Steel was neither a social nor a sociable man. His life revolved around his work. His quarters in the BOQ, the Bachelor Officer's Quarters, were small, sparsely furnished and in every sense an extension of his office in the Pentagon. Engineering texts were stacked neatly in piles on the one table in the small living room and on the table beside the metal military style cot that served as his bed. The kitchen in the quarters was small and the refrigerator and cupboards held only the foods the Captain used for his morning meal, which consisted of milk, two eggs, wheat germ and a banana whipped into a liquid concoction in an ancient electric mixer. Lunch was almost always taken at his desk, a double handful of nuts and dried fruits from a supply his Chief Yeoman kept in a drawer in his desk. Dinner was eaten at the BOQ Mess where out of long custom the stewards brought him either chicken or fish and two vegetables. He drank only water, milk, or fruit juices. Those officers who took tables near him at the evening meal refrained from smoking rather than risk his abrasive denunciation of tobacco and those who used it.

He sat at his desk after the meeting with Vice Admiral Brannon and Admiral Olsen, a pad of lined yellow paper in front of him. He lettered the name "Brannon" at the top left-hand corner of the page and slowly drew a box around the name. He could handle Brannon, he thought. It would mean calling in an IOU from the Chairman of the House Armed Services Committee. That worthy's congressional district, thanks to Captain Steel, had been awarded a lot of military installations. Brannon was only a couple of years away from mandatory retirement for age, the Congressman could find cause for his early retirement.

Admiral John Olsen was another matter. If he got rid of Brannon there was little doubt that John Olsen would succeed him. The Navy's rigid formula for promotion and succession could not be altered. John Olsen was, in Steel's opinion, more intelligent than Brannon and therefore more dangerous. He made a small box next to Brannon's name and lettered in "John Olsen," recalling the single instance when he had fenced with Olsen.

The occasion had been shortly after Olsen had been assigned as Brannon's Chief of Staff. Captain Steel had been called to Brannon's office to discuss an appropriation he had requested for additional funds to build another nuclear training school. The very fact that his appropriation was being questioned had irked Captain Steel. He wasn't accustomed to having his appropriations questioned.

During the discussion he had remarked that he had submitted the appropriation for the nuclear training school because it was logical to do so. Admiral Olsen, sitting on a sofa in Brannon's office, had smiled and said, "As Justice Oliver Wendell Holmes once wrote, and I quote, 'The life of the law has not been logic: it has been experience.'

"The Navy's experience, Captain, has been that it is not logical to build facilities when you don't have sufficient men to utilize them. We don't have enough volunteers for nuclear submarine schools to justify building another one."

Captain Steel's reply, as he remembered it, had been short.

"And I will quote to you, sir, from Thomas Henry Huxley: 'Logical consequences are the scarecrows of fools and the beacons of wise men.' "

Admiral Brannon had ended the discussion by tabling the appropriations request. That had been almost six months ago and the request was still tabled. What bothered Captain Steel was that Admiral Olsen had accurately quoted a Supreme Court chief justice. In Steel's experience seagoing naval officers didn't often read in those areas, let alone remember what they read. He drew a line between the boxes that contained the names of Brannon and Olsen. If he got rid of Brannon he'd have to contend with John Olsen. He thought a moment and then he drew an X across each box. If he moved carefully there was a possibility that he could get rid of Brannon and shunt Olsen off to another Flag job. Whoever succeeded the two men would know why they had been given the job. The Chairman of the House Armed Services Committee could take care of that small chore and the successors would know enough to stand well clear of Captain Herman Steel. He smiled gently and reached for his telephone and dialed the private line of Representative Walter W. Wendell, the venerable Congressman from Virginia and the long-time Chairman of the House Armed Services Committee.

Captain Steel met the wizened Congressman near the flame that burned at the burial site of President John F. Kennedy in Arlington National Cemetery. The two men walked among the small grave markers, Captain Steel keeping his pace slow to accomodate the old politician. Steel recounted the events from the sinking of the *Sharkfin* to the meeting with Admiral Brannon earlier that day in a succinct manner. Representative Wendell stopped at a grave marker and looked up at Steel's face.

"Can't say I disagree with what the Admiral did, Captain. Can't say that any patriotic American would disagree. Most people would probably want the Admiral to run for the Presidency. I know," he stopped and raised a veined and gnarled hand as Steel started to speak.

"I know that what he did is an open act of war and against

every rule in the book. Know that very well, sir. Know that before we get back from this little walk nuclear bombs might be falling all over the country.

"But I don't think that will happen. Roosians respect strength. They even fear it." He stopped and rubbed his chin with fingers that were misshapen from arthritis.

"And if the Roosians don't do anything at all, and I don't think they will, then your Admiral is going to be able to go to the President and while he may get his ass chewed off he ain't gonna get fired from his job, Herman. That windbag we've got for a Secretary of State, Harold dee Antoine," he pronounced the name with a downward twist of his long thin lips, "that big old windbag will get up on his hind legs and say that the Admiral done just what he would have done and the only fuss he'll make is to ask why he wasn't consulted so he could have advised the President to give orders to sink the Roosian submarine." He grinned. "Not that he would have had the guts to do that."

"That's not the point, Congressman," Captain Steel said. "Brannon has now become a dangerous man. He's committed an act of war and if he gets away with it we don't know what he'll decide to do next. He might, to use your words, he might decide to run for President. There're enough Conservatives in the country, enough worried Democrats that it might work."

"Naw," the Congressman scoffed. "You might be a genius, Herman, but you don't know beans about national politics. You got to have an organization to get elected to any job. He's got no organization. But I agree with one thing you said. If he gets away with this we don't know what he might do next and I don't like the idea of any admiral doing things with the military that I don't first approve of. When he bypasses me he ain't to be trusted, I'll agree to that."

Captain Steel walked a few yards in silence. The old Congressman looked at him out of the corner of his eye.

"Ain't forgot that you've been very helpful to me, Herman. Let me think on this a little. If we don't get burned up to a cinder by a nuclear bomb before we get back to our offices I'll think on it real hard."

"Thank you," Captain Steel said. "I'd caution you, sir, that this is something that no one should know about."

"You teaching an old dog how to suck eggs?" Congressman Wendell asked. "I got my own ways, Herman, you know that. You just go back to your office and figure out how we can scare the Roosians shitless with your nuclear submarines. Leave the politicking to me because that's what this little job is, politicking. It's something I'm pretty good at."

"The one person we have to be careful to keep this from is Moise Goldman, the President's Chief of Staff," Steel said. "He hates me."

"You boys ought to get along better," Wendell said with a sly smile. "Made a big mistake, you did, not getting next to that Jew boy. He's pretty near as smart as you are. Good politician, too. He's pure burned the ass off some people in the Congress since old Milligan decided he had too much country boy in him to be a distinguished kind of President and hired the Jew boy to make him look like a real President." He laughed silently, his thin shoulders shaking.

"Gets your cork, don't it, me using them ethnic remarks? Keep in touch, you hear?"

He walked off, shuffling along in his black high-topped shoes. Captain Herman Steel watched him, fighting back the anger he felt at the Congressman's words, realizing that the old man had deliberately baited him as part of the price he was going to have to pay to get rid of Mike Brannon.

Sophia Blovin got out of bed in an easy, fluid motion and walked to the window and scratched at the frost on the pane with a fingernail. She turned and smiled at Igor Shevenko, who was lying in bed with the down quilt pulled up to his chin.

"You're an idiot, woman," he said in an affectionate voice. "It's like the North Pole out of the bed. Come back." She smiled and walked slowly toward the bed, completely unconscious of her nudity. Shevenko watched appreciatively as she moved toward the bed, his eyes roaming over her full breasts, her rounded belly and the thick triangle of pubic hair. She slid underneath the covers and reached down and grasped him, giggling as he gasped at the coldness of her fingers.

"Make my hand warm, fill it, please," she coaxed. She reached around with her other hand and pulled his head down under the covers and put his face against one of her breasts. He nuzzled happily and she smiled.

"That's better," she murmured. "My hand is filling up with you and I'm getting all wet. Take me, now!" She pulled at him and he rolled over on top of her as she spread herself for him, clamping her long, powerful legs around his waist. She guided him into her and began to thrust with her hips, her breath coming in short gasps. She cried out suddenly and relaxed and he rolled to one side, pulling her with him, her leg over his hips. He lay there, moving gently, until she moaned and then he thrust at her savagely until she suddenly tensed and then sighed and relaxed.

"You only have to touch me and I begin to orgasm," she said softly. "If I were your wife I would drain you every night and morning. You would have no desire for Stefan."

He pulled his head away and stared at her.

"What do you mean?" he snapped.

"Stefan is, how do you say it, a homo, a queer," she murmured. She pulled his head toward her and tickled his ear with her tongue.

"You're crazy!" he said. "He's not a big strong man, frail, in fact. But not a homosexual."

"He is," she said. "I have two of those kind in my section. Brilliant analysts, both of them. They are jealous of Stefan because they think he has not one but two very powerful lovers."

Shevenko sat up in bed, ignoring the chill air on his bare chest and shoulders. "Who are his lovers?" he demanded.

"You are supposed to be one," she said. "I never believed that. The way you looked at me when I was assigned to your Directorate gave me doubts about that. Now I know you are not, you like a woman's body too much to be a pederast."

"Who is the other one supposed to be?"

"You will be angry if I tell you," she answered.

"I will be more than angry if you do not. Who is he?"

"You won't hit me if I tell you? Promise?"

"I don't hit women," he snapped. "His name."

"Admiral Zurahv."

He sank back on the pillow and pulled the quilt up to his chin, his mind racing.

"That's a very serious charge," he said slowly. "It should not be said even in jest. It should not be said unless you have solid proof."

"One of my boys was the Admiral's lover," she said. She eyed his stern face. "He was displaced by Stefan about six months ago. He hates Stefan for that."

"That's not proof," Shevenko growled. "That's nothing more than gossip."

"It is more than that. I began to check when I first heard the story. I heard little things, that the Admiral likes young men with nice round bottoms.

"I went to the old files, the military files. I have access to them, as you know, because of my classification. I found several mentions of charges that were to be brought against the Admiral and then were never carried through.

"I know a girl in the First Department of the Second Chief Directorate. She's a lesbian. They use her to compromise the wives of American diplomats and military attaches. She checked for me and found that the Admiral was accused of pederasty with young men, some of them officers on his staff. Nothing was ever done about the charges, the Admiral is too powerful."

"I suppose you and this lesbian were great friends," Shevenko said, his voice harsh.

"No," she said in a soft voice. "She tried, once, but I like what you have, not what women don't have. I understand her weakness, she understand my desires. We are just good friends, girl friends." She reached down and began to caress him gently. He felt the warmth of her tears on his shoulder.

"Sophia," he said, fighting to keep his voice gentle. "What a lesbian says is not considered to be responsible evidence. I will have to have her in, to demand the files she said she saw."

"You don't have to do that. She gave me the files and I made copies. I have them here, in my apartment."

"Why did you make copies, for what purpose?"

She moved in the bed so her right breast was against his shoulder. "Because when you had me in for my interview, before you hired me, when I first saw you my heart exploded. I wanted you for my lover. What can I bring a man such as you, a man as powerful as you are except my love, my body?

"When I first heard the gossip I thought that if I could bring you this, something that you could use to protect yourself against the Admiral—everyone knows that you two are enemies—I thought that I would be serving you."

Shevenko laid back against the big pillow, his face rocklike. She looked at him and then ducked her head under the covers and began to caress his chest and stomach with her tongue. Her head went lower and lower and he spread his legs to accommodate her and then her mouth was on him and he began to groan in ecstasy despite himself.

"And what is it you want?" he asked when she had emerged from beneath the quilt.

"Just you," she said. "As often as you can arrange to be away from your wife." She leaned over him and kissed him, her tongue searching for his.

"If you wish, I would like to be your chief aide. That would end the dangerous gossip among the pretty boys in the building that you put your manhood in Stefan's ass."

"And Stefan," he said. "What about him? He has been an efficient aide. He does a great deal of work." He ground his teeth together and she shuddered at the sound. "A great deal of work, much of it highly confidential."

"I leave that to you," she said softly "I have disturbed you, you are too tense. I am tense as well. Love me as I taught you to do last night." She pushed gently against his head, pushing it down underneath the covers. As he kissed her soft belly and then the moist area of her groin, hearing her moans of joy, he wondered if Sophia Blovin worked for him or for one of the many enemies he had made since he took over as the head of the First Chief Directorate of the KGB. She cried out in ecstasy and he shuddered. The honey trap, as he knew very well, had brought other powerful men down in disgrace.

Vice Admiral Mike Brannon flipped through his Rolodex, looking for the number of the Commander, Submarines, Pacific Fleet. He dialed the switchboard and gave the number to the operator and sat back and waited for the connection to be made. In ComSubPac's office at the Naval Base in Pearl Harbor a Chief Yeoman took the call and put it through to Vice Admiral Homer Ross.

"Hey, Mike," Admiral Ross yelled into the phone. "How are you? How's Gloria and the daughter?"

"Fine," Brannon answered. "Little Gloria isn't little any more. She's given us two grandchildren. How's your family?"

"Great. My oldest son just made XO on his destroyer. Phoebe is fine. What can I do for you, Mike?"

"A damned big favor and I have to ask you to keep it quiet. That is, I don't want you to tell anyone I asked you to do it."

"Fire away," Admiral Ross said.

"Can you call a Quiet Alert for all the submarines in your command?"

"I could. Any reason that you can tell me"

"That's the sticky part," Brannon said slowly. "I can't tell you at this time. Later."

"Okay by me. Time we had a readiness drill anyway. When do you want it called?"

"Now." Brannon said quietly.

"Will do," Admiral Ross said. "Must be important. Something big breaking?"

"Something very damned big may break," Brannon said. "I owe you one, my friend. I won't forget."

"Give my love to your lady," Ross said. "I'm due in for meetings in Washington next month. We'll have dinner?"

"On me," Brannon said. He put the handset back in its cradle.

CHAPTER 12

Captain Miller finished sticking the gummed strips of the message the *Devilfish* had received onto a sheet of paper and went into the Wardroom.

"Please tell the officers off watch to assemble here," he said to the Officer's Cook. He waited, the message face down on the green baize cloth, until the officers came in and took seats.

"We have been ordered to go on Quiet Alert," he said. "Our function in the exercise is to patrol just west of the SOSUS array off the Strait of Gibraltar. We will patrol in company with the *Orca.*"

John Carmichael, the Executive Officer of the *Devilfish*, looked at his Commanding Officer and read the warning in Captain Miller's eyes.

"I figured when they told us to get out here on the double and then threw that damned electronic dummy target at us that old Iron Mike was going to work our asses off," Carmichael said in an offhand tone. "Maybe when the drill is over we'll get to go in to a good port in Spain or Portugal."

"Electronic dummy target?" Lieutenant Rory Delahanty, the Sonar Officer, shook his head, "John, I listened to that target. I watched the screens. That was a damned submarine that we and the *Orca* were after or I'll eat my hat."

"You prefer salt and pepper or maybe some salad dressing on the hat?" Captain Miller said.

"Well, sir," Delahanty said, "I mean, I've worked with all sorts of electronic dummy targets and I've never heard anything as realistic as what we were listening to out there. It changed speeds, it even reversed course when we went to full speed to run it down and get a shot at it. At one point our computers were giving it a speed of more than fifty knots! I never heard of a dummy target that could go that fast.

"Just as the *Orca's* missiles hit the water the target's sonar transmitter started up. If that had been a submarine the sonar operator would have keyed his transmitters when he heard the missiles striking close aboard to try and confuse the missile's electronics, sir. But it wasn't a submarine so I don't know what to think." Delahanty's round Irish face was almost cherubic as he looked at Captain Miller.

"We've been away from the States for what, six months?" Captain Miller said. "We really don't know what new gadgets they've developed for us to practice with. All we have to concern ourselves with now is carrying out the rest of the exercise. I want you to tell your people in the crew that we're on the exercise and that we're in competition with *Orca*. She beat us to the target and I don't want *Orca* beating us again, at anything. And I don't want Iron Mike Brannon breathing down my neck if we fuck up. That's all, fellas."

He left the Wardroom and went to his cabin. There was a buzz of conversation after he left that Carmichael stopped with a warning frown. Carmichael finished his coffee and stood up.

"A word to the wise, gentlemen. Don't talk about this to the crew, don't talk about it among yourselves. This is an exercise, that's all. Don't speculate."

A few minutes later, sitting in Captain Miller's cabin, he looked at his Commanding Officer.

"How much longer can we keep up the charade, Captain? Damn it, Delahanty knows we were chasing a submarine. He's no fool. He can guess that the other submarine was a Russian. What's more, you don't waste two SUBROC missles on a dummy target."

"I know," Miller said. He rubbed his chin. "I just don't know what to say. We're supposed to keep this to ourselves, between you and me. I went down to the Sonar Compartment to tell the Chief and his people that they'd done one hell of a job and the Chief looked at me and the way he looked at me I know that he knows that was no dummy target. We may have to tell the Wardroom people the score. I have to think about that. I hate to think of what Iron Mike would do to me if he found out I told them."

"What do you think this Quiet Alert means, sir?"

"Oh, hell, Iron Mike is making sure that if the other side decides to strike back we're in a position to blow them out of the water," Miller said. "The Quiet Alert went out to all units, Atlantic and Pacific." He sat back in his chair, his face dark.

"I've been thinking about Captain Reinauer," he said slowly. "The Russian attack subs must carry a crew about the size of ours, a few over a hundred. I've never fired a torpedo or a missile at another ship. Neither has Reinauer. I wonder what it feels like to know you've killed that many people?"

"Submarine skippers in World War II sank a lot of ships, killed a lot of people," Carmichael said. "I don't think they worried about that."

"That was during a regular war, after Japan had pulled the sneak attack on Pearl Harbor and killed about two thousand of our people," Miller answered. "We're not at war. There's something damned funny going on, John. I wish I knew what it was."

Aboard the U.S.S. *Orca* Captain Reinauer read the message

he had run through the decoding machine and looked at his Executive Officer.

"Get all the officers into the Wardroom. Tell the OOD to turn the watch over to the Chief of the Boat." Eckert looked at him. "You going to tell the Wardroom what the score is?"

"I think I have to," Reinauer said. "ComSubLant has ordered all attack and missile submarines on a Quiet Alert. ComSubPac has done the same thing. Admiral Brannon or someone else must think the Russians might retaliate to what we did. If we're about to go to war I'm not going to keep up the pretense that we fired at a dummy target."

Captain Reinauer sat at the head of the Wardroom table, his face grim. He waited until his officers had seated themselves around the table and the Officer's Cook had served coffee.

"Leave the coffee pot on the table, Emil," he ordered. "I want the Wardroom area sealed off. No one is to go through the compartment until I say so. That includes you."

"Gentlemen," he said after the Officer's Cook had departed. "We did not fire those two missiles at a dummy target. Let me give you the background and bear in mind this is highly secret." He recited the facts succinctly and then watched the faces of his officers, looking for signs of alarm and seeing none.

"All submarine units of the Navy are now put on Quiet Alert," he said in a low voice. He looked down the table at Lieutenant Bill Reiss.

"Your suspicions about our target were well founded, Bill."

"We destroyed them," Reiss said in a low voice. "How many people aboard, a hundred or so?"

"About that, I'd think," Reinauer said.

"What happens now?" Reiss asked.

"I don't know," Reinauer answered. "All I know is that we have been assigned a patrol area off the western edge of the SOSUS network off Gibraltar. *Devilfish* will be patrolling with us. We're senior so the XO will work out the patrol area positions and co-ordinate with *Devilfish*." He drew a deep breath and let it out slowly.

"My direct orders from ComSubLant were to keep this information between the XO and myself. I have disobeyed those orders because I can't go into what might be a nuclear war with you people in ignorance. All I ask is that you give me your word that you won't blow the whistle on me when we get back to port."

Lieutenant Reiss looked at the officers around the table. "Captain," he said slowly, "I think I can speak for the rest of us and say that none of us will ever say a word about what you've just told us.

"The point is, sir, we knew. All of us here knew that wasn't any dummy target out there. None of us ever saw anything maneuver like that target did. Only another submarine could go through those maneuvers. That's all we've been talking about since we secured from General Quarters.

"I might add that the crew knows this, too, or at least they suspect it pretty strongly. Our sonar people are awfully sharp, you know. They've had too much experience with all sorts of electronic targets and with other attack submarines in drills. They know damned well that we fired at another submarine and that we hit it and they have to know that the other submarine was a Russian.

"The Chief of the Sonar Gang told me that the target was so sophisticated that its sonar operator hit his transmitting key after the missiles impacted on the surface to try and throw off the missile electronics. That's exactly what the Chief would have done if he heard missiles hitting near us, he would have keyed his transmitters at full decible rating."

Captain Reinauer nodded his head. "I know," he said. "But I've disobeyed a direct order from ComSubLant in telling you what we, the XO and myself, knew before we arrived on station. All I'm asking you is to keep it to yourselves. As far as the crew is concerned, keep up the pretense that it was a very sophisticated target that we fired at."

Lieutenant Reiss looked steadily at Reinauer. "Are we at war, sir?"

"Not that I know of," Captain Reinauer said. "I think that if we were at war all ships on station and in port would have been notified. There would have been messages for the ballistic missile submarine to unlock their missile safeguards. There have been no such transmissions. I don't know what this is all about, I don't know why the Russians sank the *Sharkfin* but I do know that we have avenged *Sharkfin*."

Down in the *Orca's* torpedo room Turk Raynor had supervised the loading of two SUBROC missiles into the torpedo tubes. He turned to one of his torpedomen.

"Old Man and the officers ain't sayin' nothin' but I'll bet a payday that we didn't fire at no damned electronic target. Did you hear the Sonar people talking over the phone circuit? Damned target was maneuvering at forty-five, fifty knots, jinking all over the fucking ocean." He turned as Lieutenant Reiss came into the torpedo room.

"Tubes are reloaded, sir," Raynor growled. "Burn separation time is set at max on the missiles."

"Very well," Reiss said. "The Skipper is pleased that the missiles worked perfectly."

"What the hell does he expect, sir? We know our jobs."

"Did you see the Captain about your transfer?" Reiss asked.

Raynor nodded. "I followed the book, sir. I talked to you first and then to the Exec and then to the Captain."

"What did the Captain say?" Reiss asked.

"He told me to think about it. I already thought about it. I want off, sir. As soon as we get back into port. Whenever that will be."

"Might be some time," Reiss said.

"We gonna go after another Russian submarine and sink it, sir?" Raynor's heavy face was grim. The people in the torpedo room tensed.

"I didn't know we had sunk a Russian submarine," Reiss said.

"Look, Mr. Reiss, you're an okay officer. You know your job and you know our jobs and you don't bullshit anyone, you shoot square. Everyone on this ship knows we fired those missiles at a submarine. We got a guy on the battle phones in every compartment, you know that. We all heard the reports from Sonar. That wasn't any electronic target we shot at."

"Are you asking me to say that we shot at a Soviet submarine when we are not at war?" Reiss's voice had suddenly become crisp, official.

"No, sir," Raynor answered. "I figure you can't do that. I'm just telling you so you can tell the Old Man that all hands knows what went on. This is a pretty damned good crew, Mr. Reiss, except for those fucking nuke people, and the crew's worried. If there's gonna be a war we'd like to know it. We figure we're entitled to know that. And if there isn't any war why in the fuck did we shoot two SUBROCS at another submarine? Longer he doesn't tell us the more the stories will grow. You know sailors, sir, they talk to each other, they try to figure out what you people in the Wardroom are doing."

"The only thing I can tell you is that we fired at a dummy target, Turk. That's it. That's final. You can pass that word along." He turned and left the torpedo room and Raynor looked at his torpedo gang.

"You heard the man," he said in his rumbling voice. "For the first time since he came aboard the son of a bitch is bullshitting the troops."

There were meetings held on every nuclear ballistic missile submarine at sea on patrol. The Commanding Officers informed their Wardrooms that all ballistic missile and attack submarines had been ordered to go on Quiet Alert. The fail-safe procedures to insure that no Commanding Officer could fire a ballistic missile without full knowledge and acquiesence of his Executive Officer and Weapons Officer were reviewed. The three officers who were issued the special keys to unlock the firing consoles made sure that their keys were hung on thongs around their necks. The precise language of the order to fire the missiles that would come from the President of the United States, or the Emergency Command Center in case the President were killed in a nuclear attack or unable to issue orders for any other reason, was gone over in detail.

The nuclear attack submarines in ports in Scotland, Japan, Guam and the United States put to sea and headed for predetermined positions to intercept any Soviet missile submarines that managed to escape the passive mine fields that were positioned to destroy enemy submarines en route to the United States.

In the Black Room of Operations Commander Fencer kept track of every Soviet submarine that had earlier gone into the Atlantic or the Pacific on patrol. The watches in the Black Room were doubled and a cot was brought in for Commander Fencer, who took up residence in the Black Room. The official word was put out that ComSubLant was conducting an all-out readiness drill for all submarine missile and attack units.

In his office Vice Admiral Brannon checked the reports that were flowing across his desk in a steady stream. He looked up at Admiral John Olsen.

"Not bad, John. We've got fairly good coverage already and in another ten hours we'll have saturation coverage with attack submarines on the Soviet routes to the Atlantic and Pacific."

"How about the Russian missile subs that were already on patrol?" Olsen asked.

"The best we can do there," Brannon said slowly, "is to assign two attack submarines to cover each one of them. That's been done. Fencer's got every one of them pinpointed. Radar units on both coasts are alerted. If they pick up any incoming missiles the bastard who fired the missiles won't last ninety seconds after he fires his last missile. We'll hit him with retaliatory anti-sub nuclear missiles from the shore."

"Same thing goes for our ballistic missile submarines," Olsen said dryly. "The Soviets can pinpoint the source of their missiles and destroy them." He got to his feet. "Submarine war isn't like it used to be when you and I fought in World War II, Mike. Now if you fire sixteen ballistic missiles at an enemy you got to know that you're dead right after your last missile is airborne. Isn't a nice thing to think about, you know?"

"I know," Brannon said. "I guess everyone on missile submarines knows that. Sometimes I wonder how we get men to serve on them, knowing that they won't live very long if they ever have to fire their missiles."

"Must be a thing called patriotism," Olsen said. "Not a popular word, now, what with Vietnam and all that. But I think it's the only thing that keeps those sailors on submarines." He looked at Brannon.

"Any word from Admiral Benson?"

"His last call to me said they had solid evidence that the Russians are in a dozen fire fights along the Chinese border. Not little fights, either, pretty good scrambles. Soviet planes are overflying Chinese territory and there's been some bombing raids on Russian posts by Chinese aircraft. Benson says it's a damned serious situation."

"The Chinese must know something," Olsen said. "Let's hope they keep nipping at the Russian heels. Might convince whoever ordered the *Sharkfin* to be sunk that they've bitten off more than they can chew." He stopped as the phone rang. Brannon picked it up and listened and grunted a "thank you" and put it down.

"Bob Wilson has told Admiral Benson that the Israeli intelligence has picked up information that the Soviet Union is going to a full submarine war alert."

CHAPTER 13

Stefan Lubutkin entered Igor Shevenko's office in response to the buzzer Shevenko had pushed, his gold Cross pen and a notebook in his hands.

"Yes, Comrade Director?"

"Is that report from Department V on the plans to disrupt the British Railway System still in the office?"

"No, sir, after you initialed it two weeks ago I sent it to Files." He looked pointedly at his wrist watch. "It's almost five, sir. The Files people shut up shop at four-thirty each day. We can't get a file until after five and with only one person on duty in Files after five that will take some time." He looked again at his watch.

"You have a date this evening?" Shevenko asked.

"Yes, sir," Lubutkin said.

"You must be a regular dog with the girls," Shevenko said, grinning. Lubutkin blushed. "Don't bother with the files, call Simonov and tell him I want to see him at once. One of these days we'll go to lunch with your girl friend, agreed? I'd like to meet her."

"As you wish, Comrade Director. I'll make the call at once and thank you for being understanding." He went into his office and Shevenko heard him talking on the telephone. Lubutkin stuck his head around the corner of the door.

"He will be here in five minutes, sir. I'll go now, and thank you again."

Anton Simonov walked into Shevenko's office and extended his hand. Shevenko shook hands with him and pulled the other man close to him.

"Go back to your office," he whispered. "Bring one of your sweepers back with you." Simonov nodded and left. He returned with a stolid man who carried a box in his hand. He nodded his head to Shevenko and put the box on Shevenko's desk and opened it. He took an electronics device out of the box and hung it around his neck and began to sweep the office for electronic bugs. When he had finished he stood in front of Shevenko's desk and packed his box.

"One tape cassette hooked up to your telephone, Comrade. The cassette is in the next office. Nothing else."

"I know about that one," Shevenko said. "I ordered it installed. Thank you." The man left and Shevenko opened the front of a dummy set of filing drawers, revealing a small General Electric refrigerator. He took two glasses and a bottle of American vodka from the refrigerator and poured two drinks.

"How does it go since the reorganization of the department?" Shevenko asked. Simonov lifted the small glass of vodka in salute.

"Good and not so good. Mostly good," Simonov answered. "Some of the holdovers from Department Thirteen, the Wet Squad people, are bored. Planning sabotage of the London subway system is not as exciting as assassinations, in their minds. Some of the people who worked on the desecration of synagogues in West Germany, that was at least ten years ago, still think that is what we should be doing today. But on the whole, things go well. And with you?"

"Like you, good and bad," Shevenko said.

"There must be some bad or you wouldn't have asked for a sweeper after your aide had left for the day."

"I have been told a reason to suspect him," Shevenko said slowly.

"Can I help?" Simonov asked.

Shevenko poured another drink and looked at the man sitting in front of his desk. He and Anton Simonov had been schoolmates when they were children and later in the Academy. Shevenko had joined the KGB several years before Simonov had been recruited and had risen within the ranks rapidly. When the Kremlin leaders decided in the mid-Sixties to eliminate the dreaded Department Thirteen because of unwanted publicity, Shevenko had prevailed upon the Politburo to shift the emphasis of the department from assassination to the planning of sabotage of military and civilian installations in the West. He also suggested that Department Thirteen be renamed Department Five and that it assume a very low profile. When those suggestions were given formal approval Shevenko had raised Anton Simonov from an administrative job in Department Thirteen to be chief of the new Department Five.

"Yes, you can help," Shevenko said. "I want a twenty-four hour surveillance put on my aide, Stefan Lubutkin. The same surveillance put on Admiral Zurahv, if you still have agents in your department who can do this without detection and who are trustworthy."

"No problem," Simonov said. He tossed off his vodka, inhaling sharply, savoring the bite of the liquor against the back of his throat. He grinned. "I had decided today to come to you tomorrow about Lubutkin."

"Why?" Shevenko said.

"First of all, he's a homosexual. You knew that, didn't you?"

"I had heard that only recently. That's why I called you. Is it common knowledge?"

"I don't think so," Simonov said.

"But you knew," Shevenko said softly. Simonov raised his hands and waved them.

"Don't misunderstand me, old friend. I was asked to do surveillance on a certain person to discover if he had normal sexual desires. I carried out the surveillance, it is still going on, and we found that this certain person does not have normal sexual desires. He prefers young men. He prefers your Stefan Lubutkin." He smiled and when he spoke his voice was very soft. "The certain person is, as you probably suspect, Admiral Zurahv."

"Why didn't you come to me when you got this request?"

Simonov shrugged his shoulders. "Comrade, the request came from very high up, too high for me to take that chance. But I did intend to ask to see you tomorrow, to warn you about Lubutkin." He sat back in his chair. "I do not concern myself with internal politics, as you know, but I have heard that you and the Admiral are not the best of friends."

"One could say that," Shevenko said. Simonov smiled faintly.

"To put it simply, Comrade Director, the Admiral is a bungholer. I looked up the proper word today, after I had decided I must come and talk to you. The Admiral is a pederast."

"And Lubutkin?" Shevenko said.

"He has the hole the Admiral bungs," Simonov said.

"You have proof of that?"

"Not the sort of proof one would need to go before a Board of Inquiry. But I have lots of circumstantial evidence. Pictures of the two of them meeting clandestinely. Lubutkin getting into the Admiral's car. Lubutkin and the Admiral getting out of the car at the Admiral's apartment and going inside. Lubutkin coming out alone hours later. Lubutkin going home to be consoled by his roommate."

"I thought he lived alone," Shevenko said.

"The housing records show he lives alone but he shares his apartment. He has two rooms and a private bath and a kitchen, with another pervert, an artist who has been in trouble before for making anti-Soviet statements. We have had microphones and a camera hidden in that apartment for two weeks. The evidence is quite interesting, if you have a strong stomach."

"Explain," Shevenko said.

"When Lubutkin comes home from the Admiral's apartment his roommate bathes him and applies some sort of salve to his asshole. The Admiral must be hung like a mule. Then your boy bungholes his roommate. Two days ago the roommate begged Lubutkin to bring his friend to their apartment for a threesome. If that were to happen . . ." Simonov left the sentence hanging.

"If that were to happen the Admiral would be commanding a shovel in Siberia," Shevenko said. "But it won't. He's too old a fox to go outside his own run." He looked at Simonov and reached for the bottle of vodka.

"You wouldn't care to tell me who ordered you to begin this surveillance of the Admiral?"

"I couldn't do that, now could I, old friend?" Simonov reached for the small glass of vodka and held it in his hand. Shevenko noticed that Simonov's hand did not tremble.

"Let me make a guess, then," Shevenko said. "Would the person who asked you to do this be older than most, one who spits a lot?"

Simonov sipped at the vodka. "In school, when we were in school," he said, "when the teacher wanted an answer and no one knew you would always guess and you were almost always right. You have not changed."

"Thank you," Shevenko said. He smiled. "You can supply me with photos, duplicates of your tapes?"

"Of course," Simonov said. "I will deliver them myself, tomorrow. We use the new camera, the one that prints the date and the time of day in one corner of the negative. How about an early lunch in that place we used to meet when you were planning the change in my department? Eleven-thirty?"

"Fine," Shevenko said. "I depend on old friends like you. I wish I had more of them. As my mother used to say, go with God."

"My mother always said that, too," Simonov said with a grin.

Isser Bernstein rocked back in his desk chair and let his eyes move from Moise Shamanski to Naomi to Lev Tolar, the top naval expert in the Mossad. Tolar, a short, squat man with a heavy beard, sat erect in his chair, holding a sheaf of papers in his hands. Bernstein turned to Naomi.

"What's the latest on the attacks by the Chinese along the Soviet border?"

Naomi looked at the notebook she held in her lap. "Our last information is timed at zero five thirty this morning, from the Moscow source. The Soviets are moving four divisions to the Chinese border. Two divisions are being pulled out of Poland, two out of East Germany. It's an airlift operation. Aviation units are also being deployed from western Russia to the border."

"Hm," Bernstein said. "Pretty big diversion of force, isn't it? Do the attacks along the border warrant that sort of diversion?"

"Our military people don't think the attacks are that serious," Naomi said. "They agree that one, perhaps two divisions would be sufficient at this time. With the caveat that if the Soviets really believe that the Chinese are going to do more than they have in the past then four divisions plus aviation units would be reasonable."

Bernstein turned to Lev Tolar.

"What's your thinking on this order from Moscow to put all their submarines on a war alert status?"

Tolar shrugged his shoulders "I wonder about the way the message was sent. It was sent in an old code, one that everyone can read. It's as if the Soviets wanted the Americans and everyone else to know what they are doing, and that isn't like them at all. If they meant serious business I think they would have used one of their top secret codes.

"Putting their submarines on war alert doesn't necessarily mean they will go to sea. Our reports show that their submarines are taking aboard stores and some torpedoes to fill out their racks. The order was issued yesterday morning but the crews of the submarines stopped work at fifteen thirty hours, the usual quitting time and crew members off duty were seen going ashore, going into town."

"What reaction do you pick up from Washington to that order?" Bernstein asked.

"The Americans have changed deployment of their attack submarines, sending two attack submarines to cover each Soviet missile submarine that is loose in the Atlantic or Pacific. But that's normal also, it's happened a number of times before when the Soviets would issue a general alert.

"There aren't very many Soviet missile submarines in the Atlantic or the Pacific," Tolar continued. "The Soviets have had quite a bit of matériel difficulty lately and their Navy seems, at times, to be on the edge of almost mutiny because of extended sea duty and very little time in port. So they've started leaving a lot of their ships in port, surface and submarine ships, to give the crews more leave time." He looked up from his notes.

"The Soviet admirals have had a policy of ten to fourteen days leave for their sailors every three years. It is a stupid policy and they've begun to realize that."

"Those Soviet submarines in port, they have to run a gauntlet of underwater listening devices and mine fields to get out to the Atlantic from the Kola Peninsula and to the Pacific from the Sea of Okhotsk, don't they?" Naomi asked.

"Yes," Tolar said. "That is, the Americans will know the minute any Soviet submarine tries to get out into the Atlantic. The net east of the Sea of Okhotsk is not as tight, the area is more open than the route from the major missile submarine base on the Kola Peninsula so a few might get out into the Pacific."

"Once they start to move out to sea the underwater listening devices pick them up and then the mines get them, is that the way it works?" Bernstein asked.

"That's the principle," Tolar said.

"I'd like your opinions of what would happen if the major powers lose their heads and begin a nuclear war. Lev, you first."

"Both sides lose," Tolar said. "Neither can neutralize the other's counterstrike capability. Both lose."

"Where does that put Israel?" Bernstein said. "Where would we be in relation to the Arab World?"

"At war," Moise Shemanski said glumly. "At war with an enemy that outnumbers us twenty or more to one. Without any doubt, most of the Third World nations would come in on the side of the Arabs."

"Japan?" Bernstein said softly.

"They'd wait, with China, until the Third World nations had mopped us up and then China would move in and dominate what was left of the world. Japan would be China's ally, without doubt." Naomi and Tolar nodded their heads in agreement.

"My assessment is that the Soviets will do nothing for a while," Bernstein said. "They have too much on their plate at the moment, no matter what their hardliners say.

"They've got this new trouble on the border with China. Their satellite states in Eastern Europe are uneasy; the invasion of Czechoslovakia is only a year old, Poland has been restless since they returned Gomulka to power back in Fifty-eight. The grain crop this year is below expectation. There are meat shortages in the countryside. They have a lot on their plate." He leaned forward and put his elbows on the desk.

"But that notwithstanding, we have to assume that the Soviets might move to retaliate against the American destruction of their submarine. Their missile submarines may not be as bottled up as the Americans think they are. When the Egyptians mined the desert approaches in the 1947 war how did we break through the mine fields? We sacrificed the lead tanks to the mines and went through the mine fields along the path of the sacrificed tanks." He looked at Lev Tolar. "Couldn't the Soviets do the same thing, run one small submarine out through the mine fields and then follow the cleared path with the rest of the missile submarines?"

"It's not quite like a desert mine field," Tolar answered. "The mines the Americans use are not mines in the true sense of the word. They are modified torpedoes that lie on the bottom, inert. They have to be activated by a sonar signal and after that is done when a ship passes over them they rise from the bottom and go to full speed and chase down the ship, using a sonar device in the nose of the torpedo that homes on the noise of the ship's propellers.

"That leaves a gap in the mine field, yes. But an American submarine lying well clear of the mine field can energize all the other passive torpedoes with sonar signals and set them free of the bottom to sink any other ships that go through the mine field."

"Interesting," Bernstein said. "Do the Soviets know of this?"

"Not to my knowledge," Tolar said. "It is a very deep secret. We found out about it when they began to modify their older torpedoes to turn them into passive mines."

Bernstein massaged his small gray goatee with the fingers of his right hand. "It might be a good idea to let the Soviets know about this," he mused. "It might be something that would give them cause to be very cautious." He looked at his people, his face grim.

"Our best national interest is quite clear. It is to prevent a nuclear war between the two superpowers. I must think about it some more but I think the Soviets should know about the torpedo mines."

"If you decide to tell them, how will you do it?" Naomi asked.

"Shevenko," Bernstein said.

"He can't be trusted," Shemanski growled.

"True," Bernstein said. He smiled faintly. "None of us can be trusted by someone from another nation, not if we think first of our own nation. But in all the years I have known Igor Shevenko I have never known him not to pay back a favor or a debt. If he has this information it will give him another lever to use in his disagreements with the Soviet admirals and their hardliner backers in the Politburo." He rose from his chair.

"Thank you," he said. "We all have work to do."

The weather in Moscow had turned unseasonably warm and a soft, misting rain was falling, blurring the sharp icy edges of the snow piled along the sides of the sidewalks. Igor Shevenko left his office and walked the two blocks between his office and the Kremlin with long, firm strides, breathing in the warm, moist air with relish. At the Kremlin he turned north and slowed his pace, heading for a worker's cafeteria near Sverdlov Square. He pushed through the door of the cafeteria and his nostrils were assaulted by the heavy, warm smells of rain-soggy clothes and the odors of cooking. He shouldered his way through the early lunch crowd and found a table back in a corner of the room. Anton Simonov entered the cafeteria a few moments later and stood looking around the room. He saw Shevenko and joined him.

"A good change," Shevenko said as Simonov sat down. "A little warm rain is better than a lot of wet snow." He looked up at the waiter who was standing near the table.

"Cabbage soup, a cold pork sandwich, and beer." The waiter looked at Simonov, who nodded and said he would have the same.

"This break in the weather probably means we will be freezing our asses off this time next week," Simonov said. "I like to see winter stay winter until it is over and done with. I don't like these little periods of warm weather."

"Did you like it in Egypt when you were there?" Shevenko grinned at the other man. He broke a piece of bread into chunks and began to chew one of the pieces.

"No. Too damned hot there. Day and night no relief from that damned muggy heat. And filth? Cairo has to be the world's dirtiest city." He pulled his chair into position as the waiter put two bowls of steaming cabbage soup on the table.

"Anything happen last night, after we talked?" Shevenko asked.

"The usual thing," Simonov said. He blew on a spoonful of soup and tested the temperature with his tongue before putting it into his mouth. "Your boy, excuse me, your aide was picked up in an alley near your office by his friend in his official car. We have pictures of that. We have pictures of the two of them getting out of the car in front of the friend's apartment. The friend must like your aide, he patted him on his ass on the way to the apartment door.

"Your aide came out of the apartment at one this morning and the friend's car took him home. The film taken at his apartment shows the same routine." He bent his head to his soup bowl and spooned up the savory liquid. He finished the soup and shoved the bowl away as the waiter put two plates, each with a thick sandwich of coarse bread and cold pork, on the table with two steins of beer.

Simonov grimaced, his open lips showing a tooth capped in stainless steel. "It's a damned disgusting business, you know that? Your aide gets buggered and then he comes home and buggers his roommate."

"Did you get pictures last night?"

"Oh, sure. We took over the apartment next door to your aide's apartment. The pictures are in my briefcase." He raised the case from the floor and put it back down. "Also cassettes, copies of the cassettes we made over the past three weeks in your aide's apartment. Turns your stomach to listen to them."

"The friend's driver," Shevenko said.

"We own him," Simonov said. "He's a sailor. Charged once with sodomy. The man he drives for got him off. I think the whole Navy is homosexual."

Shevenko grinned. "You know what Winston Churchill said when he was in charge of the English Navy? He said the quote unquote glorious days of wooden ships and iron men were really days of beatings and buggery. How do you own the driver?"

"You start following one lead and you uncover six others," Simonov said. "You know how it is. The driver has a little friend, a little fop who writes about the ballet for magazines.

We took pictures of the two of them and then leaned on the driver. He will co-operate. His boss lets your aide play with him in the back of the car. The driver knows what goes on. If necessary he'll testify to save his own skin." He looked at Shevenko as he washed down a mouthful of the coarse bread and pork with a swallow of beer.

"It's a damned dangerous situation, my old friend. With a snake in your grass such as you have you'd better be damned careful where you step." He raised his hand and the waiter brought two more steins of beer and took away the empty plates.

"If I may suggest it, old friend, let me eliminate your aide and his roommate. With apartments as scarce as they are, two animals like that don't deserve to have their own quarters. With a bath and a kitchen."

"When do you have to show your evidence to the man who asked you to do the surveillance?" Shevenko said.

"No fixed time," Simonov said. "Listen to me, Igor. Let me take care of this snake in your office. I'll arrange it so you will be in the clear, depend on me for that. You don't have to say who your aide's friend is. You can simply say that you suspected your aide and that his death came before you could bring charges against him. With both of them eliminated part of your problem goes away. With what I have got, while it's only circumstantial, the driver and the death of your aide makes what I do have damned heavy circumstantial evidence. Enough for the man who wanted the surveillance done to use his weight. And he is one who knows how to do that."

"How would you do it?" Shevenko asked.

"A simple wet job. I've got people in my department who have made a career out of that sort of thing. It would appear to be a lovers' quarrel between two homosexuals. Not uncommon, not even for Moscow."

"Weapons?" Shevenko asked.

"Probably kitchen knives. A dual stabbing. We'd wait until after your aide had buggered his friend. The medical examiner could be coached to examine the artist's bunghole for semen. Simple."

Shevenko pushed back his chair and looked at the bill the waiter had laid on the table. He put some money on top of the bill and took the briefcase Simonov handed to him. He stood up.

"Tonight," he said.

"Agreed," Simonov said. "But we may have to wait a day, wait until your aide does his job on his little friend so the medical examiner will be able to find the evidence."

"I'll owe you for this," Shevenko said as the two men walked toward the door of the cafeteria. "I always pay my debts, Anton."

"There will be no debt," Simonov said firmly. "I can never repay you what I owe you. For many things. Not the least of which is my wife's peace of mind. Her mother is safe and happy in Israel, thanks to you. She and my wife pray for you each night. Think no more about it. Think about finding someone to be your aide."

"I have someone in mind," Shevenko said as the two men walked slowly along the sidewalk. The misting rain had stopped and a cool wind was blowing. "It will freeze by tomorrow," Shevenko said.

"Who do you have in mind?" Simonov said. "I have a good man in my department who might be the man for you."

"Sophia Blovin," Shevenko said.

"Sophia?" Simonov grinned. "A man would be a fool not to bring that one along, to raise her up. And to lay her down!" He banged on Shevenko's shoulder with a heavy fist and laughed.

"You never change, old friend! You know what we used to say in the Academy, about the girls? We used to say that if you made it the first time with a girl then you could be certain that Igor had been there ahead of you!"

Shevenko shook his head, smiling. "Those were good days. Tonight, if you can."

"Leave it to me," Simonov said.

CHAPTER 14

The early morning winter winds rattled a loose window in Captain Steel's office and he went over to the window and pulled the drape across the glass, shutting out some of the cold air that came through the loose-fitting window frame and muffling the noise of the wind. He went back to his desk and sat down and watched as a Chief Electronics Technician patiently searched for hidden electronic bugs in his office. The Chief finished and packed away his gear in a box.

"Not a thing, sir," he said to Captain Steel. "Everything's as clean as a whistle." Steel nodded and the Chief left the office. He stopped at the desk of Captain Steel's Chief Yeoman, looking back over his shoulder to make sure the door to the office was closed tightly.

"What's with him, he paranoid? Every other week he wants this place swept. Who the hell is going to bug an office in this area of the Pentagon?"

"Someone did, about eight years ago. Before I got here. He found the bug under his desk. That was back when he was fighting for appropriations for his submarines. He's never forgotten it."

"Why didn't you get yourself a transfer," the Chief Electronics Technician growled. "Got to be better billets than this one for a Chief with as many years in as you got."

"It's not too bad. He's hard but he's fair. Worst thing about him is you can't drink coffee or smoke during working hours. He says coffee and cigarets are poison. He might be right. I feel a hell of a lot better, not smoking or sucking up coffee all day long."

Satisfied that his phone lines were electronically clean, Captain Steel dialed the private number of Representative Walter W. Wendell, Chairman of the House Armed Services Committee.

"Us country boys get up early," the old Congressman drawled into the phone. "Yeah, I can meet you at that place. In about twenty minutes. Can't give you too much time. Got to call a committee meeting and sort of take a fall out of one of my new members. Damned fool thinks he's gonna get a new Naval Reserve Armory for his district. Hell, the Naval Reserve is the biggest boondoggle we got and I ain't releasin' no funds for another pile of bricks. Twenty minutes."

The Congressman ordered coffee, ignoring the cold stare of disapproval from Captain Steel. He hunched over the table and dug a crumpled pack of cigarets out of his coat pocket. He pulled a cigaret out of the pack and straightened it between his arthritic fingers and lit it, not bothering to blow the smoke away from Captain Steel.

"Had one of my best bird dogs do a rundown on Brannon," he said. "The bird dog's good at his trade. He can find rich black dirt where you and me see nothin' but gravel. He couldn't find nothin' in Brannon's life, official or private, we can use against him."

"Which means?" Captain Steel rasped.

"Which means the easy way ain't there. I even had a friend ask old J. Edgar if they had anything on Brannon in J. Edgar's private files. Negative, as they say in the military."

"I gave you enough information to use, enough to haul

him before a congressional investigation committee," Steel said.

"And I told you what I thought of that information. I know what he did was wrong. General MacArthur was wrong too, but Brannon's smarter than MacArthur was. Brannon did something wrong that was so damned big and wrong that I'd say every mother's son of a voter out there in this great nation would stand up and holler that this is what we should have been doing ever since the Roosians euchered us out of half of Europe after the war." He sat back in his chair and sipped at his coffee and then he leaned forward, his elbows on the table.

"The Roosians sank one of your missile submarines. And Michael P. Brannon gave the order to sink the submarine that sank our submarine. And he got that submarine sunk. And the Roosians ain't done nothin' in return. And probably won't."

"The Soviet Navy has put all its submarines on full war alert," Captain Steel said.

"I know about that," the Congressman said. "Used an old code, didn't they? A code that everyone can read without no trouble. They want everyone to know that they're chompin' at the bit, ready to go to war.

"Well, shit! Reminds me of a bully we had in our town when I was a boy. He'd put a stick on his shoulder and dare the smaller kids to knock it off. If no one knocked it off he'd punch some of the littler kids and then laugh. Told my pappy about that and he told me that the next time it happened I should knock the stick off'n his shoulder and if I didn't he'd whop me with his belt. My daddy could whop the shit right out of you with that belt of his."

"And I suppose you knocked the chip off the bully's shoulder," Captain Steel said in a bored voice.

"I did and I purely kicked the shit out of that old boy." The old man smiled at the memory. "I don't know whether it was he couldn't really fight or if it was that I was more scared of my daddy and his belt than I was of that bigger boy. Didn't make no never mind. He never bothered us kids again." He signaled the waitress for a refill for his coffee cup and lit another cigaret.

"I know that you're an engineer, Captain, and a damned genius and you can't hardly keep your patience listenin' to me tell you that story. That's the difference between a good engineer and a good politician; politicians listen kinda close to people.

"Michael P. Brannon, Vice Admiral of our Navy, did to the Roosians what I did to that bully. He knocked the chip off their shoulder and he whupped their ass. They understand that kind of talk, Steel. The country understands that kind of talk." The faded hawklike eyes under the bushy gray eyebrows peered through the cigaret smoke at Captain Steel's ascetic face.

"Just mebbe, Captain, just mebbe you've misjudged the caliber of Michael P. Brannon. Mebbe he's a mite too tough for you. Mebbe he's got some ideas that I haven't had a chance to hear. Think that could be so?"

Captain Steel drained the large glass of orange juice he had ordered. "We're not staying on track, sir. Admiral Brannon has committed an act of war. He did so on his own. The President, the Congress of the United States, has been deliberately ignored by Brannon. That should concern you, very greatly.

"What concerns me is where does this madness of Brannon's stop? I've lost one of my ballistic missile submarines. The Soviet Union has lost one of their newest attack submarines. What is next? Will the Soviets destroy two of my missile submarines and will Brannon then retaliate by destroying two of their submarines? You know, as well as I know, that our land-based nuclear missiles can be destroyed in the first Soviet nuclear strike. If that happens our only capability for retaliation lies in my missile submarines." He leaned over the table, subjecting his sensitive nostrils to the Congressman's cigaret smoke.

"I will not allow this to go on, sir! I will not risk losing one more of my submarines! I came to you, confided in you, because I trust you. But if you cannot solve this I will be forced to take action!"

Congressman Wendell leaned back in his chair and looked at the man across the table. He smiled softly.

"Captain, I told you to let me study this and I'd solve it. This is a political matter and if you want to know something, your tit's in the wringer just as much as Brannon's is. You knew about this whole thing and you ain't done anything about it and you'll be out on your Jewish ass right alongside of Brannon.

"Now you listen to me. We can't go public with this as long as the Roosians don't make any formal protests and I'm sure that ain't gonna happen. We can't force Brannon to resign because his personal life is so clean it nauseates me. But we got that stupid asshole, that Admiral McCarty on the Joint Chiefs. He's a lightweight if I ever saw one. And like most lightweights who maneuver themselves into a nice position of power he gets worried if anyone tries to sneak anything by him. I'm havin' dinner with him tonight at my house, got to rehearse him on his testimony before my committee, that business of the Navy wantin' four more carriers. Might drop a word in his ear about how Admiral Brannon has run a sneak around the end of his line. McCarty was an aviator. They don't usually like you submarine people. If I put it to him in the right way he might force Brannon to retire early. He knows how to put pressure on Brannon."

"Tonight, then?" Steel said.

"Provided McCarty gives me the openin' I need," Congressman Wendell said. "I'll be talkin' to you soon." He rose and shuffled out of the restaurant, leaving the check to be paid by Captain Steel.

Out in the broad reaches of the Atlantic Ocean the U.S.S. *Orca* was making all possible speed westward. Far out to her starboard side the U.S.S. *Devilfish* was following a parallel course. Mission: intercept and shadow a Soviet ballistic missile submarine headed for the East Coast of the United States and sink that submarine if it gave any indication that it was opening its missile hatches to fire its nuclear missiles.

Turk Raynor relaxed in a canvas chair on the starboard side of the *Orca*'s torpedo room. He cocked an eye toward the loudspeaker as it rasped, and listened to the Quartermaster of the Watch reporting the hourly course, speed, and depth. Raynor turned to one of his torpedo gang.

"Way things are going, heading on this course, we're gettin' farther and farther from Holy Loch. Gettin' farther and farther from a chance to go up to the Personnel Office and put in for my transfer. Way things are going lately I'll never get off this fucking ship. We'll probably be on war alert and all hands will be frozen in their duty stations."

Amos Spangler, a tall, slender torpedoman with arms roped with stringy muscle, lit a cigaret. "You get any dope on why we turned west and they opened up the throttle, Turk?"

"Quartermaster told me that we're runnin' with the *Devil-fish*. She's about five miles out to starboard. Some Russian missile submarine is comin' down from the north and we're supposed to intercept her and if she makes a funny move we sink her." The senior torpedoman stretched his arms above his head until his heavy shoulder muscles creaked.

"Trouble with this fucking nuclear submarine Navy is that they don't tell you a fuck-all about what's goin' on. I'll bet those nuke poges we got aboard know all the operating dope. If you ain't been to nuke school on these damned ships then you're nothin' but slave labor."

"Until they tell you to get ready to fire. Then you're damned important. Old Man comes down here to pass the time of day and make sure we ain't fuckin' off under the sun lamp or some fuckin' thing," Spangler said.

"Don't knock the Old Man. He's good people," Raynor growled. "If it wasn't for some old hands on this tub we'd never know what was going on." He stared at his torpedomen.

"You people got to know we didn't fire at no Goddamn

electronic target when we blew them two SUBROCS out of the tubes. If you don't know, we fired at a Russian submarine."

"Why the hell did we do that? We didn't get no announcement of war starting." Spangler asked.

"*Sharkfin* is gone," Raynor said flatly. "Quartermaster said the Russian submarine we went after with the SUBROCS sank the *Sharkfin,* couple of weeks ago. Old Iron Mike, sitting there in the Pentagon, thinks he's back on a diesel boat in the war against Japan. He sent orders to *Devilfish* and us to get the Russian sub. We got her. Bam! Two SUBROCS! Now we're gonna dog this Russian missile submarine and if the skipper of that tub makes one wrong fucking move we take him out like we took out the other one."

"Jesus Christ!" Spangler said. "We're at fucking war!"

"Word I get is that no war been declared," Raynor said. "But if they keep up this silly shit you can bet your damned skivvies that if we ever get back to the States the Goddamned country will look like something that fucking cook makes in the Galley. Burned up. Like charcoal."

Captain Reinauer sat in the Wardroom, a chart of the Atlantic in front of him on the Wardroom table. Eckert, his XO, sat next to him, pointing with the tip of a pencil at the chart.

"That's the Russian's course. We're on a flat intercept, sir. Should make contact in the next eight hours if he doesn't turn to starboard and head more toward the coast. Depending on his speed, it's been varying."

Reinauer touched the chart with his forefinger. "Looks like *Devilfish* will make the first contact, she's closer to his course line if he keeps coming as he is." He looked around the table at his officers.

"The order we received specified that we do complete surveillance of the Russian missile submarine. That means silent running. He can't help knowing there's one of us here but we'd like to keep him from knowing that there are two of us after him. *Devilfish* concurs. If they contact him first they won't make any effort to go to silent running. They'll dog him, follow him, run ahead of him, drop back, run alongside, always on his starboard hand.

"We'll go to silent running and a full alert sonar status. That means we'll be doing a constant attack problem on the Russian and on the *Devilfish,* so we know where *Devilfish* is at all times. If the Russian opens his missile hatches we should be able to hear that. The word I had in Holy Loch was that the Russians use manual power to open their missile hatches. Takes them about four minutes to open a hatch and they open one or at the most two at a time.

"That gives us time to get off torpedoes, provided we have a constant firing problem in the computers. Mr. Eckert will see to it that we have a continual attack problem running. Mr. Reiss will alert the torpedo room to the problem we face." He paused and rubbed his beard. "We can't go to Battle Stations and stay there for maybe days on end, once we make contact. We'll have to play it by ear, once we find him." He looked at Reiss.

"I want you to fill in Turk Raynor. Impress on him the need for readiness to fire on a moment's notice."

"Won't we be breaking ComSubLant's order to keep this information in the Wardroom, sir?" Reiss asked.

"Oh, hell!" Reinauer snorted. "Do you think that everyone on this damned ship doesn't know we sank a Soviet submarine? Do you think the crew doesn't know that we're going to sink another one if he makes a wrong move? You can't keep that sort of information from a crew. They know." The telephone on the bulkhead buzzed and he turned and picked the handset off the bulkhead. He listened for a moment and then put the handset back.

"*Devilfish* may have made contact. Sonar reports she's put on speed and is turning northward. Let's go to Battle Stations.

We'll follow *Devilfish* into whatever she's got. Go to silent running. Mr. Eckert, start a firing plot at once." The Wardroom emptied and the soft, muted clanging of the Battle Stations alarm sounded throughout the *Orca*.

CHAPTER 15

Anton Simonov was uncomfortable. Educated by the State as a mechanical engineer he had adapted well to KGB work. He often told his wife that working for the Komitet Gosudarstvennoy Bezopasnost or working as an engineer wasn't that much different. Both jobs depended heavily on research and careful reasoning; both jobs gave one satisfaction if done well. The major drawback as he saw it was that once a man had attained some degree of rank he must, of necessity, engage in politics. Anton Simonov was not a politician.

He sat in a chair in front of Leonid Plotovsky's desk in a sparsely furnished office in a wing of the Kremlin. He watched the old man peer at the pictures Simonov had brought to the office. Plotovsky pulled the earplug for the tape recorder out of the forest of stiff hairs that stuck out of his ear and turned off the recorder.

"Disgusting," the old man said. "Revolting, absolutely revolting! To think that good men died in the Great War to save this nation from Hitler's barbarians and now we breed scum like this!" He slammed his hand down on his desk console of buttons and his secretary opened the door to his office. He hastily began to turn the pictures over.

"Tea for the two of us," he growled and she withdrew.

"I need something honest to wash the taste of this filth out of my mouth," he said. "You must need something, you've seen these things more than once."

"No more than I had to see them, Comrade," Simonov said.

"I can understand that," Plotovsky said. He thanked his secretary for the two mugs of hot tea and waited until she had left the room and closed the door.

"There are no pictures of the Admiral's face, Simonov."

"No, sir. Gaining admittance to his apartment, planting cameras and microphones and tape recorders would have been a major operation, sir. He has two servants, bodyguards, really. They never leave his apartment together. One is always there." He drew a long, slow breath.

"However, I think we have what could be called a considerable body of circumstantial evidence, Comrade. If I may be allowed, let me outline that for you.

"There are the pictures of Lubutkin waiting to be picked up by the Admiral in his official car and of the pickup. There are the pictures of the two of them leaving the car and walking to the door of the Admiral's apartment building. The lighting in that street is excellent and the number of the building can be seen very clearly. In some of those pictures the Admiral can be seen patting Lubutkin's rear end as they walk to the door of the building.

"Then there are the other pictures," Simonov continued. "Those of Lubutkin and his roommate, who, incidentally, is a dissident and is not registered as living in Lubutkin's apartment. Those pictures clearly establish that Lubutkin is a sexual pervert. He buggers his roommate, his roommate buggers him. The pictures and the tape recordings leave no doubt as to his character.

"Finally, if we have to, we can use the driver as a witness

against the Admiral. He is unwilling to give witness, as I note in my report, but he can be forced to do so."

"He's also a pervert, according to your report," Plotovsky growled. "But it would be evidence of a sort, the damned condemning the damned. I agree with you that we should not use him unless we have to do so. If we do he would have to be eliminated. Not that it would be any loss. Well, I can only say that you have done a remarkable job in a very short time, Anton Simonov. I won't forget it."

Simonov looked away from Plotovsky. To enjoy the favor of a politician was, in his estimation, almost as dangerous as being in disfavor. He turned his eyes back to the old man behind the desk.

"Thank you, Comrade. One more thing, to finish my train of thought: The pictures establish the fact that the Admiral and Lubutkin were, shall we say, companionable. The tape recordings, that section where Lubutkin's roommate asks him to have the Admiral come to their apartment for an orgy, that establishes that the Admiral's fondness for Lubutkin was based in one thing, sexual perversion."

"It's disgusting," the old man said. He turned some of the pictures over and stared at them, his thin lips curling in revulsion.

"But not uncommon," Simonov said. "I have done some research in this area, sir. I found that this sort of perversion was quite popular in ancient Greece, in old Rome and in the Mayan civilization. It was common in those nations to use young boys and young men as prostitutes."

"As nations they all went under, didn't they? Pulled down by their own excesses?"

"Yes, sir."

"We could arrest Lubutkin, make him testify about his relations with the Admiral." Plotovsky said. "We could promise him immunity and then dispose of him after the evidence had been given."

"Unfortunately, we cannot," Simonov said. He chose his

words carefully. He was skirting the quicksand now and if he didn't tread carefully he could be sucked down.

"I posted two people in an apartment we requisitioned that was next to Lubutkin's apartment. We made a peephole so the men could observe, so they would know when to film, when to activate the tape recorders. Lubutkin came home last night after seeing the Admiral and the usual perversions between the two roommates went on. After they had finished we took the film out of the camera and one of the men took it to the laboratory to process it, that was our usual procedure.

"The other man on duty heard a quarrel between Lubutkin and his roommate. This was not unusual, they often quarreled. When my man looked through the peephole a while later he saw two naked bodies on the floor. He called the office and we sent a team at once. We found both men dead. They had stabbed each other with knives from their kitchen." Simonov paused, hoping that his forehead only felt hot, that it was not in fact sweating.

"A lovers' quarrel, if I may use that expression, Comrade."

"I see," the old man said. "I suppose it could happen that way. These people are not rational." He looked at Simonov, his old eyes shrewd.

"How is it that Shevenko did not know what was going on under his nose? Do you suppose that he was sampling this slimy creature's so-called pleasures? Igor used to have a reputation for being a great man for the ladies. Could a man change, prefer young men to women, as he ages? I don't know about such things."

"Oh, no!" The words burst out of Simonov's lips. "Not Igor, sir! I don't know if he even knew about Lubutkin's perversions. I haven't talked with him about this. To have done so would have been to violate your confidence, Comrade."

"And you would never think of doing that," Plotovsky said in his dry voice. He reached out and touched a button on his desk console. His secretary opened the door between their offices and looked in.

"Summon Igor Shevenko here at once," Plotovsky said. He turned to Simonov. "I must ask you to wait in my secretary's office while Shevenko is here. She will get you some fresh tea and some cakes."

When Shevenko arrived at Plotovsky's office the pictures were in a neat pile at one side of the desk, a piece of paper covering the top photograph. Shevenko entered the office and shook hands with the old Communist leader and sat down in the chair where Simonov had been sitting.

"I wanted to talk to you about this business of the Admiral," Plotovosky began. "But before we get to that, did your aide, that nice young man, what's his name, Lubutkin? Yes. Did he report for work this morning?"

"No sir, he did not. It is the first absence he has been guilty of since he began working for me two years ago."

"Do you know why he didn't come to work?"

"Yes, sir, I do. The State Medical Examiner called me not an hour ago. He is dead. The Medical Examiner told me that he and his roommate, I didn't know he shared his apartment and my office is checking now with the Housing Administration to see if his roomer was registered, the Medical Examiner told me that he and his roomer apparently had a fight and killed each other. The Medical Examiner also confirmed what I had learned two days ago, that Lubutkin was a pervert. If you will permit me sir, it is distasteful, the Medical Examiner found semen in each of the dead men's rectums."

Plotovsky nodded his head. "You learned of his perversion two days ago?"

"Yes, sir. I asked Internal Security to begin a surveillance of Lubutkin yesterday. The surveillance was to have begun today. The paperwork, you know, Internal Security has to have everything down in writing and in triplicate, that took some time." His heavy face took on a somber cast.

"I was perhaps derelict, Comrade, in not suspecting him earlier. But he was such an efficient aide. I considered myself lucky to have such an eager worker."

"I can understand that," Plotovsky said. "These days the young people don't know the meaning of work and sacrifice. They live for pleasure." He looked up, his hooded lizardlike eyes half hidden behind their drooping eyelids.

"Now you have to look for another eager young man, don't you? Someone who is willing to work long hours and keep a tight mouth about what he knows of your work."

Shevenko paused. The conversation was taking a turn he didn't like. Apparently the old man had known of Lubutkin's death. The question was, how much did he know? He looked at the floor and then up at Leonid Plotovsky.

"I won't run the same risk this time. I have decided to promote Sophia Blovin to the position of my aide. I gain in two ways if I do that. I have her expertise on the American psychology close at hand and I am more familiar with feminine appetites than those of perverts."

"Blovin," the old man said. He made motions with his hands, indicating Sophia's generous bosom endowment. "I remember her from the meeting we had. I think she's a good choice." He grinned slyly. "Now all you have to worry about is her falling into bed with some CIA agent or an Israeli agent. Maybe you had better take care of those appetites yourself, Igor. You used to have quite a name for that sort of thing at one time."

"Comrade, you shock me," Shevenko said with a small smile. "I'm a happily married man."

"Hah!" Plotovsky said. "I knew your mother-in-law before you did. Like mother like daughter. If the daughter is like the mother you live with an Arctic ocean iceberg."

"Did my honored friend seduce my mother-in-law?"

"Before she married your late father-in-law, who must have died of frustration," Plotovsky said. He leaned back in his chair. "Your wife's mother was a handsome woman, still is. I was younger then, full of piss. That was before the Great War and I didn't seduce her, she seduced me. She told me she believed it her duty to give solace to a hero of the Soviet Union." He shuddered at the memory. "A bad experience. I never went back. Enough of that, let's get to the business at hand. Did you know the Admiral was servicing your late aide?"

"No, sir," Shevenko said with a straight face. "Are you sure?"

"Very sure," Plotovsky said. "What sort of information could your late aide have passed on to the Admiral?"

"Not much," Shevenko said slowly. "I told him as little as possible. He didn't know I went to Israel, as you did because I told you. I told him only enough so that he could do his job."

"But he did have access to your office files," the old man persisted. "He could have gone into the files at night, when you were not there."

"I keep confidential material in a safe, sir. The safe is fixed to sound an alarm and spray the intruder with an indelible red dye if the safeguards are not first deactivated. He did not know about those safeguards."

The old street fighter put his gnarled hands on his desk top and studied them. "Lubutkin's death seemed to have happened most opportunely. Now that his lover is dead the Admiral has no chance to know what our strategy will be to oppose him unless there is some other leak in your organization. Is that possible?"

"I don't think so, sir," Shevenko said. He watched Plotovsky carefully. Sophia had told him earlier that Simonov had been summoned to see Plotovsky. Had Anton said anything? He thought not.

"I think that's enough of that subject," Plotovsky said suddenly. "Thank you for coming on such short notice." Shevenko stood up and walked to the coat tree and put on his coat and muffler and settled a fur hat on his head. After Shevenko had left the office Plotovsky buzzed for his secretary.

"Ask Comrade Simonov to come back in, please."

Simonov entered from the secretary's office and stood before Plotovsky's desk. "Your secretary arranged for me to hear what was said in your conversation with Comrade Shevenko," he said in a low voice.

"And?"

"I cannot believe anything bad about Comrade Shevenko, sir. We have been friends since our school days. You know that. He promoted me to my present position, sir. I admire him and trust him."

The old man nodded. "I know all that. I approved of your promotion. You do your work well and you have a tight mouth." He nodded his head slowly on his stalklike neck. "I know, too, that he arranged for your wife's mother to emigrate to Israel." He raised his hand as Simonov started to speak.

"I arranged for her passport, Anton," he said. "She is an old lady. She could do no harm. I have nothing against the Jews. I fought beside Jews in the Revolution. They were good men, good fighters. Our Communist theorists think they know everything. They don't. But I do. Almost everything. That is one of the advantages of age, Simonov, what you don't know you know how to find out. That's all. My thanks for your good work." He lowered his head and hawked and spat into the cuspidor that stood beside his chair.

He sat quietly for a few moments after Simonov had left and then he carefully turned over the pictures and sorted through them, looking at each picture with care.

"The naval defender of the Soviet Union!" he rasped. "What a farce!"

Vice Admiral Brannon's Chief Yeoman came into the Admiral's office and closed the door behind him.

"Permission to speak off the record, in confidence, sir?"

"Of course, Chief, what's on your mind?"

"I had lunch today with a chief I served with when he was first class. I got him his hat. He told me, his exact words, sir, were, quote a certain four-striper is out to hang Mike Brannon's ass unquote."

"Nothing very new in that, Chief. That certain captain has been after my ass ever since I was assigned to this billet."

"I know that, sir, but that captain hasn't been using his big guns. Now he's loading up for a broadside, sir."

"What's the caliber of his broadside guns, Chief?"

"Pretty heavy, sir. This chief told me that it's a congressman. A powerful congressman. Powerful enough to already have run a check on your private and official life sir. His caliber is big enough so that he went into the FBI's secret files to try and find something against you. That came up a blank so now, this chief tells me, they're gonna get at you through Admiral McCarty of the Joint Chiefs. They figure he can find a way to push you into retirement, sir."

"Interesting," Mike Brannon said. "I owe you my thanks, Chief. Both of us know that carrying tales is never good duty."

"I don't consider this to be tale-carrying," the Chief Yeoman said. "You shoot square with all hands, Admiral. This other chief and me, we hate to see someone playing dirty games to get at you, sir."

"You've paid me a compliment, Chief," Brannon said with a grin. "And I'll accept it. And I thank you for the scuttlebutt."

"Sir," the Chief Yeoman said in a strained voice, "sir, it isn't scuttlebutt! It's the straight poop!"

"I'll treat it as such," Brannon said.

CHAPTER 16

The Soviet ballistic missile submarine cruised steadily at 15 knots, running at 200 feet below the surface of the Atlantic. The crew was relaxed, a patrol station off Washington, D.C., even in winter, was better than the previous patrol area, which had been conducted under the ice near the North Pole. That had been almost seven weeks of complete discomfort, the ship wrapped in a numbing cold that the ship's heaters could never dispel, the crew swathed in sweaters, heavy boots and gloves day and night. The Atlantic in the Washington latitude would be chilly but not as cold as the far North. The great winter storms that often raged off the American coast were of no consequence to the submarine. It could submerge below the storm action and wait until the weather front had passed.

Captain Malenkov stood in the Command Center of his submarine and studied the chart his Navigator had placed on the work table. He nodded approval of the course line and the ETA on station. The chart showed that the patrol area would be 350 miles east of the American coast line, just east of the sharp drop where the Continental Shelf descended into an area noted on the chart as the Hatteras Abyssal Plain. The water in the patrol area was deep, almost 2,000 fathoms. Farther to the west, over the Continental Shelf, the chart showed depths of 12 to 24 fathoms. He turned his face upward as the loud-speaker rasped.

"Contact! Sonar reports fast screws bearing two three zero degrees. Contact is below our depth."

Captain Malenkov turned to his Navigator. "We have a visitor, Alexy. Our information was that the Americans didn't have any of their submarines out here. Like all our intelligence, it was apparently wrong." He stared at the chart.

"We'll stay on course, maintain speed. He will probably nose around like a dog at a garbage heap and then go away."

"Contact is making very fast turns," the loudspeaker rasped. "Contact is changing course to our stern."

"Range on the contact, get his distance and give me a triangulation on his depth," Captain Malenkov ordered.

"Range is two thousand yards. Target's speed is approximately forty knots. Target is definitely coming around our stern. Depth is three hundred feet."

The Soviet Captain watched as his Navigator swiftly drew in the plot on the chart. He snapped his head around to stare at the Navigator as the clangor of the other submarine's sonar beams echoed through his ship.

"He's letting us know he's there," Malenkov grunted. "He must be hitting us with his full decibel range. What the hell is he up to?"

"Target is now bearing one eight zero and moving to our starboard . . . Target is now changing course to run up our starboard side. It's very hard to get accurate bearings, sir. He's ranging on us with everything he's got."

"To hell with him," Captain Malenkov grunted. "Let him play his game. Let him make all the noise he wants. This is the open sea. We have a right to be here."

"And a duty," his Navigator murmured. He drew in a line on the chart to show the position of the other submarine. He looked at his Commanding Officer.

"Two can play at this game, Comrade. We could range on him."

"Let's do that," Captain Malenkov said. He picked up the telephone. "Sonar Room, I want full decibel ranging on the target. Let's find out which of us is the noisier."

Aboard the *Orca* Captain Reinauer and his XO studied the computer video screens in the Control Room. "He's locked in on him," he said to Eckert. "Look at the rate he's closing at, he must be doing thirty knots or better. Looks like he's going to sweep around his stern." He turned his head as the loudspeaker on the port bulkhead began to rattle and then blare.

"He's hitting him with all the power in his sonar transmitters," Ecker said. "Those Russians must think they're inside a boiler factory, all that noise hitting them."

Captain Reinauer studied the screen closely. "We've lost *Devilfish* on the passive. He must be around on the Russian's starboard side." He touched the helmsman on his shoulder.

"Six hundred feet. Let's do it quickly. I want to be able to hear both of them."

The *Orca* slanted downward sharply until it was well below the other submarines. The two white dots on the video screens now showed clearly.

"Looks like he's only about five hundred yards off the Russian's beam," Eckert said. The loudspeakers began to scream and Captain Reinauer, annoyance showing on his face, reached for the telephone. He stopped as the loudspeakers went suddenly quiet and the voice of the Sonar Chief on watch came over the speakers.

"Both targets are hitting each other with full decibel range, Control. I'll turn down the volume so it won't ruin your ears. They're making so much noise out there I don't think they can hear anything at all, Control."

"Affirmative," Captain Reinauer said into the telephone. "I want one quick echo range on the nearest target, that's a Russian submarine."

"Will do," the loudspeaker said. Reinauer waited.

"Range to the nearest target is two zero zero zero yards, Control."

"Very well," Reinauer said. "Helm, come left to three zero zero." He looked at the video screen.

"That puts us on a closing course with him," he said to Eckert. He turned to Lieutenant Bill Reiss, the weapons officer.

"Give me a time of direct closing," he said quietly. Reiss punched the keys on his computer console.

"At this speed, twenty knots, we'll be at collision point in three minutes, sir," Reiss said. "He's running at two feet, sir. *Devilfish* is on his starboard beam at the same depth."

"Very well," Reinauer said. "Maintain present speed."

"What do you intend to do?" Eckert said.

Captain Reinauer grinned, his white teeth showing in his thick black beard.

"We've got a reinforced sail on this lovely baby of ours. We can break through six feet of pack ice if we have to. I'm going to try and slide up underneath that bastard and give him a nudge. ComSubLant said to do a bump and run if possible. We'll bump the bastard!" He held down the talk button on his telephone.

"Sonar, this is the Captain. You think there's any chance either of those targets out there can hear us?"

"Not a chance, sir. They're making so much noise I don't think they can hear anything at all, sir."

"Very well," Reinauer said. He looked at the screen again and raised his eyes to Bill Reiss.

"Go to computer navigation to close on the nearest target. I want to come up underneath him and do it at dead slow." The helmsman leaned back in his padded chair as three lights flared on his console, indicating that depth, course and speed were now being controlled by the computers. Reinauer and Eckert watched the video screen as the white dot that was the *Orca* closed rapidly on the nearest of the other two white dots.

"Depth is three hundred feet, sir," the helmsman said.

"Up bubble of five degrees. Speed slowing to five knots, sir. Up bubble now two degrees, sir."

"Very well," Reinauer said. He looked upward instinctively as the sound of the Soviet submarine's screw echoed through the hull of his ship.

"Relative positions," Reinauer snapped.

"We're coming into him just aft of his bow," Reiss said. "Eighty degree port angle on the bow for us."

"Give me a vertical range!" Reinauer snapped.

"Target is fifty, repeat five zero feet above us, sir!" The sonar operator's voice was cracking with excitement.

"Close on a collision course!" Reinauer ordered. "One bump and then flood down and come hard left rudder after the bump." He turned to Eckert.

"I hope that bastard's got a solid keel, I don't want the son of a bitch draped around our neck!" He pressed the button on his telephone set.

"All hands, stand by for a collision. Helm, stand by for hard left rudder and turn for forty knots as soon as we hit. Flood manifold, stand by for quick flood and deep depth after the bump." He waited, watching the two white dots merge on the screen. Bill Reiss, standing in front of his computer console keyboards, cleared his throat.

"Expect collision in twenty-one seconds, sir. Override for helm on speed and depth is go, sir."

The *Orca* closed relentlessly on its target. The American submarine's bow slid just beneath the hull of the Soviet submarine and the heavily reinforced top of the *Orca*'s sail slammed into the Soviet submarine's keel with a loud crash. The crew members on watch in the forward section of the Soviet submarine were thrown off their feet by the force of the collision and amidships, in the Command Center, Captain Malenkov went to his knees, clutching at the work table in front of him to keep from falling.

"Collision!" the Navigator screamed. "Rig all compartments for collision! Make a report on damage!"

Aboard the *Devilfish* Captain Miller ordered his Sonar Room to stop ranging on the Soviet submarine.

"Ranging stopped, Control," the Sonar Room reported. "The target has stopped ranging, sir."

Captain Miller studied his video screens. John Carmichael, standing beside him, pointed at the screen. "That second blip, that must be the *Orca*. What the hell did he do? Look, he's turning away, going deep, increasing speed. Both the damn blips were one piece when I looked at it the first time."

"I think that son of a bitchin' Reinauer sneaked in on the Russian while all the noise was going on and gave him a bump and run," Captain Miller said. "Bastard never did tell me what he intended to do if we caught up with the Soviet sub. All he asked me to do was to get on its starboard side if we were both to port when we picked up the Soviet sub and to make a lot of noise. Bastard!" There was a tone of admiration in his voice. "Look, he's well clear of the Soviet now and he's turning back, coming up to depth." He winced as the loudspeakers on the bulkhead blared with the sound of the *Orca*'s echo-ranging transmitters.

"He's giving him hell from the other side. Commence full decibel ranging on the target. We'll make that bastard go out of his mind with noise!"

The initial confusion aboard the Soviet submarine was over in less than a minute as the crew, meticulously trained for emergencies, found that there were no leaks and that the ship was still answering its helm. Captain Malenkov looked at his Navigator.

"Two submarines after us," he said. "One deliberately came up underneath us and hit us! They're madmen! What in the hell is going on? We've done nothing wrong. Are these bastards going to risk an international incident?" He jumped as the *Orcas*'s sound transmitters hit the port side of his ship with a devastating roar of noise. Seconds later the noise doubled as the *Devilfish* joined in from the starboard side with its own shattering sound waves.

"Surface!" Captain Malenkov ordered. "I'm not going to stay down here with two madmen on each side of us. We'll go up and if they come up we'll find out what the hell they're up to." He grabbed at the work table for support as the submarine slanted upward sharply.

"He's going up," *Orca*'s Sonar Room reported. "He's blowing ballast tanks, Control. He's at one hundred feet and going up, sir."

"Surface," Captain Reinauer ordered. "Let's go up with him and see what happens. Tell *Devilfish* we're surfacing and suggest they do the same."

The Soviet submarine broke through the surface of the Atlantic and wallowed in the long deep-water swells, its rounded hull almost submerged. On either side of it the smaller American attack submarines burst through the surface, throwing spray as the sleek hulls reared half out of the water and then settled back. Captain Malenkov climbed into the upper part of his submarine's sail and took a bullhorn from his quartermaster. He watched and saw figures come into view in the top part of the sails on the two submarines that were now stationed on his port and starboard beams, less than one hundred yards away.

"What is the meaning of this madness?" Malenkov said into the bullhorn mouthpiece. "This is Captain Malenkov of the Soviet Navy. I demand to know why you are interfering with my ship in international waters."

Captain Reinauer raised his bullhorn to his mouth. "No one has interfered with you, Captain. We were trying to protect you from some American whales that make their home in these waters."

"Whales?" Captain Malenkov's voice was almost a scream. "You rammed my ship! You may have damaged my hull. I'll have you before an international court of inquiry! Who am I speaking to?"

"Captain Richard Reinauer, United States Navy, commanding the U.S.S. *Orca*, Fleet Attack Submarine. The ship on your starboard hand is the U.S.S. *Devilfish*, commanded by Captain Robert Miller, United States Navy.

"No one rammed your ship, Captain. It was the whales. They don't like Russian ships, Captain. They ram every Soviet ship they see. Very dangerous animals, those whales. Your commercial fishermen kill lots of their relatives and they want revenge. We tried to save you from the whales by making a lot of noise with our sonar gear but we didn't have much luck."

"You are insane!" Captain Malenkov roared into his bullhorn. "If I am interfered with again I will retaliate."

"You mean you have harpoons aboard and a harpooner?" Captain Reinauer replied. "I wouldn't do that if I were you, sir. A cornered pod of whales can be very dangerous. You could lose your ship, Captain."

Melenkov turned to his Navigator. "There's something very wrong here and these fools know what is going on and we don't. So we'll play their game and see what happens." He raised the bullhorn.

"We appreciate your concern for us, Captain. Do you have any suggestions about how we should handle these whales?"

"He's getting cute," Reinauer muttered to Eckert. "So we'll get cute." He cleared his throat and raised his bullhorn.

"I'd suggest you stay on the surface and ask for instructions from your headquarters, Captain. We'll submerge and try to herd the whales away from you."

"Very good of you," Malenkov answered. "Are you acting as fellow submariners or do you have orders to help us in this situation?"

"We are acting under orders, Captain. I strongly suggest you stay on the surface and contact your headquarters. We'll go down and look for the whales."

Captain Malenkov saw Reinauer's head disappear and then the submarines on either side of his ship began to slowly descend. He watched until the two submarines had disappeared. "Get me a sonar report on what they are doing," he snapped.

"Sonar reports contacts on either beam, sir," the loudspeaker on the bridge rasped. "Both contacts appear to be moving very slowly away from us. Depth of both contacts is now one hundred feet."

"Are we going to dive?" his Navigator asked.

"Dive? And be rammed or worse? Don't be a fool. There's something going on here that we know nothing about. I am not going to risk this ship. We stay on the surface and make a full report to Polyarnyy and wait for instructions. While we wait I want a man over the side in shallow-water diving gear to make an inspection of our bottom, up forward, where they rammed us." He stood in the ship's sail, his pale blue eyes scanning the empty sea.

"I will say one thing for those people," he said, "they must be superb seamen to be able to hit us as they did without losing their own ship."

"Or lucky," his Navigator said. "Madmen are often lucky, our own folklore teaches us that."

"Not lucky," Captain Malenkov said. "Seamen of the highest order. And clever. If we submerge we will be attacked. No ballistic missile submarine can fight off two attack submarines. Up here, on the surface, we are safe. At least for a while. Until Polyarnyy tells us what to do."

"Up here on the surface we are no longer a ballistic missile submarine," his Navigator said. "We cannot fire our missiles while we are on the surface."

"That's what I meant when I said they were clever," Captain Malenkov said. "That's why I suspect something very serious is going on politically. They have frustrated us for the moment. Polyarnyy must be informed at once. Perhaps others of our fleet have been frustrated in the same manner."

"Do you suspect we might be close to war, Comrade Captain?"

"Yes," Captain Malenkov said. "I'm going below and draft the message. You have the bridge and the watch. I want a constant sonar watch kept and I want the positions of both those submarines charted at all times." He dropped through the hatch and climbed down the ladders to the Command Center, thinking about the message he had to send. The Command at Polyarnyy would not be pleased with the way his ship's nuclear missile effectiveness had been so neatly neutralized. He pulled a pad of paper across the work table and took a pen out of his pocket. What was to be would be. He began to write.

CHAPTER 17

"What's the tactical situation?" Mike Brannon asked. John Olsen walked over to the big chart that covered almost all of one wall of Vice Admiral Brannon's office.

"The Russians have four nuclear missile submarines in the Atlantic. Here, here, here, and here. All of them are being covered by two or more of our attack submarines. They've got six of their missile subs out in the Pacific. Three of them near Pearl, one off Alaska and two near the West Coast. Each of those subs is covered by two attack submarines. The skippers of all our attack ships have let the Russians know they're there, that they're riding herd on them. We've got our own missile submarines in attack position. If they start anything we can incinerate damned near the whole of the Soviet Union."

Brannon walked back to his desk. "How about the passive mine arrays?"

"We're covering them with two submarines at each line of listening devices and mines. If they try to come out without notifying us we can blow them away. We've sent messages to the Soviet Admiralty notifying them that we're holding submerged exercises in those areas and to notify us, as per international custom, if they intend to send any submarines through those areas."

"They won't believe that for a moment."

"Maybe not, but they probably know what we're talking about." Olsen lowered his lean length into the cushions of one of the two sofas in the office and nodded his thanks for the cup of coffee Mike Brannon had put on the coffee table in front of the sofa.

"Joan gave me some scuttlebutt last night," he said, his voice carefully noncommittal. "She was at the weekly bridge party for junior officers' wives yesterday. Said one of the wives let it slip that Admiral McCarty is after your scalp. And mine. You hear anything about that?"

"Yes," Brannon said. "I got the word last evening from the Chief Yeoman. He told me about it."

"What gives?" Olsen asked.

"Our friend Captain Herman Steel is feeling his oats. He's enlisted old Representative Walter Wendell on his side. Wendell wants a new carrier built in the shipyard in his district. Captain Steel's testimony before Appropriations could help. Steel's been responsible for giving Wendell more damned Navy stuff than you can shake a stick at."

"So Wendell's paying back the IOU?"

"That's the way it works around here," Brannon said. "The Chief told me that Wendell had already run a check on my personal life and my military record and couldn't find anything to hit me with. He's even run a check on J. Edgar's private files. They can't find anything to use as a lever to force me into retirement so they're trying to get Admiral McCarty to do their work for them."

Olsen let out a low whistle. "Heavy guns, Mike. If the Joint Chiefs of Staff tell you to turn in your hat you turn in your hat. Or do you?"

"No, I don't," Brannon snapped. "Two people can play at Steel's little game. He's got the Chairman of the House Armed

Services Committee on his side. I've got a couple of guns on my side."

"You wouldn't care to tell me the caliber of the guns? Seeing as how if you get forced out I'll probably be carrying your seabag and mine?"

"Moise Goldman," Brannon said.

"The President's advisor?" Olsen's voice was incredulous. "He's supposed to be untouchable, he's the, what do you call it, the President's 'Eminence grise'?"

"The false Cardinal? I guess so," Brannon said. "He's got more power than a chairman of a congressional committee if it comes down to a fire fight. Or the Joint Chiefs of Staff."

"He's Jewish too, isn't he?" Olsen said. A grin was beginning to form on his lips.

Brannon nodded. "Yes. I came into this job just after President Milligan was elected. When the President began to get a lot of criticism in the press for his, let's say his countrified ways, he reached out for help to the *New York Times*, asked their managing editor if he'd come aboard as Chief of Staff for the President.

"It's a hell of an honor. Every newspaperman I've ever known thinks he can run the country better than the President. Or run the military better than the generals and admirals. So he took the job." He looked at John Olsen over the rim of his coffee cup.

"By the time he came aboard Captain Steel was already trying to open my sea valves, sink me. He thought that Goldman would be the man to do the job. But he and Goldman didn't hit it off. They're like flint and steel. Every time they meet there's fireworks. So I moved in and cultivated Goldman, did him some favors. He came to trust me, in time. I've never called in my IOUs from him."

"You think he'd help now? If Admiral McCarty is after your scalp Goldman wouldn't go to bat for you without knowing something about the score of the ball game."

"He knows the score," Brannon said softly. "I've kept him

informed. He's a hell of a good man. Keeps his mouth shut."

"He knows about the *Sharkfin*, about the sinking of the Soviet attack sub?"

Brannon nodded. "Remember back in the old days, in the war? When the Japanese destroyers had us pinned down and we were hunting for a heavy layer of salt water to hide under, so they couldn't hear us on their sonar?

"Goldman's my heavy layer of salt water. When I got home last night, after the Chief had tipped me off about Captain Steel and Admiral McCarty, Goldman called me to tell me what was going on. So don't pack your seabag yet."

"What will he do, force Steel to retire? That would be the best thing that could happen, as far as we're concerned."

"No!" Brannon snapped. "The Navy needs Steel. We need him. All we have to do is to box him in and let him know who's in charge, who's really in charge. I figure that Goldman can do that if he has to, if I can't do it."

"How?" Olsen asked.

"The Russians haven't made a move since we blasted their attack submarine," Brannon said slowly. "Every missile submarine they have in the Atlantic and Pacific is being dogged by our attack submarines.

"That means the skippers of those submarines are going to report to their headquarters that they're under constant surveillance. No ballistic submarine in the world can hope to survive if they're attacked by two attack submarines. I figure it this way." He leaned his elbows on his desk.

"As soon as they realize they're stymied they'll begin working out something to ease the pressure. If I'm right I think they'll get Brezhnev to call the President."

"That still leaves you holding a hell of a big sack, Mike. You'll have to explain to the President why you didn't tell him."

"That will be tough," Brannon said. "I won't be able to tell the President that I kept Goldman informed. But Goldman will argue our case for us in private. He gave me that assurance."

"And if Brezhnev doesn't call?"

"Goldman thinks that if that happens then we, I, go to the President and tell him everything and let him announce it publicly. It would be a hell of a feather in his hat, he could take credit for a hardline retaliation to Communist aggression and he's been accused of being soft on the Communists so often that Goldman thinks he'd jump at the chance."

"Looks like we've got the other side looking down the barrel of a gun," Olsen said cheerfully.

"Don't underestimate Captain Steel or Representative Wendell," Brannon said. "Or Admiral McCarty. He may not be the brightest admiral we've ever had but he's always been a hell of a good seaman and he's got a good nose for heavy weather."

A white-faced aide brought the message from the ballistic missile submarine that had been bumped by the *Orca* into Admiral Zurahv's office. The aide laid the decoded message on the Admiral's desk and retreated as fast as his dignity would allow before the storm broke.

Igor Shevenko read the message that had come by diplomatic pouch from Israel and touched a button on his desk console. Sophia Blovin came into his office.

"Get me Comrade Plotovsky on the phone, please," Shevenko said. He sat, scanning his copy of the *New York Times*, until his desk buzzer sounded. The rasping voice of the old Communist leader inquired politely after his health and then paused.

"I have a piece of information, sir," Shevenko said slowly. "The source is absolutely solid. The Americans have set up passive underwater listening networks that cover the exit of our submarines to the Atlantic and Pacific Oceans, as you are doubtless aware. I am also informed that just beyond those listening networks the Americans have laid an extensive network of mines that are something different, something new.

"The mines are torpedoes that lay inert on the bottom. If they are activated, this is done by an American submarine using sonar, the torpedoes will rise from the bottom when a ship passes over them and chase down the ship, homing in on its propeller, and sink it."

"Which means?" Plotovsky said.

"It means that we cannot put our submarine fleet at sea to neutralize the American ballistic missile submarine threat," Shevenko said. "No matter how effective any land-based missile attack might be against the North American continent we would suffer the same devastation. Perhaps worse."

"Hell of a piece of news to be told first thing in the morning," Plotovsky growled.

"That's not all, Comrade. The same source informs us that every one of our ballistic missile submarines now at sea is being shadowed by two or more American attack submarines."

"The Admiral has put us in an untenable position," Plotovsky rasped. "You'll be in your office all day? I'll call you." The phone went dead and Shevenko sat back in his chair and reread the message from Dr. Saul. Sophia came in with a tray covered with a snowy napkin and holding a pot of tea and a plate of pastry. She put the tray down on his desk and drew a chair up in front of the desk and sat down. Shevenko looked at her and smiled.

"Coffee and pastry with you across the desk is much better on my eyes than looking at Stefan each morning. Did you sleep well?"

"No," she said primly. "I don't sleep well alone after having you in my bed. When I wake up in the morning there is no one beside me to cherish. I think you should send your wife away for a vacation."

"Don't start that again," he grumbled. "I told you once, she goes on her yearly vacation to the Black Sea in July. She'll be gone a month. I can't make any changes in those plans. Be patient."

She shrugged and poured a cup of tea for him and put a pastry on a paper napkin and placed the food and drink in front of him. She poured her own tea and bit into a crusty croissant with relish.

"The messages this morning are good," she said. "The intercept of the message to the Admiral about the collision at sea with the American submarine, the information from Israel. All good for your cause."

He nodded. "Good for us, good for the rest of the world. Old Potato Nose Khrushchev was right, you know. Our grandchildren will bury the West. Not with nuclear bombs, that is madness. We can do it with economics. Ours is a controlled economic system, theirs is free enterprise. No free enterprise system can compete with a controlled state economy in a world market. We can undersell them, cause them to lose money and markets."

"If we had the technology to match them in producing goods," Sophia said.

"We'll get that from the West itself," he grinned. "Capitalists always have to make money. We buy their technology and then improve on it, simplify it so it can be produced more cheaply and fuck them with their own shaft." She grinned at him lasciviously.

"Stop using love words during business hours, bull of the bed. I'm liable to lock the doors and rape you."

"Not before I've read the *Times*," he said. "You wouldn't do that to your boss, would you?"

"Fuck the *New York Times*," she said in a half whisper. "I can wait until this evening. Then I'll show you what is more important, the football page or pages I can give you to read." She reached across the desk and picked up the telephone as it began to ring.

"Comrade Director Shevenko's office, First Directorate," she said. "Thank you, Comrade. He will be there."

"Plotovsky's office harridan, the old witch," she said as

she raised her cup of tea. "He wants you at his office as soon as you can be there. She said it will be a private meeting." He nodded and finished his pastry and wiped his lips with a Kleenex. Sophia stood up and looked to make sure the door to the hall was closed. She came around the desk and bent and kissed him, her tongue probing his mouth, her hand fondling his crotch.

"Stop it," he growled. "You want me to walk into his office with a hard-on?"

She giggled. "It might give him a heart attack. I don't think he's had it up in ten years."

"Don't be too sure," Shevenko said. "Old, old Communists are the sneakiest fuckers of all."

Leonid Plotovsky had the copies of the messages from Shevenko's office on his desk when Shevenko walked in. The old man hawked loudly and spat into his cuspidor and waved Shevenko to a chair in front of the desk.

"I don't hate the Americans," Plotovsky growled. "You know that, Igor. They gave us a great deal of help after the war of 1914, kept us from starving. Kept a lot of us from starving. Herbert Hoover.

"I admire their industry and their technology but damn it, they are going too far! This!" He waved a liver-spotted hand over the stack of messages.

"This is very close to open war, my friend. Very close!"

"It wouldn't have come to this if the Admiral hadn't ordered the test of his new torpedo," Shevenko said.

"I know that," the old man muttered. "Now we have to get out of this mess and get out gracefully. He looked at Shevenko, his old lizard's eyes half covered by his eyelids.

"You know the folk tale of the Commissar on his way home in a sleigh with the wolves howling behind him. He saved his family by throwing one of the servants in the sleigh to the wolves." Plotovsky's lined face was serene. "The question is, which faithful servant will be thrown to the American wolves?"

"The Admiral seems to have placed himself at the rear of the sleigh," Shevenko said.

"Do you know where the Admiral is right now?" Plotovsky asked.

"No, sir."

"He's asked for a meeting with Brezhnev. He's seeing him now." He rocked back in his chair and laced his thin fingers across his lean belly.

"If I were to guess I'd say that he was maneuvering to put someone else close to the rear of the sleigh. Someone named Shevenko."

Shevenko felt a cold chill. "The evidence of the Admiral's perversion, his infiltration of my office with Lubutkin, whom we know was a sexual pervert, that has been put to one side?"

"No," Plotovsky said. "It will be used. But it is of such a nature that it can only be used as a last resort. To face him with such things would be to destroy the effectiveness of the evidence. He would laugh in our faces." He paused. "The Admiral is a clever man. He knows how to fight a rear-guard action. He knew when he cultivated your aide that he might be caught, that the aide might be caught. He prepared defenses. I am sure of that. But I don't know what defenses he has." His eyes narrowed.

"Your life has not been blameless, Igor." He shook his head as Shevenko started to speak. "Don't misunderstand me, I don't disapprove of your screwing women. I still do it myself." A sly grin crossed his face. "Not that you or your bloodhounds would ever be able to prove that. But there are other things; your contact with the Israelis, for one. Who knows what the Politburo would think of that?"

"To maintain such a confidential contact is important to our national security," Shevenko protested. "It gives us an opening to the West that is to our advantage. Those dispatches from Dr. Saul this morning, that is proof."

"Granted," the old Politburo member said in a soft voice. "But what would my fellow members of the Politburo think of your meeting in Israel with the American CIA agent named Bob Wilson, of drinking coffee with him, and giving him cigars and admitting to him that we were guilty of a criminal act in the sinking of the American submarine? There would be an immediate suspicion that you were a double agent."

Shevenko felt the cold chill spread through his legs. He shook his head from side to side.

"No!" he said in a low whisper. "No! I would never betray my country!"

"Let us say that I believe you," the old man across the desk said. "You were educated in America, you know their idioms. Let us play ball together, you and I. Now here is what I want you to do." He leaned across the desk and began to speak slowly and carefully in a voice barely above a whisper.

CHAPTER 18

Admiral Benson and Bob Wilson left the Director's office on the top floor of the seven-story CIA headquarters building and walked into a private elevator and descended to the basement of the building. A driver stood waiting beside a long, black Cadillac with heavily tinted bulletproof windows. The two men got into the back seat of the car and locked the doors and the car eased out of the quarter-mile long tunnel that extended out of the back of the building. The driver made his way along a narrow roadway that wound through a thick stand of trees. A guard at the high, electrified fence opened a gate and waved the car through. As the car drove down the road toward Langley it passed a faded sign that read "Research Station, U.S. Government," a pseudonym known to every intelligence agency in the world as the headquarters of the CIA. The car picked up speed and reached the Roosevelt Bridge and crossed the Potomac River, leaving Virginia behind.

Admiral Benson read through the report that Wilson had written, passing each page to Wilson as he finished reading.

Wilson took the last page of the report and put it away in his attache case.

"Things are getting to the critical stage," he said to Admiral Benson. "That memo from Admiral Brannon about one of his attack submarines bumping, is that what he called it, bumping? Running into the Russian ballistic missile submarine. That's pretty risky, isn't it? You make the tiniest mistake and you both go down. Hell of a way to let the other side know you aren't fooling around."

"I think Admiral Brannon may be going a little bit too far," Benson said. "We've lost one submarine and we've sunk one of theirs in return and it's being kept a pretty damned good secret. If we lose another submarine because of some tactic like this, keeping it a secret will be damned near impossible."

"I don't think the secret is being that well kept," Wilson said. He reached in his coat pocket for a cigaret and lit it. "You hear the latest? Captain Steel is making his move. And to do that he has to tell some other people about what's been going on."

"No, I didn't hear about that," Benson said.

"Steel has a buddy in the House," Wilson said. "Representative Wendell, the Chairman of the Housed Armed Services Committee. I got a tip yesterday that one of Wendell's bird dogs—he's got some damned tough investigative people on his personal staff. One of his bird dogs went to the FBI yesterday and asked to see J. Edgar's private files on Vice Admiral Brannon.

"The guy who tipped me said there is no file on Admiral Brannon in J. Edgar's safe. So Captain Steel is moving in another direction. Wendell wants the contract for building a new nuclear carrier to go to a shipyard in his district. Captain Steel can help a lot. So Wendell is going to lean on Admiral McCarty of the Joint Chiefs of Staff to force Admiral Brannon to retire. Now, or damned soon, before Brannon reaches the mandatory retirement age."

"That's dirty pool," Admiral Benson said.

"Yeah, but it's the way they play hard ball in this town," Wilson said. "They made a mistake in leaving their tracks in the FBI. We've got good sources there. I could have told them they wouldn't find anything kinky about Brannon."

"How would you know?"

"I like to know what kind of people I'm dealing with," Wilson said. "I ran a check on Brannon early on. He's as clean as a whistle. Got a good marriage to a good woman and he doesn't play around. Good Irish Catholic type. He's got one daughter. She's clean. Married to a Navy officer who's on a submarine out in Pearl Harbor. The daughter's out there with her husband. But this new angle, the Joint Chiefs of Staff thing, this Admiral McCarty could force Brannon to retire?"

"I would think so," Admiral Benson said. "The Joint Chiefs of Staff are pretty powerful in the military. All Admiral McCarty would have to do is to tell Admiral Brannon that he had a younger man he wanted in Brannon's duty station and tell him his retirement was required for the good of the Service. Brannon must be about sixty-three years old. He'd have a hard time fighting something like that."

A carafe of hot coffee and a platter of doughnuts were on the coffee table in front of the larger sofa in Admiral Brannon's office when Benson and Wilson walked into the office. Rear Admiral John Olsen turned from the window and smiled a greeting and the four men sat down around the coffee table and filled their cups.

"The reason I asked for this meeting," Admiral Benson began, "is because Bob has some new information from his contact in Israeli intelligence that you should know about." He turned to Wilson.

"The Navy has listening devices on the ocean bottom so that if any of the Russian submarines go into the Atlantic or

Pacific you people know about it?" Wilson looked at Mike Brannon, who nodded assent.

"You've also mined the areas just outside of the listening devices, that right?"

"Yes," John Olsen said. "It's called a passive mine defense. It has to be activated before the mines will work."

"The mines are torpedoes, that right?"

"Modified torpedoes," Olsen said. "But that's not supposed to be talked about, Bob. It's classified as highly confidential information."

"Israeli intelligence knows about it," Wilson said. "And they've told the KGB about those modified torpedoes and how they work." There was a silence in the office.

"What are you trying to tell me?" Brannon snapped. "That the Israeli intelligence is on the side of the Soviet Union?"

"What I'm saying is that the KGB is on our side, your side, in this mess," Wilson said. "The KGB doesn't want a nuclear war. They don't want any upset in international relations at all. It screws up their operations. The Mossad knows this and they don't want a nuclear war either. If that comes they go down the drain because the Third World nations would survive a nuclear war and they'd be on the side of the Arabs and that would be the end of the Jews." He watched as John Olsen selected a cruller crusted with dark chocolate frosting from the platter on the coffee table.

"I've been on the other side of the KGB ever since I've been in the Company," Wilson said slowly. "When you've been at it as long as I have you begin to develop a sense of what the other side is doing. My contact in the Mossad has damned good penetration in the Soviet Union, way better than any other intelligence service. He tells me everything he can, that is, everything he can tell me as long as it's in his best national interest. The Mossad people are professionals.

"The KGB are professionals. Like us, they've got more than one intelligence service and like us those intelligence services are more often than not fighting each other.

"In the Soviet Union there are two big intelligence services, the KGB and the GRU. The GRU is Army intelligence. They don't get along with the KGB. The GRU and the military think that the United States can be pushed and pushed and that we won't hit back. That's why they tested that new torpedo and sank the *Sharkfin*. They didn't give a real damn about the torpedo, that was just an excuse. What the GRU was trying to prove was that it was right and the KGB was wrong, that Uncle Sam doesn't have any teeth any more." He took a long drink from his cup of cooling coffee.

"If the GRU had been right the next move would have been something a hell of a lot more serious than sinking one of our submarines."

"Such as?" Olsen prompted.

"I don't know, not exactly, sir," Wilson answered. "Maybe they'd try a move into the Middle East. The Soviet Army rearmed Israel, you know, after the Forty-seven War. They played their cards wrong after they gave Israel all new weapons and we moved in and played the right cards and froze them out of Israel.

"But the rest of the Middle East is wide open to Soviet expansion. Iraq, Syria, North and South Yemen, even the Emirates down in the south end of the Gulf are all targets for the Russians. About the only strong power base we have in the Middle East right now is Israel and Iran. And I'm not too sure of Iran. I was on the team that helped put that bastard of a Shah back on his Peacock Throne and he's turned into a real son of a bitch. The bastard kills more of his people each year with torture and that sort of thing than any nation in the world. One of these days they're going to throw his ass out of there in a revolution and when that comes Iran will be up for grabs. The Soviets know this and if they have a power base in the Middle East before that happens then they can move in." He paused and shrugged his powerful shoulders.

"I'm sorry. I didn't mean to give a lecture. Let me get back to business.

"The GRU and the KGB are at each other's throats most of the time. The GRU has won this round. They put enough pressure on in the Politburo through the hardliners they own there to force Brezhnev to not vote when the motion came before the Politburo to test the torpedo. The Mossad guy tells me that if Brezhnev had voted it would have been a tie vote and the motion would have been tabled. He didn't feel he had the power, I guess, to force the issue to a tie so he didn't vote. The GRU won the poker hand and you, we, lost the *Sharkfin*.

"Your response," Wilson looked directly at Vice Admiral Brannon, "that changed things. The KGB is working on the Politburo members who voted against the test of the torpedo. We don't know how that will end up, the Mossad doesn't know. So the Mossad fed the KGB the information about the passive mines to give them an ace in the hole, a card they could play if push comes to shove." He reached for the carafe and refilled his cup.

"The reading I get from the Mossad is that it's touch and go in the Politburo right now. There's a showdown coming. The guy the Mossad is worried about is a Soviet admiral named Zurahv. He's the front man for the hardliners and the GRU and he's got a lot of power."

"I know the name," Brannon said. He went to his desk and opened a drawer and pulled out a file. He came back to his chair and sat down and riffled through the papers in the file folder.

"Yes, here he is. His father was a captain in the Soviet Navy. His ship went down and the father drowned in 1905, in the Battle of Tshushima Straits." He looked up at the other men.

"That was in the war between Japan and Russia, the old Russia. The Russian Navy thought they could whip the Japanese but the Japs smashed the Russian battle fleet to bits. That ended Russia as a major sea power and they are just now beginning to make a move toward becoming a world sea power again.

My file on Admiral Zurahv says that he didn't see much action in World War II but that's understandable, the Soviet Navy didn't have much opportunity to do anything. Since then, since World War II, Admiral Zurahv has made a big name for himself in building up the Soviet Navy and the file says he's accumulated a lot of political power. That reinforces what you've just said, Bob."

"Which leaves us where?" John Olsen asked.

"Where we are now," Brannon said. "As I mentioned in my memo, Admiral Benson, we're dogging every Soviet ballistic missile submarine that's now out in the open sea. We've got two or more attack submarines on each Soviet submarine. The skippers of our attack subs have let the Soviet sub skippers know they're being dogged. They'll report that to their commands." He stopped and closed the file folder he was holding.

"We've intercepted some traffic from the Soviet submarines, they're hollering for instructions on what to do, telling their bosses that we're riding herd on them." A grin came and went on his heavy face. "I'll have a copy made of the message that skipper sent after he got bumped by the *Orca*. He's asking for orders to be sent back home. He's got some minor damage to his hull up forward and he's scared out of his wits. At last report he was on the surface and waiting to be told what to do."

"It sounds pretty good but you're playing a hell of a dangerous game, Mike," Admiral Benson said. "Bob told me this morning on the way over that Captain Steel is playing dirty. Sooner or later you're going to have to go to the President with this whole business, you know that."

"I know about Captain Steel," Mike Brannon said. "And I know about Wendell and about Admiral McCarty. We haven't fired all our tubes yet, we've got some torpedoes they don't know we've got." He stood up and the others rose.

"I want to thank you, gentlemen, for coming over, for the information, Bob. It helps."

Admiral Benson brushed a doughnut crumb from his immaculate jacket. He looked at Mike Brannon, his face serious.

"I liked it better when I was at sea, Mike, didn't you?"

"I don't know," Mike Brannon said. "It's like being in World War II again, sort of."

"Except that you aren't sure who the enemy is," Admiral Benson said.

CHAPTER 19

By the time Admiral Zurahv had disposed of a stack of paperwork that had accumulated on his desk the message from the submarine that had been bumped by the U.S.S. *Orca* was at the bottom of a small stack of messages from other Soviet submarine commanders. The Admiral picked up the stack of messages and began to read them, his beefy face beginning to glow with rage as he read messages from his submarine commanders that told of harassment of Soviet ballistic missile submarines by American attack submarines. The tone of each message was the same: worry. The submarine commanders, unused to being constantly followed, unable to understand why they were periodically subjected to high decibel blasts of sonar beams from the American submarines, wanted information. What was going on? Why were the Americans interfering with them in the open sea? Was there any change in the world political situation?

When he reached the message at the bottom of the stack and read it he smashed the palm of his big right hand against his desk and bellowed for his aide. The naval officer came in and stood at attention.

"I want a meeting of my staff at once," the Admiral snapped. "They are to drop whatever they are doing and come here at once." The aide saluted and left and Admiral Zurahv picked up the stack of messages and read through them again, slowly.

The staff officers arrived in a group within five minutes. They sat down in chairs in front of the Admiral's desk and listened to his reading of the messages. When he came to the last message he stopped.

"Pay particular attention to this message. It gives evidence of an attack on one of our ships by an American submarine while our ship was in international waters." He read the message slowly.

"He has sustained some minor damage to his hull, so far as his diver could see," the Admiral rumbled. "That is not cause to bring him home to base but the state of his mind is more than cause to order him home. That will be done at once." He nodded at his aide who made notes on a pad he held in his lap. "Bring him home and relieve him of command." A captain sitting at the right end of the line of chairs cleared his throat.

"Comrade Admiral, I understand your feelings. The man is obviously frightened. But if we relieve him of command who do we put in his place? We are very short of qualified nuclear commanding officers, sir. Bring him home, yes, put his ship in drydock and get a good estimate of whatever damage was done and then, if I may suggest it Comrade, a private audience with you should put enough starch in his backbone to overcome this uncertainty he now feels."

"He doesn't need starch, he needs steel in his backbone," the Admiral growled. "But I agree, we are short of nuclear skippers. Bring him home and get clearance for immediate entry to the drydock for his ship. I'll handle him personally.

"Now we come to the heart of this business. The Americans have to be taught a lesson. Let's discuss what form that lesson will take."

"What form would you suggest, Comrade?" the captain who had spoken before said.

"What I'd like to do is to give them a full broadside of ballistic missiles, Captain Bogomolets," the Admiral growled. "Incinerate the bastards! And then give the same dose to China and have an end to this bullshit about who is the major power in the world."

"Unfortunately," Captain Bogomolets said, "that course of action, while it is one I approve of, would require permission from the Politburo."

Admiral Zurahv leaned back in his chair and the chair creaked in protest against his great weight. "I have information, Captain, that the entire American retaliation that we have experienced and are now experiencing is being conducted by an American admiral by the name of Brannon and without the knowledge of his president or his Congress." He paused as his aide cleared his throat.

"With all due respect, Comrade Admiral," the aide said. "Our land-based nuclear missiles are under the direct command of the Army, and the Army . . ."

"And the damned Army is afraid of its own shadow!" Admiral Zurahv snapped. "A few Chinese begin firing off rifles along the border and the Army shifts troops halfway across Russia to reinforce the border and transfers planes thousands of miles to stand by. In the name of Lenin, they ordered planes to the airfields along the damned border with China and there are no bombs at those airfields to arm the planes!" His big hand touched a stack of paper.

"I have an urgent request in this pile from the Army asking me to ship food from Vladivostok to the Army bases along the border because they don't have enough food there to feed the troops they're bringing in. I have never seen such a mess in my life. Let one Chinese peasant piss toward our border and the damned Army goes into a panic."

"All very true, sir," Captain Bogomolets said, "but the fact remains that if the Army is that shaky the last thing they would do is to follow orders from us, even from you, sir, to begin a nuclear attack against North America. They would go running to the Politburo to get endorsement of the order."

"So we'll get the order from the Politburo," Zurahv growled. "I'll take care of that. Captain Bogomolets, I want you to shift armed naval units to within close distance of each missile site. Find some excuse to do that, maneuvers or whatever. As soon as I have made my case to the Politburo that we must strike now I want to be sure that the orders will be followed. Your units will see to that." He stood up.

"Dismissed," he snapped. He remained standing until the last of his staff had left his office and sat down. He put the messages from the submarine commanders into a neat pile and then put them in a folder. His aide came in and stood at attention in front of his desk.

"By telephone, just now, sir," the aide said. "An order from Comrade Plotovsky that you see him at once in his office. I am to call his office and assure him that you will do so, sir."

"Tell him I'm on my way over," Admiral Zurahv said. "I might as well take care of him, get him out of the way before I ask for an emergency meeting of the Politburo."

"If I may suggest it, sir," the aide said, "Comrade Plotovsky is not one to be taken lightly. He is very close to Comrade Brezhnev. He has a great name."

Admiral Zurahv grinned, his tobacco-stained teeth showing, "But not close enough to the great man to convince him to vote when we asked for the weapons test, my young friend. I, too, have a great name. My father had a great name. The old man, Plotovsky, has grown very old, too old to make decisions in these times. It requires vigor and patriotism to make decisions today. By the way, did you send the memorial wreath to that grave as I ordered?"

"That was done, sir," the aide intoned. "Without any name on the wreath, as you ordered."

"As I told you," the Admiral said. "I knew the young man's father at one time. We were not friends. But that is no reason why the dead should not have a wreath on the grave. Call Comrade Plotovsky's office and tell him I will be there within the next half hour."

Moise Goldman walked into Admiral Brannon's office and stuck out his hand. Brannon shook it warmly and waved Goldman to a chair in front of his desk. The former *New York Times* Managing Editor sat down in the chair and crossed his legs and combed his fingers through his black beard.

"What's new, Admiral?" he asked. Brannon succinctly itemized the actions he had taken against the Soviet ballistic missile submarines. Goldman pulled a pipe out of his coat pocket and filled and lit it.

"Any indication of how the Soviets are reacting, sir?"

"They are advising their submarines that there is no change in the world political situation," Brannon answered, "and that the Americans are undoubtedly crazy and that a protest would be filed, which means nothing."

"It could mean that they're stalling for time because the hardliners in the Politburo haven't got their act together," Goldman said. He relit his pipe. "I sure as hell don't want our side to start dropping nuclear warheads on the Soviet Union. I've got grandparents in a little town just outside of Leningrad."

"I don't think anyone is going to drop anything," Brannon said.

"I wish I were that sure," Goldman repiled. "I did two years as the Moscow Bureau Chief for the *Times.* The Russians don't think like we do."

"I didn't know you had been in Moscow," Brannon said. Goldman nodded, puffing hard at his pipe to keep it lit.

"Tough duty, to use your phraseology, Admiral. I speak the language and I can read and write it and that made it a little easier for me but it wasn't a good two years. You earn your money."

"Then let me ask you," Brannon said cautiously, "do you think Brezhnev will call the President?"

"No," Goldman said shortly. "He'd lose a lot of face. He's a Ukranian and they're proud people. He's a proud man." He drew on his pipe. "On the other hand he's a hell of a politician; you don't come as far as he's come, hold the jobs he's held without being one of the world's better wheelers and dealers. If he can't see any profit in being stiff-necked he might make that call. As I said, the Russians don't think like we do. You can't figure them out, not even one Russian can figure out another Russian. But every day that goes by means something."

"What?" Brannon asked.

Goldman grinned around his pipe stem. "What do you think it means?"

"I have to think that each day they don't do something means that we're getting closer and closer to standoff and that Brezhnev will make the call."

"I wouldn't be too sure," Goldman said. He took a pocketknife out of his pocket and opened the blade and cleaned out his pipe in an ashtray on Brannon's desk.

"State Department intelligence says they have word that there's a showdown coming in the Politburo. They don't know what's responsible for the showdown and they're making a lot of silly-assed guesses about grain production and the shortage of meat in the countryside. I think the showdown is between the hard and softliners in the Politburo." He uncrossed his legs and sat up a little straighter in his chair.

"Give me your military estimate of what would happen if a nuclear war starts, Admiral."

Brannon rubbed his face with one hand. "It's pretty well known, Moise. If they launch first we'd knock down some of their missiles but enough would get through to wipe out about ninety percent of our land-based missiles. And most of our cities."

"How about our air strike capability?"

"Overrated, in my opinion. They could get most of the planes before they got to their target area." He reached for the coffee carafe and poured two cups of coffee.

"If they launch first they'd put a big percentage of their civilian population in their air raid shelters. Russia has a first rate civil defense system. All of their important people would be deep underground where we couldn't touch them with nuclear missiles. But there is one factor they can't get around."

"Such as?"

"If they launch first we wouldn't respond with submarine missiles immediately, Moise. The submarine skippers would get the word that they'd launched. They'd then move into launch position, those that weren't already there, and wait for three weeks. The psychologists have told us that two weeks is about the absolute limit you can keep people in deep shelters before psychological disturbances begin to take place. We'd wait out that period and then wait another week and then we'd launch from the submarines." His normally cheerful face was somber.

"Our estimates show that we'd eliminate the Soviet Union as a nation."

"Cheerful thought," Goldman said. "Now I've got a cheerful thought for you, Admiral. I think we'd better go in and talk to the President, tell him everything."

"That wasn't what we had decided on," Brannon said.

"I know that," Goldman said. "But there's another factor in the equation. Your friend Captain Steel has gone to Representative Wendell. The word I get is that Captain Steel wants your ass in a basket and he's using Wendell to satisfy that want.

"Now old Wendell is a pretty cute operator but he can't do what Steel wants unless he lets a few facts out that aren't supposed to be let out. And that means that those things will get back to the President. And if that happens then your ass isn't going to be in a basket, it's going to be hanging from a yardarm, if they still have yardarms in the Navy. So I think it's time that the two of us go to the Old Man and tell him what's gone on."

"I've trusted you, Moise," Brannon said slowly. "I hoped that you would trust me, let me work this thing out. And I think it will work out."

"I trust you," Goldman said. "But I know a little more about how politics is played than you do, I think, and I've got a feeling in my tokus that if you don't sit down and tell the President everything you're going to find yourself in a pissing contest with a skunk—and my daddy used to warn me never to get into that sort of a contest."

"When?" Brannon asked.

Goldman looked at his wrist watch. "He's waiting for you now, Admiral. I've got a car and driver out back, near the service entry."

Brannon rose and went to the coat tree and got his uniform overcoat and hat.

"What's your reading on how he'll respond?"

"Politically," Goldman said. "He's a political creature. Just let me do the preliminary talking, set it up. Then you speak your piece, tell him everything that's happened. Don't give him reasons why you didn't tell him or the Joint Chiefs about the sinking of the *Sharkfin*. Then I'll jump in and give him my opinion of where he stands politically."

"And then?" Brannon asked as he buttoned his coat.

"Then he'll ask you why you didn't tell him as soon as the *Sharkfin* was attacked and sunk and you're on your own, Admiral." He held the office door open, a grin on his face.

The office of Leonid I. Brezhnev, First Secretary of the Communist Party of the Soviet Union, reflected the life style the burly Communist leader preferred. The desk he sat behind was made of solid walnut. Its vast surface shone with a deep gleam that spoke of hours of patient hand rubbing and polishing. Thick rugs covered the floor and large, comfortable sofas were arranged along two walls of the spacious office. Small tables inlaid in intricate patterns of rare woods stood in front of the sofas. In front of the desk there were three chairs upholstered in a pale gold leather that complemented the muted colors of the fabric-covered walls.

The chair in back of the desk was a present from an American ambassador, a "senator's chair," large, comfortable, with a high back. The chair was covered in a black leather that had been carefully selected to be blemish-free. The First Secretary took pleasure in pointing out to visitors the perfection of the leather upholstery, explaining that the Americans took the precaution of raising animals for such purpose, keeping the cows in enclosures that contained no barbed wire or sharp corners that might possibly cause a scar in the animal's hide.

Igor Shevenko walked into the First Secretary's anteroom in response to the summons he had received a half hour previously. An aide to Brezhnev rose from behind his desk, looking at his wrist watch.

"You are ten minutes early, Comrade Shevenko."

"A bad habit of mine," Shevenko said. "My father taught me to always be ahead of an appointment. That way I would never be late." He grinned at the aide who looked again at his watch and sat down. The aide turned suddenly, his face stricken, as the door behind his desk opened and two men came into the anteroom. Shevenko recognized them at once. Lieutenant General Mishikoff, head of the GRU, the Glavnoye Rezvedyvatelnoye Upravleniye, the Army Intelligence Service, and his aide, Brigadier General Koslin. The two Army officers, the silver stars on their gold shoulder boards glittering in the harsh fluorescent lights, nodded solemnly at Shevenko as they walked past him and out of the anteroom.

"I should have been on time," Shevenko said to the aide in a soft voice.

"It would have been better," the aide replied. He picked up the phone and spoke briefly and then rose. "The Secretary will see you now, Comrade Shevenko." He turned and opened the door for Shevenko who walked into the inner office and stood waiting, watching Brezhnev as he read a report on his desk. The sharp eyes beneath the massive eyebrows raised suddenly and Brezhnev nodded and indicated that Shevenko should take a chair in front of the desk.

"Thank you for coming, Igor," Brezhnev said. "You are well, I hope?"

"Yes, thank you, sir. And you?"

"Oh, those damned doctors keep telling me I should stop smoking but they give me nothing to take the place of tobacco." He shook a cigaret out of a package and lit it. He inhaled deeply and put the cigaret in an ashtray and touched the papers on his desk.

"This report from the GRU, it's contradictory to the report you sent me this morning. I wonder who is right, the KGB or the GRU?"

"What did General Mishikoff say, if I may ask, Comrade Secretary?"

"He says the United States is about to launch a nuclear missile attack against us from land, sea, and air. You said in your report that this was a possibility, it has always been a possibility so there was nothing new in that, but you did not indicate that such an attack was imminent. You'd better explain your reasoning a little better, Comrade Shevenko." The First Secretary leaned back in his high-backed chair and the cold eyes stared at Shevenko.

"My report reviewed what I see as a crisis, sir. It is my firm conviction that it is a grave crisis. My agents in Washington and information from other sources tell me that one or two admirals in Washington have begun a course of retaliation to our test of the new torpedo against one of their submarines.

"I am informed that President Milligan does not know that he has lost a submarine, that he does not know that the retaliation has taken place. The last piece of information I received before coming over, sir, was that each of the ten missile submarines we have on patrol in the Atlantic and Pacific Oceans are now being hounded by at least two American attack submarines. I am not a naval expert, but I have made inquiries and am told that no missile submarine being hounded in this manner can hope to fire more than one missile before being sunk." Shevenko settled a little deeper into the comfortable leather chair.

"Our sources indicate that the American admirals are acting completely on their own. My analysis of this would be that they are hardliners who are dissatisfied with the course of detente that now exists between the Soviet Union and the United States." He paused, searching for the right words.

"If I may say it this way, sir, the Americans see our weapons test as a grave provocation, literally an act of war. They retaliated in the same manner."

"And?" Brezhnev said.

"They are now waiting for what they see as a reasonable reaction from us."

"Which is?"

"With all due respect, sir, I am advised that the American admirals expect you to call President Milligan and explain to him that a terrible mistake has happened, that it won't happen again, that the submarine crew that committed the mistake is being punished." He sat up straighter, waiting for the reaction.

"I apologize to no one!" Brezhnev snapped.

"If you will allow me to continue to take the part of the devil's advocate, Comrade, the American admirals who have acted in this insane manner would not see your call as an apology. President Milligan would know only what you had told him, what his renegade admirals tell him; that one of our submarine commanders went crazy, that it would not happen again."

"What advantage could they get?" Brezhnev asked.

"Possibly a withdrawal from the state of detente," Shevenko answered. "I think that would satisfy them. If the President took a hard line the American military would be in a position to demand more spending for weapons."

Brezhnev rocked forward in his chair. "If I do as you say they want me to do it would solve nothing. The faction within the Politburo that wants to smash North America and Mainland China now, at once, would still be there. The American admirals who have created this impasse would still be there. There is no political gain for either side." He stopped and lit another cigaret.

"I inherited a dissident Politburo from Nikita. You know that as well as I do. The feeling was, still is, that Khrushchev went too far toward the West, that he undermined our struggle for world leadership." He drew on his cigaret and sent a plume of smoke toward the ceiling.

"I saved Nikita from liquidation, did you know that?"

"Yes, sir. I knew that."

"Now I must save the Soviet Union from nuclear attack."

"You are the First Secretary, sir," Shevenko said.

"Who is at the mercy of the Politburo if it turns against me," Brezhnev snapped. "Admiral Zurahv, General Mishikoff, are both advocating an immediate nuclear strike against the United States and Mainland China. They have called for an emergency meeting of the Politburo at four tomorrow afternoon. Comrade Plotovsky has told me that he has asked you to be there as a witness for his side."

"Yes, sir, he has asked me to do that."

"What do you hope to gain?"

"With all due respect, sir, at best a majority vote to discontinue the weapons testing program. At worst, a defeat by no more than one vote with the hope, my and Comrade Plotovsky's hope, sir, that you will cast a vote on Comrade Plotovsky's side and create a tie and table the matter."

"That's Plotovsky's thinking," Brezhnev said. "He's a rare bird, that old man. A street fighter who turned into a politician and forgot nothing of his street fighting tricks." He stubbed out his cigaret in a glass ashtray and reached for the cigaret package.

"And if Plotovsky's side, your side, wins how do we go about cleaning up this mess? Have you thought about that? I am not going to apologize, Igor!"

"There is a way," Shevenko said slowly. "I could reach the head of the CIA through Israel, let him know the crisis is over. He could go to the President, tell him what happened and assure him that everything is normal. If it can be done that way the American admirals who are playing president would be forced out of the Navy."

"They've lost one of their submarines," Brezhnev said.

"The loss has not been announced, sir. It could be laid to unknown causes. The history of the sea is full of such incidents, sir. Just as we would, in due time, announce the loss of our submarine to the same cause."

"It always comes down to politics," Brezhnev said. "And politics are the same all over the world. Only the penalty for failure differs." He leaned back in the big chair, the eyes under the bristling eyebrows steady on Shevenko.

"I knew your father, as you know, Igor. We were great friends. His death in the great patriotic war was a blow to me, almost as much a blow as it was to you and your family. For his sake I hope you are well prepared for the meeting."

"My father used to talk a lot about you, sir," Shevenko said. "He said you were a man who never forgot a friend. I will do my best."

"That's a nice thing to have said about yourself," Brezhnev said. He got out of his chair and walked around the desk and put his heavy hand on Shevenko's shoulder.

"I'm afraid that in those days friendship was based on trust. Those were the days when we were fighting a common enemy and there was no room for politics."

Admiral Zurahv paced the floor of his office. His chief naval aide, Captain Bogomolets, watched him from a chair as he sipped at a mug of hot tea.

"The old man, Plotovsky, saw the First Secretary this morning, early. Then Brezhnev called for the two generals, Mishikoff and Koslin."

"Understandable," the Captain said. "Brezhnev is a cautious man, a politician. He would listen to one side and then the other. The full Politburo will be at the meeting. If we don't win, if we get a tie vote, then it is up to Brezhnev to break the tie with his vote."

"If he chooses to vote. He didn't, the other time."

"He can't ride that horse a second time," Captain Bogomolets said patiently. "We've talked about that earlier. He will have to vote. The fact that he called in Plotovsky and then the GRU is an indication that he may believe that the vote will be a tie."

The Admiral stopped pacing and faced his aide. "Mishikoff reported to me that when he and Koslin left the First Secretary's office Igor Shevenko was sitting in the anteroom. I don't like the sound of that, my friend."

"The foolishness with that boy," Captain Bogomolets said softly. "Shevenko's aide. A pity."

"Shevenko had him murdered!" Admiral Zurahv snapped. "And don't call it foolishness, you had the same appetites years ago."

"Admitted," the naval Captain said.

"So what do you think Shevenko told Brezhnev, that I was a sodomist and therefore couldn't be trusted?"

"The conversation between them, as I am told by Brezhnev's aide, did not cover that subject, my friend. In fact, Brezhnev did not give Shevenko any encouragement in his role as a witness tomorrow. Rather, he warned him to do well."

"How reliable is that damned aide?" Zurahv growled.

"Reliable enough," Captain Bogomolets said. "What we have to do now is to figure some way to impress on the opposition that it is imperative that we move in our direction and at once."

Admiral Zurahv lowered his massive hams onto the edge of his desk and rubbed his belly. "Yes. Here's how we will do it. We will watch closely during the meeting. If we see signs of doubt in those we think we are sure of, there's at least one who could play the role of turncoat. We'll play our trump card, we'll say we have absolute information that the United States and Peking have decided to launch a simultaneous nuclear attack on the Soviet Union."

"Not a very strong trump card," Bogomolets said. "Proof will be demanded."

"The GRU will manufacture that proof," Admiral Zurahv said. "We'll only use it if we have to, if Plotovsky has succeeded in turning old Arekelyan to his side. I don't think Brezhnev will dare to vote with Plotovsky if we raise the issue of national security." The Navy Captain shook his grizzled head.

"I still think it's a chancy thing."

Admiral Zurahv shrugged. "Here is what I want you to do. Get off messages to all our missile submarines now at sea. Tell them to take stations and revise targets for missiles to hit at all hard-based missile sites in the United States." He paused and shifted his position a bit to better accommodate his bulk.

"In the same message tell them to stand by for a firing order. Send the messages in Code Zebra Seven. We have no evidence that the Americans have cracked that code."

Captain Bogomolets stood up and smoothed his uniform tunic. "You intend to begin the attack no matter what the results of the meeting?"

"I intend to save my country from nuclear death," Admiral Zurahv said.

CHAPTER 20

Admiral Brannon and Moise Goldman walked down the hall in the White House to the door of the Oval Office. The Marine sentry on duty outside the door came to attention and snapped off a salute to Admiral Brannon.

"Is the President here yet?" Goldman asked the Marine.

"Inside sir. Not alone."

"Oh?" Goldman said. "Who's with him?"

"Captain Steel and Representative Wendell, sir. They got here about fifteen minutes ago. Admiral Benson and his aide are also inside."

"Thank you," Goldman said. He touched Mike Brannon's arm and the two men walked a few yards down the hall.

"We've been euchred, Admiral. I might not be able to do any preliminary talking. Play it by ear, sir. Don't say anything you don't have to say." He turned and went back up the hall and the sentry knocked softly on the door and opened it.

The lights were on in the Oval Office to offset the gloom of the winter day outside. Inside the historic room three men were seated at an oblong table. John Milligan, the President of the United States, a big man whose sloping shoulders and barrel chest were the despair of tailors who tried to fit his suits, sat at the head of the table. At his left hand was Representative Walter W. Wendell and next to him Captain Herman Steel. The President smiled at Goldman and motioned to him to sit in the chair at his right. Mike Brannon took the chair next to Goldman, directly across the table from Captain Steel. Near the end of the table Admiral Benson and Bob Wilson were standing, closing their attache cases.

"Thank you for the excellent briefing, Admiral Benson, Mr. Wilson," the President said. "Please keep me informed." He waited until the sentry had closed the door after Benson and Wilson left the room and turned to Mike Brannon.

"Are all admirals insane?" the President asked, looking at Mike Brannon. "This Russian admiral, Zurahv, who Wilson said is leading the hardliners in the Politburo, he must be insane to even think about starting a war." He put his hands on the table and Mike Brannon noticed that the hands, despite the expert care of a manicurist, showed the signs of the President's childhood and early manhood on a Kansas farm.

"You might be a little insane yourself, Admiral," the President said softly. "Just a little bit. Captain Steel says you are completely mad but I don't think that's true." The somber eyes beneath the thick graying eyebrows fixed on Mike Brannon.

"Why didn't you notify me at once when you knew we had lost a submarine? Why didn't you notify me as soon as you had determined that our submarine had been sunk by the Russians? I'm the Commander in Chief of the Armed Forces of this country, in case you've forgotten."

"I haven't forgotten, sir," Brannon answered.

"Then why didn't you inform me at once?" He locked his two hands together on the table. "Let me say this to you, Admiral. I told these other gentlemen and the two who left that I wanted the truth, the damned bone truth to be spoken in this meeting and what's said in this office doesn't go out of this office and no matter what you say I won't use it against you."

"Very well, sir," Brannon answered. "I'll level with you.

I figured that if we didn't do something in retaliation for the sinking of the *Sharkfin* and do it damned fast the Russians might do something even worse than sinking one of our submarines.

"I reasoned that if I came to you that your hands would be tied, so far as taking any retaliatory action. You'd have to notify congressional committees and the National Security Council and by the time all the arguing and speech-making was over the story would be in the newspapers and on television and then you wouldn't be able to do a thing." His dark blue eyes stared at the President.

"I issued the orders to destroy the Russian submarine that had sunk the *Sharkfin* because I am convinced that swift and terrible retaliation is the only language that the Russians understand. I was sure in my own mind that it was the only way to prevent a nuclear war, sir."

"It's a reasonable rationale, Admiral, but you'd better explain why you believe that the Soviet Union was or is ready to attack us."

Admiral Brannon looked across the table at Captain Steel and then turned to look at the President.

"I do not cry wolf, sir," he began. "My military record will bear that out. But there is a school of thought about how a nuclear war could begin that I think is soundly based. I'll cover it as quickly as I can.

"The assumption is, sir, that if the Soviet Union should decide to start a nuclear war they would strike first at our hardened missile sites, at our land-based missile silos. As soon as their missiles were launched at those targets Mr. Brezhnev or whoever is head of the Soviet government, would call you on the hot line and tell you the missiles were underway, that they would hit their targets in about fifty minutes and that loss of American life would be minimal—most of our land missile sites are away from heavily populated areas, as you know, sir.

"You would be given the choice of surrendering at once, unconditionally, or the next missiles would be launched within minutes at our biggest cities. The probable death toll from that strike could be fifty million or more American lives." Brannon paused and looked around the table and then back at the President.

"The assumption, sir, is that you would have no choice but to surrender and save at least fifty million Americans from death."

"Horse shit!" the President said. "Anyone who thinks that I, that any American president who sits in this White House would surrender without firing a shot is crazy!" He balled a large hand into a fist and struck the table.

"We'd fire our own missiles in retaliation." He looked down the table at Captain Steel.

"You told me, you testified before the Congress, that your submarine missiles can hit a pickle barrel at three thousand miles. Isn't that so?" He turned back to Mike Brannon.

"Admiral, the Russians *have* to know that they'd be wiped out! They wouldn't be as stupid as that."

"If missile accuracy was what it's supposed to be I would agree with you, sir," Mike Brannon said.

The President nodded his head toward Captain Steel. "Let me hear it again, Captain, tell Admiral Brannon here what you told me and the Congress about how accurate our missiles really are."

Captain Steel nodded his head. "Sir," he began, "the accuracy of our missiles is based on firing under optimum conditions. We have never fired a missile under less than optimum conditions."

"Let me put it this way, sir. Each target in the Soviet Union is to be hit by three or more nuclear missiles. We have never fired more than one missile in any test. We don't have any knowledge of what would happen to the incoming missiles after the first missile exploded, if the incoming missiles would be blown apart in mid-air or blown away from the target. We just don't know. We've never been given permission to make such a test, sir."

The President slowly began to crack the knuckles on his

right hand with the fingers of his left hand. The popping sound filled the quiet room.

"You said that your accuracy figures were based on firing under optimum conditions. Correct me if I'm wrong but optimum, if I remember the word, means ideal, perfect?"

"That's right, sir," Captain Steel said. "We have no accuracy figures on missiles fired from polar or near polar waters, sir. We don't know what effect the polar winds, the temperatures over the Soviet Union would have on missiles."

"My God!" the President said. "Go on, Captain."

"We have no accuracy figures for land-based missiles, sir, other than those fired from the West Coast to island targets to the west. Obviously, we have never test-fired a missile across the North Pole toward the Soviet Union. We don't have any accuracy components for those areas, sir." His ascetic face was tight and drawn.

"What you're telling me," President Milligan said slowly, "is that you and the rest of the fucking military chiefs have been lying! I have been told, sworn to on a stack of Bibles, that even if they attack us first we can literally destroy the Soviet Union. That's been the rationale behind your nuclear missile submarine programs and all the rest of our nuclear weapons programs—that neither side can dare risk starting a nuclear war. Now you sit here and tell me that our missiles aren't accurate enough to justify that rationale! God damn it, where's the truth in you people?"

"Everyone knows that our figures on accuracy are based on optimum conditions. It's just that no one ever had the brains to ask about accuracy under unfavorable conditions," Steel responded. "Nobody tried to pull the hat down over your eyes or over any president's eyes, it's just that we can't test under the conditions of war so we do the best we can. And that's the truth, Mr. President." He leaned back and hooked one elbow over the back of his chair.

"The truth is hard to find in this world, Mr. President."

Representative Wendell spoke up suddenly. "The information given to you was given in good faith, sir, in good faith. It's a matter of politics." The old Congressman's wrinkled face was placid.

"You know perfectly well, Mr. President, that if the military people went before the Appropriations Committee and said well, we know the Roosians are building missiles and we've got to match them there but we can't tell you how accurate the missiles we build will be they wouldn't get a damned dime! What they'd get is such a whoopin' and hollerin' from the press that they'd all be out on their asses.

"There's another truth, sir, and that's that the Roosians know we ain't as accurate with our missiles as we say we are—and what's more they know that we know that they ain't accurate either. In fact, they're worse shots with missiles under the best of conditions than we ever were or will be!

"What's important, Mr. President, is that the Roosians made a move, figuring that we'd never have the guts to do anything about it. This Admiral across the table from me, he hit back. That's what important! They sucker-punched us and Admiral Brannon hit 'em back, slammed them one right in their damned balls! And the Roosians ain't done one thing since that time. That's what's important."

Captain Herman Steel half turned in his chair and stared at the Congressman, his face horrified.

"Captain Steel," the President's voice was low, soft. Steel turned away from staring at Representative Wendell with an effort and looked at the President.

"I want you to do something for me. I want your best estimate of our nuclear missile accuracy under the conditions we're likely to face if we have to use those missiles. I understand that it's never been done but I think that you're the best man I could ask to do that. I want to see your figures as soon as you can pull them together. Now if you'll excuse us, I have to do some talking to Admiral Brannon." Captain Steel nodded and rose. He looked down at the old Congressman, who smiled up at him, turned, and left the room. The President turned to Admiral Brannon as the door closed behind Captain Steel.

"Okay, Admiral, what else have you done that I don't know about?"

Brannon rubbed his chin. "Well, sir, I put two of our attack submarines on every Soviet missile submarine at sea. I gave them orders to bird dog the Soviet submarines and harass them in any way they could.

"That's brought some results. Every one of the Soviet ballistic missile subs, there are ten of them at sea, sir, every one of them has been screaming to their bases, asking to know why we're bird dogging them, asking if the world political situation has changed, which is another way of asking if a war has started. Moscow has been telling them to cool it, that no war has started." He looked across the table at Representative Wendell.

"I think the Russians have read the message. They know that they'll lose every missile submarine they have at sea the minute they open their missile hatches to fire."

The President nodded and turned to Wendell. "Walter, give me your opinion of what the public reaction would have been if the Admiral had come to me and told me what had happened and what he wanted to do and I had bypassed the Congress and told him to go ahead and then made it public?"

Wendell moved his lower jaw back and forth, seating his dentures firmly. "The Congress would have been sore-assed, Mr. President. But not so much they wouldn't sit there and take it because every damned voter in this country would be hollerin' that we should have been doing this ever since the Roosians made their move to take over half of Europe after the war. No doubt about it, sir."

"You've put me in a bad bind, Admiral," the President said. "Admiral Benson told me that his aide, Wilson, let the KGB know that the whole mess could be cleared up if Brezhnev would call me and apologize. He hasn't called."

"I know, sir." Brannon said.

"Mr. President," Wendell said. "We ain't in the same political party but I think you know that you can depend on me to help you out when things get a little dark brown around the edges. Why don't we just sort of wait around a bit more and see what the Roosians do? Give 'em until tomorrow morning and if they don't do nothin' by then you could mebbe get on the hot line yourself and tell ol' Brezhnev that you know what's happened and you sure as hell don't want no nuclear war and he'd better not want one either. Sound reasonable to you, sir?"

"Maybe," the President said. He looked at Mike Brannon. "What's your reasoning on what the Soviets will do next?"

"I don't honestly know," Brannon said. "The last word I had from Bob Wilson was that the Politburo is in a crisis situation—a fight between the hardliners and the faction that wants to maintain the status quo, detente, sir. The Israeli intelligence people are on top of the situation in Moscow. They've apparently got agents deep inside the Kremlin. Israeli intelligence has been feeding information to the KGB about our intentions to retaliate with all we have in the hope this would give the softliners some ammunition to use, sir."

"That's what Mr. Wilson told me before you arrived," the President said. He leaned back from the table. "If the hardliners win there'd a hell of a risk of a nuclear war. If the concept you mentioned earlier happens, if they call me and tell me they've fired at our missile bases, I will not surrender! I'll fight!"

"I think they know that, sir," Brannon said softly.

"Mmm," the President said through closed lips. "But if the softliners win then we've got to clear up this mess. Make an announcement that we've lost a submarine and we don't know how we lost it. And we've got to do something about the crews of those two submarines that sank the Russian submarine."

"That can be handled, sir," Brannon said quietly. "That's my job."

"I know you can swear the officers to secrecy and make it stick," the President replied, "but I know from my own experience in the Marine Corps during World War II that you can't keep things of importance from the troops. They probably know they sank a Russian submarine."

"I would guess they do, sir," Brannon answered. "We can order them to never say a word about it but some of them will talk. Sometime or other some of them will talk."

"I don't think that will do any harm." Moise Goldman spoke for the first time since he had sat down at the table. "It will make a little flurry in the press but there's no way anyone can prove anything and it'll die down after a few days. I think that overseas the story will be believed and that won't hurt our foreign policy, sir; we've got too many of our allies saying that we're too soft on the Soviet Union, because of Vietnam. A story like this gets out and it won't hurt us."

"You might be right," the President said. He turned his head toward Representative Wendell. "You have anything else, any other thoughts, Walter?"

"Only that if you're thinkin' about making a call to Brezhnev that you got to remember there's a seven hour time difference. That Wilson fellow said that he had word that the Politburo is goin' to meet at four tomorrow afternoon. That's nine in the mornin', our time, Mr. President."

"Thank you for reminding me," President Milligan said.

Riding back to the Pentagon in Goldman's car, Mike Brannon turned to the President's Chief of Staff.

"Did you see the look that Captain Steel gave Wendell when he said that I had hit the Russians in the balls?"

"He just lost his war, Admiral," Goldman answered. "The Congressman was his ace in the hole for riding you out of the Navy. Now, as far as he knows, you're still in the driver's seat and he's sucking wind. Might be interesting to see what he does. I'll keep you posted if I hear anything."

Admiral Brannon's Chief Yeoman stopped him as he

walked toward his office door. "Captain Steel is in your office, sir."

"Very well, Chief," Brannon said. He walked into his office and saw Captain Steel standing by the window. The lean Captain turned and laid a sheet of paper on Brannon's desk.

"My request for retirement, Admiral," Captain Steel said. "Effective as soon as I can carry out the request the President made of me. Sir."

Mike Brannon read the paper and then twisted it into a ball and tossed it in the wastebasket.

"Request denied, Captain," he said. "The Navy needs you. I need you. Get the hell out of my office. I've got work to do."

CHAPTER 21

Far out in the mid-Atlantic a Soviet Golf Command and Control submarine nosed cautiously to the surface and extended its massive communications array above its Conning Tower. In the Radio Room of the communications submarine an operator began to tap out a long signal to the Soviet ballistic missile submarines in the Atlantic. When he had finished his transmission he turned on his receiver and listened for the acknowledgments.

"All ships acknowledge, sir," he said to the Radio Officer who stood beside him.

"Good," the Radio Officer said. He went out of the radio room and found the submarine's Commanding Officer drinking tea in the ship's tiny galley. The Commanding Officer looked at his wrist watch.

"It's zero three hundred," he said. "We've got almost two hours until dawn. Tell the Watch Officer we'll dive fifteen minutes before false dawn. How's the weather topside?"

"Clear night, Comrade Captain. Lots of stars. No moon. No wind. Sea is calm."

The ship's Captain nodded. "Pass the word to those people still awake that they can go up on deck for fifteen minutes at a time. Five men in each party. No smoking."

Aboard the *Orca,* 400 miles off the East Coast of the United States, Captain Dick Reinauer studied a chart on the work table in the ship's Control Room.

"There's going to be hell to pay," he muttered to his XO. "If we don't find that son of a bitchin' Russian submarine old Iron Mike is going to have me for breakfast. Of all the damned times to get a glitch in the sonar gear!"

"Maybe *Devilfish* is still with him," Eckert volunteered. "He sure went to high speed and went down damned deep before the glitch happened. *Devilfish* should have been able to stay in contact." Both men looked toward the loudspeaker on the port bulkhead as it rasped.

"Sonar report for the Officer of the Deck and the Captain. Sonar gear is now in full operation and we have contact with the target. Target has apparently reversed course and is coming toward us at high speed. Target depth is seven zero zero repeat seven hundred feet. Range is three zero, repeat thirty miles, sir."

Captain Reinauer reached for the telephone and dialed the Sonar Room.

"I want a full report on the glitch," he said into the telephone. "And I want a footprint confirmation that we're on the same target. I don't want to begin following some damned electronic dummy that bastard might have fired to fool us."

"We can confirm this is the same target, Captain," the voice on the loudspeaker said. "We're tracking a Soviet Yankee One Class ballistic missile submarine, sir. He's making the same screw noise pattern and one of his circulating water pumps has got a bad bearing. We confirm same target, sir."

"Very well," Reinauer said. He turned to Eckert. "What

the hell is he doing on a reverse course? He told us yesterday evening that he was ordered home. Now he's coming back toward us. Why?"

"We know he got off a long message when he was surfaced," Eckert said. He looked at the twenty-four hour clock on the bulkhead. "We're due to surface in an hour for radio traffic. Maybe we'll find out what the hell is going on."

Reinauer nodded, studying the chart in front of him. "Let's start a war problem on him. I want to run outboard of him and stay out in front of him. We'll assume *Devilfish* is inboard and near him. Tell Communications to stand by for satellite transmission ten minutes before we go up. I want to go up and down as fast as we can. We lose too much time on the surface so work out the problem to stay well ahead of him, at least twenty thousand yards. By the time we go up and down we should still have some lead on him and then we'll close on him and start staying close to the bastard." He thanked the watch messenger for a cup of coffee and a fresh doughnut.

"I want the torpedo room on full alert, XO. If we hear that bastard opening his missile hatches we nail the son of a bitch!"

Sophia Blovin walked into Igor Shevenko's office with a sealed envelope in her hand. She put it on the desk.

"This is a message the Navy sent," she said. "One of Comrade Simonov's men delivered it just now."

Shevenko put a blunt thumb under the flap of the envelope and ripped it open. He read the message and Sophia saw his face harden.

"The bastard!" Shevenko muttered.

"Who?"

"Zurahv, that's who!" he said. He tapped the message. "He's ordered all ballistic missile submarines to stand by for an order to fire their missiles at Alpha Targets at fifteen hundred hours and thirty minutes, Greenwich Time."

"Alpha Targets are what?" Sophia Blovin inquired.

"Military targets. Hardened missile sites in the United States." Shevenko picked up a ball-point pen and began to make notes on a piece of paper.

"Fifteen thirty hours Greenwich Time, that's five-thirty in the afternoon, our time. Today. An hour and a half after the Politburo meeting begins. If he wins the vote this afternoon he can do as he pleases. If he loses the vote . . ." He paused.

"If he loses then he's going to start a war anyway, is that it?" she asked.

Shevenko nodded. With the pen he drew a recognizable sketch of an atomic explosion. "And that is how it will end!"

"Unless you and Comrade Plotovsky can stop it," she said softly. "I do not want to die now, not since I've found you."

"Nor do I," Shevenko said. "Get me through to Dr. Saul in Israel. I want a clear line, no taping. As fast as you can. If he's not near a phone tell whoever answers that it is of utmost importance that he communicate with me at once." Sophia Blovin nodded and left the office. She came back in five minutes.

"He is not in his office. They said they can reach him and have him return the call within the half hour."

He nodded and dialed a number on his telephone. He listened to the phone ring at the other end, feeling the sweat gathering in his armpits. The ringing stopped.

"Comrade Plotovsky, please," he said, crossing two fingers of his left hand as he said it, hoping that the old man would be in his office. He relaxed slightly as he heard the raspy voice on the line.

"Shevenko, Comrade. I must see you at once, sir. Yes, very important. Do I have your permission to have an overseas call placed to your private line? Good. I will be there in twenty minutes."

He put the phone back in its cradle and turned to Sophia Blovin. "Get back to the person you talked to in Israel. Give them Comrade Plotovsky's private line number. Tell them whose number it is, they know of him. Have Dr. Saul call me at that number thirty minutes from now. If he can't do that let me know at once." He got out of his chair and went to the coat tree and put on his coat and hat. His grin was lopsided as he looked at Sophia Blovin.

"I never thought I would be getting into bed with the Jews to save my good Russian ass," he said.

"You are a big enough man to do that, but Comrade Plotovsky?"

"He doesn't hate Jews," Shevenko said as he buttoned his coat. "He had a team of dynamiters during the Revolution. That was over fifty years ago. All of them were Jews. They blew up a lot of the Tsar's troops. Now we'll see if we can blow up Admiral Zurahv with the help of the Jews."

"What are you going to ask the Israelis to do?" she half whispered. He stopped at the door and looked at her.

"I don't know," he said. "I just don't know."

Isser Bernstein put down the telephone and ran his hand over his bald head. He read the notes he had made during his talk with Shevenko and carefully rewrote the notes, fleshing out his self-taught shorthand. His aide came into his office in response to his buzzer.

"Get me Mr. Wilson of the CIA at once, please," he said. He looked at his wrist watch. "It's ten-thirty here. Seven hours time difference, three-thirty in the morning there. He should be at home. If he is not, get me Admiral Benson. If he isn't home get me Admiral Brannon."

"Bob Wilson better be home in his own bed," Naomi said primly. She left the room and Isser heard her talking to the operator on the Mossad switchboard. He settled back in his chair and waited, looking at his watch from time to time. The light on his telephone console suddenly began to blink and he picked up the receiver and heard Bob Wilson's sleepy voice.

"Dr. Saul here," Isser boomed out. "Wake up. You have

a notepad and pen near your bed? Ah, always prepared, are you? Take this down carefully.

"The Soviet Union will launch ballistic missiles from submarines at fifteen thirty hours Greenwich time. Repeat fifteen hundred hours plus thirty minutes Greenwich time. Targets will be hardened missile sites in the United States.

"The attack will be launched ninety repeat ninety minutes after the Politburo goes into emergency session to resolve the differences between the hard and softliners."

Bob Wilson sat on the edge of his bed, fully awake, the hair on the back of his neck raising. He looked at his notes and took a deep breath to calm himself and then carefully read back what Isser Bernstein had said to him.

"Source?" he said into the mouthpiece.

"Shevenko. He tried to reach me. I was out. His aide called back and gave Naomi instructions I should call him at once. He was not in his office. He was in the office of Leonid Plotovsky of the Politburo. Plotovsky has been the leader of the softliners in the Politburo."

"Credence?" Wilson said.

"I believe Shevenko is telling the truth, Bob. He wouldn't dare lie from that old man's office. Plotovsky would have him hung up by, how do you say it, by his balls. Yes. I would appreciate you calling me back as soon as you have information of what action your side will take." He listened a moment, swiveling back and forth in his chair.

"For what it is worth, my old friend, and I give you this because I owe you so much: If the attack is launched you may tell your President that Israel will attack the Arab states within minutes after the first missiles leave Russia. We are not going to sit here and be taken by madmen like Nasser and Qaddaffi as if we were rabbits in a pen. Make sure your President knows that." He put the telephone back on its cradle. He buzzed for Naomi.

"Get me the Prime Minister, please," he said. Naomi came back into his office in two minutes.

"Her schedule for today reads like she is to attend a meeting of the Knesset, sir. That's going on now. It's a closed meeting, the subject matter is the Egyptian aggressions."

"Hm," Isser said. "Phone the Chief of Security at the Knesset. Tell him I have to talk to the Prime Minister at once. Tell him the conversation must be conducted over a safe phone." Naomi left and Isser Bernstein sat, drumming his fingers on his desk top. The telephone rang.

In Washington a sleepy Vice Admiral Mike Brannon was jolted wide awake by the call from Rear Admiral Mike Benson. He dressed as swiftly as he could as his wife made him a cup of strong coffee. He gulped the hot black liquid down and pulled on a heavy overcoat. He stopped at the door and kissed Gloria Brannon and held her close. He heard the single, muted sound of the automobile horn outside and he suddenly hugged her more tightly and kissed her again and trotted down the front steps to the car.

"The White House," he ordered the driver. He craned his neck, looking out the car window and saw his wife's ample form outlined against the lights in the living room of his quarters and wondered if he would ever see her again.

CHAPTER 22

Admiral Brannon thanked the Marine Sergeant who opened the door of the Oval Office for him, and walked inside, hearing the door click closed behind him. A mess steward, immaculate at that hour of the morning in a white starched jacket and blue trousers, was putting a tray of cups and saucers and carafes of hot coffee on the sideboard. He finished and left the room and Mike Brannon nodded to the three men who were seated at the long table.

Admiral Benson was wearing a pair of slacks and a sport shirt covered by a pullover sweater. Bob Wilson had apparently put on the first clothes he grabbed out of his closet; his trousers were wrinkled and paint-stained and he had on a gray sweatshirt. Captain Herman Steel was in full uniform, his black tie knotted neatly between the collar wings of his starched white shirt. Brannon walked to the sideboard and filled three cups with coffee and brought them to the table. He nodded at Captain Steel, who barely acknowledged the gesture.

Moise Goldman, dressed in faded blue jeans and a black turtleneck sweater walked into the office followed by the President, who had on a red dressing gown with the Presidential Seal embroidered on the left breast pocket. Goldman got coffee for the President and himself.

"Let's go over this one more time," the President said. He sipped at his coffee, his eyes turning toward Bob Wilson. "Start at the beginning, Bob. Moise, take notes, please." "I asked for his source, sir. He told me it was Igor Shevenko, chief of the First Directorate of the KGB."

"What's the First Directorate?" the President asked.

"That's the KGB division that is responsible for all intelligence operations outside of the Soviet Union, sir."

"Do you know anything about this Shevenko?" Goldman asked.

"Yes, sir. I know him. He's tried to kill me several times. I've tried to kill him."

"Uh, huh," Goldman said. He doodled a little square on his notepad. "Since you both obviously failed what sort of relationship do you have? A sort of mutual admiration society? Do you talk to each other through Israel?"

"I've met Shevenko face to face in the past." Wilson's voice was edged. "Don't get me wrong, Mr. Goldman. He's the enemy. I respect him. He'll lie as easily as he breathes but I don't think he's lying now. We know that the KGB doesn't want a nuclear war. I believe that. Isser Bernstein believes it."

"Go on," the President said.

"Bernstein told me that Shevenko's personal aide had called his office. He was out but Naomi, Bernstein's right hand girl, told Shevenko's aide that she could have him return the call in a half an hour. Five minutes later Shevenko's aide called again and asked to have Bernstein make the call to Leonid Plotovsky's private office. The number for that phone was given to Bernstein's aide."

"I know Plotovsky," Goldman said quietly. "I met him when I was in the *Times* Bureau in Moscow. He's an old man now but still powerful in the Politburo. One of the original great heroes of the Communist Revolution. A very hard case.

He's a moderate who often runs counter to the policies of the Party."

"In what way?" Captain Steel spoke for the first time since the meeting began.

"He doesn't dislike Jews, for one thing, and he's spoken out against persecution of the Jewish intellectuals." Goldman said. "He fought beside Jews in the Revolution and found out they could fight as well as any other Russian.

"He doesn't hate the United States. He distrusts us but he doesn't hate us. He believes the Khrushchev Doctrine that a controlled state economy can, in time, undermine capitalism and that the world will fall into the Soviet Union's lap if they are just patient." He stopped and nodded at Wilson to continue.

"Bernstein told me he believed Shevenko was telling the truth," Wilson said. He looked again at his notes. "He said when he made the call to Plotovsky's office that Plotovsky answered the telephone himself and then put Shevenko on the line. Bernstein doesn't believe that Plotovsky would be a party to a nuclear attack and he doesn't believe Shevenko would dare lie with Plotovsky listening, that he'd be hung by his balls. Exact quote, sir," he said looking at the President.

"Bernstein also said that I should tell you, Mr. President, that if the Soviet Union launches a nuclear attack against the United States Israel would attack the Arab States within minutes."

"That would be difficult," Captain Steel said. "The last reports I saw showed that the Israeli Army is tied up with the border incidents that Egypt is carrying out against Israel. To attack the Arab states, he used the plural? That would require a call-up of all reserves and that would take weeks."

"How long does it take to roll back the covers of underground silos and fire nuclear rockets?" Wilson said in a dry tone of voice. "How long does it take to put nuclear bombs on aircraft and get them airborne?"

"Israel has never admitted it has the capacity to make nuclear weapons but we know they have and we know they've got nuclear weapons." He put his notes back in his shirt pocket and looked around the table.

"Isser Bernstein also said that Israel was not going to sit there and be taken over by, quote and unquote, madmen like Nasser and Qaddaffi as if we were rabbits in a pen. Make sure your President knows that."

The President looked at the clock on the wall of the Oval Office. "It's four-thirty in the morning," he said slowly. "What time is it in Moscow and in Greenwich?"

"Eleven-thirty A.M. in Moscow, sir. Nine-thirty A.M. at Greenwich." Mike Brannon said. "To put it another way, we've got six hours to their launch time."

The President began to crack the knuckles of his right hand with the fingers of his left. "Six hours. If we can believe this report and I think we'd better damned well believe it. Except that they might begin firing before the launch time they've set. They're capable of that."

"Capable but I don't think they will, sir," Goldman said slowly. "I don't think the hardliners would dare start a nuclear war before the Politburo met. The way I read this from what I know about the workings of the Politburo and the Soviet mind, and I'd appreciate your feedback Admiral Benson, Mr. Wilson, is that the hardliners are gambling on carrying the vote for all-out nuclear war against us, against Red China. I read the voting as iffy with maybe Brezhnev casting the vote to break a tie.

"If the hardliners get the votes they'll launch at the designated time. The information we have is supposed to be secret. That right, Admiral Benson? We're not supposed to know they're planning an attack? If they do launch, Brezhnev would be on the phone to the President with an ultimatum, unconditional surrender or what did you say in the last meeting Admiral Brannon? We lose fifty million people within an hour? That ultimatum would be followed by a strike against Red China. How do you see it Admiral Benson, Mr. Wilson?"

Benson nodded his head slowly. "I have to agree, sir." He looked sideways at Bob Wilson who nodded his head in confirmation.

"And that means that within minutes after the Soviets launch, Israel will launch and the whole damned world will be in flames!" the President said. "Damn that woman! When I called her to congratulate her on her election as Prime Minister she swore to me on the head of her grandchildren that Israel had no nuclear weapons and would never countenance nuclear weapons anywhere in the Middle East."

"Six hours to holocaust unless we can figure out some way to stop it," Goldman said softly. He looked up as a quiet knock sounded on the door of the Oval Office. Captain Steel rose and went to the door and opened it and took the salute of the Marine Sergeant on duty outside the door.

"The switchboard has an urgent call for Mr. Wilson, sir. I am instructed to say that it is of the highest priority and that he must answer it at once, sir." Captain Steel nodded and closed the door and Goldman motioned to Wilson to take the call at a phone on the sideboard. He put a pad of paper and a pen down beside the phone as Wilson picked up the receiver.

"Press the button on the far left if you're getting a scrambled call," he said. Wilson nodded, listened for a moment and pressed the button. He wrote quickly, scrawling the words in large letters, thanked the person at the other end of the line, and hung up and walked back to the table and sat down.

"That was Isser Bernstein in Israel," Wilson said. He put his notes on the table and looked at them.

"He said they had just received a message from an agent in Moscow. There was a second part to the information they gave us earlier this morning about the time of the missile strike. Right after that message was sent another message was sent to all Soviet ballistic missile submarines on station. Those submarines are ordered to be in a positoin to receive incoming messages between fourteen and fifteen hundred hours, that's Greenwich Time, today. At that time they will be given a go or no go order on the missiles." Wilson pushed the paper over to Admiral Benson, who smoothed it out and studied it.

The President looked at Mike Brannon. "That sound authentic to you? Would that be what they would do if they were thinking about firing their missiles?"

"It's not what we would do," Brannon said slowly. "Our procedures are different. The naval officer with the Football, with your up to date codes for ordering our submarines to fire, would give you the black book and you'd prepare the firing order.

"I don't know what their procedures are. I don't think anyone knows. We've always assumed that they would operate somewhat as we do."

"I've been around Khrushchev when he was out of the Soviet Union and I never saw anyone with anything like our Football procedure," Goldman said. "When he visited the United States he wasn't even in communication with Moscow for days at a time." He pulled his pipe and tobacco pouch out of his trouser pocket and carefully filled the pipe.

"It might be," he said in a thoughtful voice, "it just might be that Admiral Zurahv is covering his retreat. If the Politburo meeting goes badly for his side he'd have time to call off the missile launch."

"Or he could order the operation to go forward even if his side loses this afternoon and then take over the government," Captain Steel said in his harsh voice. "It would be a fait accompli situation."

"No," the President said. "I don't think so. Brezhnev would have him shot within minutes."

"Maybe, Mr. President," Goldman said. "Maybe Admiral Zurahv wouldn't have to take over the Soviet government. Brezhnev is a politician, with all due respect, sir. If Zurahv told him that an order had been given to fire the submarine missiles and that it couldn't be recalled because the subs had gone to deep submergence, and that Brezhnev had no other course but to call and tell you that within the hour our land-based missile sites would be hit, and if you didn't surrender all our cities would be hit . . ." He stopped as the President spread both his hands on the polished table.

"I don't like the way this meeting is going, damn it," the President grunted. "I know what you're going to say, Moise. If Brezhnev looked at that sort of thing he could see himself as ruling the entire world if we caved in." He began to pound softly on the table with his right hand.

"What I want now, God damn it, is what do we do? Brannon, you're the damned Admiral, what in the hell do we do?"

Mike Brannon looked at his Commander in Chief, his deep blue eyes calm.

"We fight back, sir. We've got four, four and a half hours until the Soviet submarines will begin to come close to the surface to raise their antennas to pick up their go or no go orders. That's time enough if we move fast."

"Time enough to do what?"

"We know the location of every Soviet missile submarine, sir. Each one is being covered by two of our attack submarines. We can drop sonar buoys from planes in the areas where their submarines are cruising and where our submarines are watching them. The message bouys will begin broadcasting sonar messages over and over."

"Saying what, Admiral?"

"I'd suggest that the message say that if the Soviet submarines return to submerged cruising depths our submarines attack immediately and destroy them, sir. The message could also say that if the Soviet submarines surface and remain surfaced—they can't fire their missiles while they are on the surface—that they won't be harmed. The Soviet subs will read the messages and if they don't our submarines could be instructed to relay the messages to them.

"Then you could get on the hot line to Brezhnev and tell him you know what's going on and the first Soviet missile submarine that submerges will be destroyed and that will be a signal for an all-out ICBM attack on the Soviet Union from our land-based and our submarine missiles." He sat back, his hands in his lap.

"How long would it take to do that, to get the messages made, get the sonar buoys made, have them dropped?"

"Two hours, I'd guess. No more." Mike Brannon looked across the table at Captain Steel. "What's the exact range of the SSN–Six missiles the Yankee One class of Soviet submarines carry, Herman?"

"Two thousand nine hundred and fifty kilometers, Admiral. That's about sixteen hundred nautical miles. Their submarines would have to be fairly close inshore to be able to reach the northern areas of the Midwest, where we have a lot of hardened missile sites, sir."

Mike Brannon turned his head toward the President. "No problem, sir. We could have the message buoys prepared within an hour. Another half hour to load the planes. We could drop at least an hour and a half to two hours before the Soviet subs have to come up to receive their go or no go message."

"Do it!" the President said. He waved his hand toward the telephone on the sideboard. Moise Goldman uncapped his pen and handed it to Brannon with a pad of paper. Brannon wrote rapidly for a moment and then rose and went to the telephone. He waited while the White House operator connected him with the War Room deep within the Pentagon and then he began to talk, enunciating each word carefully. He finished and asked that the message be read back.

"End of message," the voice on the other end of the telephone line said. "As you know, Admiral Brannon, this sort of alert requires the personal endorsement of the President of the United States, sir."

"He's here in the Oval Office with me," Brannon said. "I'll put him on."

"Negative, sir," the officer in the War Room said. "We'll call the Oval Office and ask to speak first with Football and then with the President."

"I don't know where Football is," Brannon said.

"I'd suggest you find him sir. If this situation is a Red Alert, Football should be within close reach of the President and I must advise you that our conversation is being taped, sir. I'll call the Oval Office in two minutes, sir."

Brannon hung up the telephone and turned to face the table. Goldman was getting out of his chair and walking toward the door.

"Football should be in the hall," he said to Brannon. "I'll get him." He opened the door and spoke to the Marine Sergeant outside, who beckoned and a tall naval Commander came into the room carrying the black attache case that was called "The Football."

The telephone rang and Moise Goldman picked it up at once. He identified himself and motioned to the Navy Commander, who placed his attache case on the sideboard and used a key to open it. He took the telephone from Goldman.

"Commander Stanley Baker here. I.D. number is Football six four three eight six one. Code one four three. I.D. number for this day as of midnight is Baker six one. Yes the President is here. I'll put him on."

President Milligan rose from his chair and took the telephone from Commander Baker, who held out a small black book opened at the proper page.

"This is the President," he said in a slow, strong voice. "I am reading the code from the book Football is holding. President's code for Red Alert and ultimate defense is Able Zebra nine four two." He waited a moment.

"Execute the orders given you by Vice Admiral Brannon at once," he said. "Report to me in the Oval Office as soon as the buoys are dropped." He squinted at the black book that Commander Baker was holding. "Send Red Alert and standby warnings to all missile submarines on station. Thank you."

He placed the telephone on its cradle and padded back to the table, his slippers making soft noises against the rug.

"That's it," the President said. "Now we wait."

CHAPTER 23

The conference room in the Kremlin was buzzing softly with a hum of low conversation. On one side of the room Leonid Plotovsky stood, surrounded by four of the Politburo members who backed his stand of moderation toward the West. On the other side of the room the five hardliners huddled, talking softly, planning their strategy. The talking stopped as a door opened and Leonid Brezhnev walked in and took his seat at the head of the table. The two groups moved to the table and sat down, facing each other across the table. A male secretary, his face devoid of expression, slipped into the room and sat down at a small desk within earshot of the conference table and arranged his pens and a thick pad of paper in front of him.

In an anteroom Igor Shevenko sat in a hard chair, looking at his wrist watch from time to time.

"Almost time to start," he said to Anton Simonov, who sat beside him. Simonov nodded.

"How do you think it will go, Igor?" he asked. Shevenko rolled his eyes up in the direction of the ventilation duct in the wall and Simonov nodded in understanding.

"It will go as it should go," Shevenko said in a clear voice.

"What is best for the nation will be done. That is all any citizen could ask."

In an adjoining anteroom Admiral Aleksandr Zurahv sat with an Army general. He opened his mouth to say something and caught the general's warning shake of his head and closed his mouth.

Leonid Plotovsky coughed and cleared his throat and raised a large handkerchief to his mouth.

"We are here, Comrade First Secretary," he said, his eyes on Brezhnev, "to review the situation we now face. We all know the circumstances.

"We are divided, which is not a bad thing of itself. Out of division comes compromise for the good of the nation and co-operation."

"Understood," Brezhnev said. "We will vote now." He looked down the table at the group. "All those who favor changing our position on this matter will please raise their hands." Plotovsky and the four men on his side of the table raised their hands.

"All in favor of continuing the policy will raise their hands." The five men across the table from the Plotovsky group raised their hands.

"A tie," Brezhnev said. "As I expected. Before I cast my vote we will hear from the advocates from both sides and whatever witnesses each side desires to call. Comrade Plotovsky, as the senior member of the Politburo in terms of age and service, will speak first."

"I request that Comrades Igor Shevenko and Anton Simonov be called, Comrade," Plotovsky said. Brezhnev nodded and the secretary went to the door that led into the anteroom where Shevenko and Simonov were waiting and summoned both men. He led them to the table and seated them at the foot of the table, facing Brezhnev, who nodded and smiled his greeting.

Sergei Pomonvitz, the leader of the opposition, raised his hand.

"I request that Admiral Zurahv and his party be present,

Comrade Secretary." The aide went to the door of the other anteroom and ushered Admiral Zurahv and General Mishicoff into the room. The secretary brought two chairs to the table and Shevenko and Simonov shifted their chairs so they were aligned on Plotovsky's side. Admiral Zurahv and General Mishicoff sat opposite them. Brezhnev smiled at the Admiral and the General and turned to Plotovsky.

"We will hear your arguments first, Comrade Plotovsky." He looked down at the table. "The witnesses will respond when asked to do so."

"We, my group, are convinced that the present policy of pushing the United States and the West into a corner from which they cannot extricate themselves by means other than nuclear war or surrender is needlessly dangerous," Plotovsky began. The fierce lizard eyes darted a glance at Admiral Zurahv.

"We find ourselves in the position where our policy is being dictated by the military. The United States has struck back without the knowledge of its president or its Congress because of the actions of an American admiral. We have lost an attack submarine, one of our newest and finest. The United States has lost one of its ballistic missile submarines.

"We submit this has gone far enough. It is time to call a halt. It is our opinion that this can be done with honor. We do not advocate relaxing the vigilance we must always exert to survive in this world. We do not argue that it is wrong to attack if we are in danger but we argue that this is not the time, not the way, that such an attack should be started." He leaned back in his chair, his eyes on the group across the table.

"Comrade," Sergei Pomonvitz said, "we all know that the Soviet Union lives constantly under the danger of a surprise attack from the Americans and the Chinese. The Chinese have already begun their campaign of harassment along our borders, serious incidents that require the use of a great deal of manpower and equipment to hold at bay.

"We, our military experts," he nodded his head toward Admiral Zurahv and General Mishicoff, "have ample, more than ample evidence that the border strikes by the Chinese are a diversionary tactic to blind us to the true intentions of the United States. We do not believe the American retaliation to our weapons test was done without the knowledge of President Milligan. We all know what the mood is in the United States toward the Soviet Union. They are our enemies, Comrades! They mean to divert us with the Chinese and then smash us, burn us, with nuclear missiles! And when that is done they will send in the Chinese hordes to suffer the residual nuclear radiation poisoning while they clean up the wreckage of what was once the Soviet Union." He turned to Admiral Zurahv.

"I request that Admiral Zurahv give us his thoughts, Comrades."

The bulky Admiral frowned, his small eyes almost hidden in the puffy rolls of flesh of his face.

"There is no doubt in our minds that the retaliation taken by the United States was done with the full knowledge of the American president." He leaned back in his chair.

"We are asked to believe that one American admiral, not the top admiral in the American Navy, mind you, we are asked to believe that this one American admiral took it upon himself to enter into a state of war with the Soviet Union without informing his president or the Congress of the United States.

"That, Comrades, I submit is impossible! Could I do such a thing? Of course not! This admiral, his name is Brannon, is an anachronism. He commands the submarines of the American Atlantic Fleet yet he is not qualified to even command one of his nuclear submarines! He is a political admiral and as such would not dare to take the retaliatory step that was taken.

"I therefore submit, and my opinion is backed by General Mishicoff and the GRU, that the United States president initiated this retaliatory action because . . ." His heavy hand slapped the table in front of him. "Because the warmongers in the United States, the munitions manufacturers and the Soviet Union

haters used the loss of one of their submarines due to unknown causes to provoke a war against us. They produced a
faked photograph to prove that their submarine had been attacked. They produced faked evidence that only one of our
submarines could have been the attacker." His hand curled into
a fist and he pounded the table gently.

"The photograph that Comrade Shevenko gave to me as
proof that the Americans knew how their submarine was lost
is a fake! The American submarine is on the bottom in twelve
thousand feet of water and our experts say, without fear of
contradiction, Comrades, that it is impossible to take photographs of anything at that depth!"

Leonid Plotovsky spat into his handkerchief. "Admiral,
what do you take us for? Dogs that salivate when you ring
your bell? Who are you, who are we to say that the Americans
cannot take pictures of the ocean floor at whatever depth? Do
we know this? No! We presume it because we cannot do it at
this time.

"What you are forgetting is that Israeli Intelligence working
in co-operation with Comrade Shevenko because the Israelis
are not fools and fear a nuclear war, have documented every
step the Americans have taken. Documented it, Admiral! Everything Israeli Intelligence has told Comrade Shevenko has been
borne out!"

"Jews!" The word came out of General Mishicoff's mouth
as if it were a wad of spit. "Jews! Who can believe them? They
are hand in glove with the American imperialists. If we are
destroyed they rule the Middle East and Africa. Their evidence
is worthless!"

Leonid Plotovsky, his lined face calm, turned to Igor Shevenko. "You all know Comrade Shevenko, you know his record
as Chief of the First Directorate of the KGB. I submit that
Comrade Shevenko's loyalty, his patriotism, is beyond question.
I equate it with my own. Comrade Shevenko?"

"Comrades," Shevenko said in his deep voice. "I appreciate
the kind words from Comrade Plotovsky,. I am grateful I am

allowed, by your permission, to serve my country as I do. I have little to say other than what I have learned in my contacts with the Israeli intelligence service which, I must add, is excellent. Almost as good as our own.

"The Israelis have at least one or more deep moles within the American defense establishment. Their information is detailed and very accurate. As Comrade Plotovsky has pointed out, in this particular case they have warned us of events to come and those warnings have been borne out.

"I would not say that the Israelis are giving us this intelligence thinking that if we are attacked and crippled or destroyed they can take over more than one hundred million Arabs." He frowned. "That is a large mouthful for a nation of about four million people to chew, Comrades. The Israelis fear a nuclear war because if it happens they will be swallowed up by the Arab states." He put his large, square hands on the table in front of him and studied them with his eyes. He looked up.

"I received some additional intelligence from the Mossad before the meeting, Comrades. I gave it to Comrade Plotovsky."

Brezhnev looked at the old street fighter. Plotovsky took some papers from his inner jacket pocket and spread them on the table in front of him.

"Our good friend, Admiral Zurahv, a little while ago said that the American admiral could not possibly have acted on his own in ordering the destruction of our attack submarine. To reinforce this statement Admiral Zurahv said—please correct me if I am wrong, Admiral—you said quote could I do something like this? unquote. Is that not right, Comrade?"

"That is correct," Admiral Zurahv said. "I am obedient to the wishes of the Politburo. Just as Admiral Brannon must obey the wishes of his rulers."

"Then why, Admiral," Plotovsky said, his eyes on the papers in front of him, "why did you send an order to all Soviet ballistic missile submarines now on station off the coasts of North America to stand by to fire missiles at military targets within the United States this afternoon, ninety minutes after this meeting was convened?"

There was a dead silence in the room. The hardliners at the table stared at each other and then turned their heads to look at Admiral Zurahv.

"Before you answer that question, Admiral, why did you also send a message to each of our submarines to come to the surface this afternoon and receive an order to launch missiles or not to launch?" The old man sat back, his hooded eyes sharp.

"Comrade Secretary, with your permission I will continue." His bony hand raised and a long, arthritic-knobbed forefinger pointed at Admiral Zurahv.

"For your information, Admiral Zurahv, the Americans read your messages. They have warned the commanders of our submarines that if they submerge after receiving your message to launch or not to launch they will be immediately destroyed by the American attack submarines that are now close by to each of our ships. And one more thing, Admiral. You spoke of faked photographs. If you wish to make an issue of faked photographs I am prepared to place on this table for all to see some photographs that are not faked." He sat back in his chair and seemed to collapse inward upon himself.

There was absolute silence in the room that was broken by the sharp note of the buzzer on the telephone at Brezhnev's elbow. He picked up the telephone. He listened for a moment and asked the person on the other end of the line to wait a moment.

"I must ask all of you to retire to your respective anterooms," Brezhnev said. "I will call you when I am finished with this telephone call."

Aboard the U.S.S. *Orca* Captain Reinauer stood in the Control Room and studied the electronic plot on the video screen.

"We have a constant firing solution, sir," Lieutenant Reiss said in a low voice. "Range is eleven miles. Target bears zero zero four. *Sharkfin* is ten miles dead ahead of the target, sir."

"Very well," Reinauer said. He picked up the telephone handset.

"Sonar, make the following message to the target as soon as the sonar buoy stops transmitting.

" 'Ivan, when you surface to receive your orders we advise you to stay on the surface. I am under orders to destroy you if you go back down to operating depth. End message.' " He put down the telephone and heard his ship's sonar beam vibrate the *Orca's* hull. Two minutes later the loudspeaker rasped.

"Message sent and receipted for, Captain. Target sent us a message. Quote, I read you stop What is going on question mark. End message, sir"

Captain Reinauer picked up the telephone. "Make this reply: 'I presume our leaders are quarreling. I urge you as a fellow submariner to advise your headquarters of my orders. End message.' " He put down the telephone and waited.

"Message receipted for just before the sonar buoy started sending its message again, sir," the Sonar Room operator reported over the loudspeaker. Reinauer acknowledged the message and turned to his XO.

"Things are getting damned tight, my friend." He turned as the loudspeaker began to rasp.

"Sonar to the Captain. Target has increased propeller speed and is heading for the surface. We read him at three zero zero, repeat three hundred feet and going up."

"Very well," Captain Reinauer said. He looked at Lieutenant Bill Reiss. "Advise the torpedo room to stand by for a SUBROC firing run. If that bastard starts back down to depth we blast him." He picked up the telephone and punched a button that would let him talk to all compartments in the ship via loudspeakers.

"This is the Captain. Now hear this. We are facing a critical situation that none of us know much about. We may be firing

SUBROC missiles at a Soviet missile submarine. If we have to do that it will mean a nuclear war between the United States and the Soviet Union has started. Those of you who pray should do so now. Pray that we won't have to fire. May God be with us."

Isser Bernstein stood in a Communications Room that had been built deep beneath the ground. He looked up as the officer in charge moved toward him.

"We are picking up radio traffic from Soviet submarines to Moscow via satellite, sir. They are talking in plain language, asking for instructions, telling their headquarters they are threatened by several American attack submarines. I find it odd that they are not sending these messages in code."

"I don't," Isser Bernstein said. "If you are in danger of being blown out of the water or down to the ocean bottom, I don't think you'd bother with coded messages. You'd get the word out as swiftly as you could and as plainly as possible about what you face." Both men turned as one of the women sitting at a receiving unit suddenly rose and hastened toward them.

"Urgent message from Agent Little Fox, sir. Little Fox reports that the Politburo is in session and the first vote was a tie."

"Thank you," Bernstein said. He looked at the Communications Officer. "If we are lucky, my cousin, Brezhnev will cast his vote against starting a war."

"And if he does not?"

"Then it begins," Isser Bernstein said with a sigh. "The final holocaust from which there will be no survivors."

CHAPTER 24

The mess stewards cleared away the plates and the remains of the meal that had been brought to the Oval Office and refilled the coffee carafes with steaming hot coffee. President Milligan rubbed the stubble on his chin with his hand and looked at the clock on the wall.

"Nine o'clock," he said slowly. "That's four in the afternoon in Moscow. What's the agenda at this time?"

Vice Admiral Mike Brannon looked at his notes. "Two things should happen at this hour, sir. The Politburo should be convening and the Soviet missile submarines should be coming close enough to the surface to extend antennas to receive a go or no go order on firing missiles."

"You think they've read the sonar buoy messages by now?" the President asked.

"Yes, sir," Brannon replied. "By now our attack submarines have taken firing position, that is, they are now ten miles from their targets. They have to keep that distance because the blast effect of the SUBROC nuclear missile warheads is so powerful."

"So damned much depends on them reading those sonar buoy messages," the President said. "I wish we could be sure they got the message."

"I think we can assume they know what will happen if they go back down to firing depth, sir," Brannon said. "Captain Steel's suggestion that we build in a five minute delay between repetitions of the sonar buoy messages lets our own submarines contact their targets. It gives us two ways of reaching them. I figure that when the Soviet subs go up to get their go or no go message they'll be telling their headquarters what the score is and asking for orders."

"I agree with Admiral Brannon, Mr. President," Captain Steel said. "Those Russian submarine captains know that if they go back down to firing depth they will be destroyed. Ignoring the sonar buoy message, returning to firing depth means the destruction of their ships. I don't think Russian submarine commanders are that much different from our own ship commanders. They won't deliberately risk the loss of their ships because of what must seem to them to be a big foul-up in orders."

"Suppose they're told to submerge and fire their missiles? Would they do that? Moise, you spent a lot of time in Moscow. Would they be likely to follow that kind of an order even if it meant they would be sunk?"

"I don't know," Goldman said. "It's like being told to commit suicide. Russian tank commanders at Stalingrad did exactly that, sir. They followed orders to attack the Germans and they attacked in the face of anti-tank guns that fired shells that went through their tanks as if they were made of paper.

"I just don't know. You could spend your life in Moscow, in Russia and not really know how the Russian mind works." He stopped as a loud rap sounded on the door. Captain Steel rose and went to the door and took a sealed envelope from the Marine Sergeant. He closed the door and handed the envelope to the President who ripped it open with his thumb.

"The War Room reports radio traffic in plain language

from Russian submarines off our coast," he said. He laid the page aside and swiftly read the second page.

"The first two messages translated tell the Soviet High Naval Command that Soviet submarines have been warned not to submerge after receiving radio traffic on pain of being attacked by four to six American attack submarines and they are asking for instructions."

"They're laying it on pretty thick," Goldman said. "Four to six attack submarines? We've only got two attack submarines on each Soviet, haven't we, Admiral?"

"Two," Mike Brannon said. "That's enough. The question now is, will the Politburo get those messages? Supposing the Soviet command doesn't choose to let the Politburo know about the messages? The Politburo is in session right now."

"I can make sure of that," President Milligan said. He rose and went to the sideboard where the telephones stood.

"Moise, get on that other phone and double-check on our interpreter and theirs when I talk. Tell the War Room switchboard that I want the hot line activated and I want to talk to Brezhnev. If the other end says he's busy the interpreter is to tell them that I want him on that telephone no matter what."

"The terminology is 'President Red Alert,' sir," Goldman said. "That calls for getting the First Secretary on the line no matter what he's doing."

"Whatever it takes," President Milligan said. "Get that son of a bitch on the line."

The members of the Politburo filed out of their respective anterooms and took their seats. Leonid Plotovsky nodded his head politely to Leonid Brezhnev.

"As the senior member of the assembly, second only to you, Comrade, I request that if the telephone call that caused you to ask for a recess has any bearing on the business at hand we be informed of the contents of the call."

The cold eyes under the heavy black brows looked up and down the table. "The call was from the President of the United States," Brezhnev said. He turned to look at Plotovsky and the old man's lizard eyes stared back at him, unblinking.

"May we be privileged to know what President Milligan talked about?" Plotovsky asked.

Leonid Brezhnev reached for a cigaret and lit it. He inhaled deeply and let the smoke stream out of his nostrils.

"The President of the United States has advised me that we have ten missile submarines on station off both coasts of North America. Each of those submarines has been told and have receipted for the messages, that they will be destroyed if they submerge to their . . ." He paused and looked down at the notes the interpreter had written.

"Our submarines have been ordered to surface for a message instructing them to either fire or not fire their missiles at military targets in the United States. They have been told that if they submerge after receiving the message they will be destroyed by one or more of several American attack submarines now in position to carry out that destruction." He inhaled his cigaret again and coughed, his heavy face reddening.

"The President told me that several of our submarines have already sent messages that they have been warned of what will happen if they don't obey the American orders and have asked our Naval High Command for instructions. Are you aware of this, Admiral Zurahv?"

"No, Comrade," Zurahv said. "I have received no messages of that sort."

Brezhnev pointed at the telephone. "I suggest you call your communications center and find out if such messages have been received, Admiral. If they have not we can assume that the President of the United States is a liar."

Admiral Zurahv rose and walked to the telephone. As he picked up the handset Brezhnev's aide picked up his telephone at a signal from the First Secretary. Admiral Zurahv looked at the cold-eyed aide and dialed. He looked again at the aide as he put the receiver back on its cradle.

"Comrade," he said slowly, "my communications people tell me that all of our missile submarines on station off the coasts of North America have surfaced as ordered and have notified our command that they are in immediate danger of being destroyed by numbers of American attack submarines if they submerge." He drew a deep breath.

"I am advised that all of our submarines have notified us that they will remain on the surface until further clarification of their orders, Comrade."

"Check and mate," Leonid Plotovsy said in a soft voice.

"What were their orders," Brezhnev asked. "What were their precise orders, Admiral?"

"To commence firing missiles at seventeen thirty hours, Comrade." The words came from Admiral Zurahv's lips in a half whisper.

There was no change of expression on Brezhnev's face. "Countermand that order at once, Admiral. Order all of our submarines to return to base at once. Send the orders in plain language so the Americans can read them." He watched as the bulky Admiral rose again from his chair and went to the telephone and gave the orders.

"It is done, Comrade First Secretary."

"Thank you," Brezhnev said. "Is a vote necessary to settle our course of action for the near future? I agree with your faces, Comrades. We need not vote. Comrade Plotovsky, my old and trusted friend, my thanks. My thanks also to you, Comrades Shevenko, Simonov. I will see Admiral Zurahv alone. My thanks to all of you."

As the Politburo members filed out into the hall outside the conference room Plotovsky was heard to murmur "Check and mate and game." Sergei Pomonvitz, the leader of the hardliner faction, grinned wolfishly at Plotovsky.

"One game does not make a tournament, old one. There will be other games."

"Granted," the old man said. "But before you set your board for the next game you will need a new bishop to lead your attack, Comrade."

"I don't think so," Pomonvitz said. "I don't envy the Admiral the tongue lashing he is getting right now but his position is secure."

"It won't be after the First Secretary gets through throwing up, as I know he will do when he sees the photographs of the Admiral and listens to the tape recordings I left with him," Plotovsky said.

Sergei Pomonvitz shrugged. "I can guess what they are, my friend. I hoped he would be careful but apparently he wasn't. So he goes off the board. Time will take care of providing a new piece. As it will take care of you."

Plotovsky grinned as the two men stepped into the elevator. "Never count on what seems inevitable, Sergei. Hitler made that mistake when he thought that time would take care of the British. They outlasted him, as I have outlasted a dozen like you." He smiled again, broadly, his small lizardlike eyes crinkling.

Sophia Blovin brought hot tea and a platter of pastry to Igor Shevenko's desk. She pulled up a chair and poured the tea and placed a pastry on a paper napkin in front of Shevenko.

"It went well?" she asked, her voice anxious.

"Yes," he nodded. "It went as it had to go. I think mainly to the efforts of our friends in Israel who kept the lines of communication open. I must think about what sort of present to send to Dr. Saul to show my gratitude."

"What will happen to those who were on the side of starting a war?" she asked.

"Nothing will happen to the members of the Politburo," Shevenko said. "I think Admiral Zurahv, will be retired. He can spend his time at his dacha trying to seduce young men."

"You can be sure of that?"

He nodded as he bit into a cream-filled Napoleon. "I am sure. I didn't want to use the photographs that Anton got for me but Plotovsky insisted that I give them to him so he could give them to Brezhnev.

"You know Brezhnev, he's a puritan at heart. He'll get sick at the stomach when he sees the pictures, listens to the tapes, and reads the report that Anton put together. The Admiral will be out on his fat ass so fast he won't know what hit him."

"Thank God," Sophia said in a low voice. Shevenko grinned at her. "I share your feeling, I think He had a lot to do with our success. But don't celebrate too much, the opposition will find someone else to take his place." He drained his cup and she refilled it.

"I feel like celebrating. I always do after a hard fight. Why don't you make the arrangements to come with me to the United States? I can't get you a ticket to the Super Bowl game but other than the few hours that will take and a couple of more hours or so for business there we could have a week together, just the two of us. A night in Havana, another night in Mexico City, two or three nights in Miami. It could be fun."

"I would have you to myself," she grinned at him. "No wife to worry about, no emptiness in the bed when you have to leave at midnight, as you do here. I'd love to go to Miami with you. I've never been there. New York, Washington, yes, not Miami. What sort of clothes will I need there in winter?"

"It will be warm in Miami," he said. He reached for her and she came around the desk and bent over him, her breasts crushing against his face.

"I may even," he said in a muffled voice, "I might even defect once I get there. It might be worth it if I could have you with me. Would you defect if I asked you?"

She lowered her head and her mouth found his and opened as she breathed in deeply through her nostrils.

"Yes," she said. "Oh, yes!"

CHAPTER 25

The U.S.S. *Orca* trailed the Soviet Yankee One Class ballistic missile submarine. The *Orca* was running at 100 feet, easily keeping pace with the Soviet submarine as it wallowed along on the surface. Captain Reinauer studied the chart in front of him and motioned to his XO.

"They're running out of our patrol area and into the New London zone," he said. "Let's send them a message. Tell them they're running out of our area and that they'll be covered by other submarines until they get near their home base. Tell them"—he paused and his beard split in a grin—"tell them we wish them a safe journey home and Godspeed. And tell Raynor I want to see him."

The burly torpedoman knocked on the bulkhead outside the Captain's cabin and went inside the tiny compartment in response to Captain Reinauer's order.

"We're headed home," Captain Reinauer said. "I wanted to know about your request. Do you still want a transfer?"

The torpedoman shifted his feet, his eyes on the bulkhead above the Captain's head.

"Well, sir, I kind of, well, you know, this past week or so, all the trouble and the tension . . ." His voice trailed off.

"Yes?" Reinauer said in a soft voice.

"Well, sir, that torpedo gang of mine, good as they are, sir, they aren't good enough if I'm not there at Battle Stations. I mean, sir, that you'd have to get a damned good man to replace me and I ain't blowin' my own horn, sir."

"That's what's been worrying me all along," Reinauer said. "There's just no substitute for experience. And I mean that. I put experience above going to a specialty school any time."

"Too bad the selection board doesn't feel that way," the torpedoman said. "I'll go out on twenty a first class petty officer because I don't have that damned nuke school in my record."

"I wouldn't say that," Captain Reinauer said. "I'll make you a proposition. I've been ordered to see Vice Admiral Brannon as soon as we get into port. He's not a nuke man, you know. I intend to ask him for permission to advance four of my first class petty officers to Chief Petty Officer regardless of the fact they haven't been to nuclear schools. The Admiral is World War II. I think he might listen to me." He looked at the enlisted man in front of him.

"You think that you could hold off your request for transfer until after I see the Admiral, see how I make out?"

"Captain," the torpedoman said slowly, "you bust through that damned nuke school requirement to make Chief and you're gonna raise the morale in the non-nuke submarine sailors up to about as high as it can get. Hell, yes, I'll go along with you, sir." He grinned at his Commanding Officer, who smiled back at him.

The air conditioning in the hotel suite in the Fontaine-bleau Hotel in Miami Beach hummed with remorseless efficiency, fluttering the heavy drapes over the windows that blocked out the red ball of the sun rising out of the Atlantic Ocean.

Sophia Blovin rolled over in the king-sized bed and slid her hand down under the sheet. Igor Shevenko awoke.

"No," he said.

"Why not?" she asked, giggling. "You didn't mind last night."

"It's morning, I have things to do today."

"It was morning two days ago in Mexico City and you had things to do there and you didn't mind." Her hand was insistent. He reached his right hand down under the sheet and grasped her wrist and squeezed until she gasped in pain.

"Business comes first when you are in enemy territory," he said. "I have to see some people, make some decisions. When that is over we will celebrate. A big dinner with wine and then love as you want it as long as I last." He leaned over and kissed her lightly on the tip of her nose.

"Can we have breakfast here, in the room?" she asked.

"Not room, my dear, suite. The prices these capitalists charge for a sitting room and a bedroom make it imperative that you call this a suite, not a room. What would you like for breakfast?" He sat up in bed and reached for the telephone on the bedside table.

"You order for me, please."

"Eggs Benedict? Coffee? Tea? Your pleasure, lovely one."

"Not Eggs Benedict. That is only good if one has champagne with it and then makes love and love is not to be made this morning."

"What, then?"

"Mmmm. Orange juice, a big glass. Three eggs, scrambled with lots of toast and butter and marmalade. A lot of coffee." He smiled and dialed the room service number and gave the order, ordering an omelet for himself.

"It will take twenty minutes," he said. "Enough time for me to take a shower." He sprang out of bed and she laughed. He turned, his face serious.

"You have no fanny," she giggled. He grinned and went into the bathroom.

The room service waiter knocked gently at the door, remembering that one did not bang loudly on the door of a suite that rented for $200 a day. He nodded and smiled at the man who opened the door and averted his eyes from the gorgeous blonde who was sitting up in bed with the sheet pulled above her breasts. He laid out the breakfast quickly and expertly and left the room. Igor double-bolted the door and sat down at the table. Sophia threw off the sheet and jumped out of bed.

"You are beautiful in the nude," Igor said in a soft voice.

"Pour my coffee so it will cool a little," she said. "I just want to brush my teeth before I eat. I am going to eat in the nude and give you an appetite." She disappeared into the bathroom and closed the door. Shevenko reached into his trouser pocket and took out a small tin box. He shook a white pill out into his hand and replaced the box in his pocket. He crumbled the pill in her cup and poured hot coffee over it. She came back into the room, combing her hair with her fingers.

"I think this climate is good for me," she said. "I feel alive, alive all over. Not like at home at this time of year when I freeze day and night." She drank her orange juice in three long swallows and spread orange marmalade on a piece of toast and chewed vigorously. "Um, very good marmalade. Try some."

"I will," he said. She nodded and attacked her eggs. All her appetites are natural, he thought to himself as he watched her eat. She eats as if she will never eat again and she enjoys eating. She makes love the same way. He sighed gently and she looked at him over the rim of her coffee cup.

"It's strong coffee," she said. "It needs more cream. Why do you look so sad? Is something wrong?"

"No," he said. "I don't look forward to the first order of business today. I have to deal with some of those damned Cuban Communists. They're the worst kind, always wanting to start a revolution in Miami, attack the government, all sorts of silly things. Convincing them to keep a low profile is almost impossible."

"Will you be through with them in time to go to the game?" she asked.

"If I'm not someone will be sorry," he said. He refilled her coffee cup and lit a cigaret, marveling at the superbly modeled flesh across the table.

"Must I wait here?" she asked. "Can I go down into the arcade, look in the shops?"

"I don't see why not," he said. "I should be back well before dinner."

"I'll only be out for an hour or so and not out of the hotel," she said. She explored her teeth with her tongue, searching for bits of food and then suddenly yawned hugely.

"Oh, I'm sorry!" She blushed and stood up. "I'm sleepy. You kept me up too late." She yawned again and he moved quickly, catching her as she slumped. He half dragged her over to the bed and laid her down and pulled the sheet up over her body. He went to his attache case and took out a leather case that contained a plastic syringe, a needle, and a tiny vial of clear liquid. He filled the syringe from the vial and very gently inserted the needle into the flesh of her shoulder and pressed the plunger home with a steady thumb.

"Eight hours," he said to himself. "Six this evening. But she's so damned healthy I'd better be sure." He took a pair of handcuffs made of a plastic as strong as fine steel from a pocket in his attache case and snapped one ring around her wrist, the other around the bed post near her head. He left the room and hung a "Don't Disturb" sign on the outside door knob.

The Orange Bowl was a maelstrom of noise as the Baltimore Colts left the field and the Dallas Cowboys trotted on to limber up. Shevenko turned his head as a man sat down in the seat beside him.

"Thought you'd never get here, Bob," Shevenko said, grinning at Wilson's grim face. "Who do you like in the game? A little bet would make things more interesting, don't you think?"

"You're the visitor," Wilson said. "You get the choice."

"Colts," Shevenko said. "I would feel better about it if it were the New York Jets with Joe Namath throwing that football like he did here two years ago. But I can't see the Colts losing twice in a row in this stadium. How much can your expense account stand, for a bet I mean?"

"How about ten bucks and it's not from my expense account."

"Fine," Shevenko said. "Do you know how long it's been since I've seen a real football game? Over eight years. I watched a couple of your service teams in Korea three years ago but that doesn't count. That's not the Super Bowl." He waved at a passing vendor and bought two hot dogs and two paper cups of an orange colored drink.

"I am the visitor but I am also the host," he said. "I bet not even the Company could get seats as good as these, right on the fifty yard line." He fell silent as the pre-game ceremonies began and when the Marine color guard marched down the field to the flagpole he stood with the crowd and sang the words of the "Star Spangled Banner" in a deep bass voice. Wilson looked at him curiously and then joined in, self-consciously, his voice low.

The two men stayed close together as they left the Orange Bowl, Shevenko moving through the dense crowd with an expert use of shoulder and hip. Outside of the stadium Wilson stopped and took out his billfold and extracted a ten-dollar bill. Shevenko shoved it in his pocket.

"At least I won something out of this rotten business," he said. "I have one more favor to ask of you, my friend. Will you come back to the hotel with me?"

"Sure," Wilson said. He led the way down the street to a house where cars were parked on the front lawn.

"Fifteen bucks to park your car on their damned grass," he said as he started the engine and backed into the street. "Damned people around this stadium make enough money during the football season to pay their year's taxes."

"The joys of capitalism," Shevenko said. "When you get to the hotel it will cost you five dollars for a Cuban refugee to park your car and another five dollars to the same Cuban to get it back for you and for all you know the Cuban might be a Communist. You think it's better to be free and pay for everything. I think I like it best under our system. But each to his own, I guess." He paused and offered a cigaret to Wilson and took one for himself and lit it.

"I'd like to trade you some information, Bob."

"Shoot," Wilson said.

"Our admiral, the asshole who started this whole business, has been forced into retirement. He's lucky Papa Brezhnev didn't have him shot. He knows that and the people who backed him know it, too. I think we will have a period of some peace for quite a while now. What about your admiral, the one who ordered our submarine attacked and sunk?"

"You know the name Captain Steel, Herman Steel?" Wilson said.

"Yes. The father of your nuclear Navy. A difficult man to get along with, I am told."

"That's right," Wilson said. "He and Vice Admiral Brannon, he's the one who issued the orders to get your submarine, he's been fighting Admiral Brannon tooth and nail for almost three years.

"When Brezhnev called the President and said he'd ordered his missile submarines to return to base and it was confirmed by our submarines, Admiral Brannon offered the President his resignation. Captain Steel stood up on his hind feet and hollored his head off, said if the President accepted Admiral Brannon's resignation he'd have to accept his own resignation."

"So your mad admiral stays on duty?" Shevenko said in a soft voice.

"He's not mad," Wilson said, his voice sharp. "He knows how to play hard ball with you people."

"God help us all if the rest of your military, or ours, learn that lesson," Shevenko said. The two men got out of the car at the door of the hotel and Wilson gave a five-dollar bill to the Cuban valet parker. As they stood waiting for the elevator Wilson looked at the Russian.

"We both owe one hell of a debt to Dr. Saul, do you agree?"

"I do," Shevenko said. "I have in mind how I will repay him."

He unlocked the door of his suite and went in, followed by Wilson. The CIA man looked at the unconscious form of Sophia Blovin on the bed, his eyes moving from the bare breasts of the sleeping girl to her handcuffed wrist. Shevenko went to the bed and unlocked the handcuffs and put them in his jacket pocket. He picked up his bag and turned around.

"That is Sophia Blovin," he said, nodding his head toward the bed. "Also known as Little Fox. My personal aide in my Directorate for the past few weeks. Before that she worked for the Directorate as our expert in American psychology. I give her to you for safe keeping, Bob. It's my way of repaying Dr. Saul."

"I don't understand," Wilson said.

Shevenko walked toward the door of the suite. "How did you think that Dr. Saul knew everything that was going on in my operation? Sophia is a deep mole. She works for Dr. Saul." He looked at Sophia's sleeping form with affection in his eyes.

"She doesn't know I found out about her but if I was able to do that, in time, someone else in my organization would also find out. Lubianka prison is not a place for Sophia." He paused at the door, his hand on the knob.

"The drug I gave her is harmless, no side effects. She'll

wake up by six." He turned the knob and opened the door.

"Send her back to Dr. Saul with my compliments. Tell him he owes me one." He went through the door and closed it behind him.

Author *Harry Homewood* was a qualified submariner before he was seventeen years old, having lied to the Navy about his age. He served in a little "S"-boat in the old Asiatic Fleet. After Pearl Harbor he re-enlisted and made eleven war patrols in the Southwest Pacific. He later became Chicago Bureau Chief for *Newsweek,* chief editorial writer for the *Chicago Sun-Times,* and for eleven years had his own weekly news program syndicated to thirty-two PBS television stations.